Was this how her luck, her attention to detail, was going to run out?

After the better part of a decade studying and training for this kind of situation, she was going to be outdone by a jammed door?

No. Freaking. Way.

Summoning every ounce of focus and strength she had, Nika moved the car's collapsed front and side air bags out of her way. Using her left hand, she scrambled for the door handle again, but panic threatened as her fingers pulled at it with no luck.

Lean against the door.

She let gravity use her body weight and finally the door moved a fraction of an inch. Metal against metal. Bracing herself to shove her shoulder against it, she breathed in—and the door was yanked open. She fell out of the car, knowing the ground was going to be hard and cold. Instead she was caught in midair. The icy field below her face was still, her body secure.

"I've got you, Nika."

Mitch.

She'd fallen into Mitch's arms.

* * *

We hope you enjoy the Silver Valley P.D. miniseries. Be sure to look for more stories in 2017!

* * *

If you're on Twitter, tell us what you think of Harlequin Romantic Suspense! #harlequinromsuspense

Dear Reader,

Thank you for taking the time to visit Silver Valley, Pennsylvania. Since the Silver Valley P.D. series has launched, you've been overwhelmingly supportive, and it tickles me each time you ask, "When's the next one coming out?" I can't thank you enough for your emails, Facebook posts and your attendance at my book signings.

Her Christmas Protector and *Wedding Takedown* set the stage for Silver Valley's fight against a disbanded cult that's determined to regroup in their cherished community. In *Her Secret Christmas Agent*, the True Believer cult has reached its tentacles into Silver Valley High School. I had to have the strongest hero and heroine possible to face this danger together. I think you'll enjoy the result.

Again, no writer works alone, and I'm no exception. While many solitary hours are spent at my computer, I rely on the real-life everyday heroes who walk among us to inspire the Silver Valley series. I remain indebted to my local law enforcement and the many other law enforcement agents I've interviewed along the way.

Please continue the conversation with me on each story and character. Whether you prefer Facebook, the blog on my website, Twitter, Instagram, Pinterest or good old-fashioned email, you can reach me. And please sign up for my newsletter so you won't miss out on the many contests I run. It's all on my website, www.gerikrotow.com.

Until the next Silver Valley P.D. story—

Peace,

Geri

HER SECRET
CHRISTMAS AGENT

—

Geri Krotow

HARLEQUIN® ROMANTIC SUSPENSE

Recycling programs
for this product may
not exist in your area.

ISBN-13: 978-0-373-28207-4

Her Secret Christmas Agent

Copyright © 2016 by Geri Krotow

Printed in U.S.A.

Former naval intelligence officer and US Naval Academy graduate **Geri Krotow** draws inspiration from the global situations she's experienced. Geri loves to hear from her readers. You can email her via her website and blog, gerikrotow.com.

Books by Geri Krotow

Harlequin Romantic Suspense

Silver Valley P.D.

Her Christmas Protector
Wedding Takedown
Her Secret Christmas Agent

Harlequin Superromance

What Family Means
Sasha's Dad

Whidbey Island

Navy Rules
Navy Orders
Navy Rescue
Navy Christmas
Navy Justice

Harlequin Anthology

Coming Home for Christmas
Navy Joy

Harlequin Everlasting Love

A Rendezvous to Remember

Visit the Author Profile page at
Harlequin.com for more titles.

A girl can't have too many sister-friends!
To Cathy Maxwell, thank you for the love and
real-time support. To Lena Zharichenko, thank you
for encouraging me to write romantic suspense.

Chapter 1

You are going to die.

Mitch Everlock stared at the message written on butcher paper and taped across the chemistry classroom's high-tech SMART Board. Its red letters were dripping as if they'd been drawn with blood. Judging from the unmistakable scarlet hue and the metallic tang permeating his classroom, it *was* blood. His arms were full as he held his travel coffee mug in one hand, his laptop bag slung over his shoulder, and a pile of heavy books in the other hand. All of which he wanted to hurl at the red-lettered message. As former Special Forces and a current Trail Hikers secret operative, he wasn't afraid of or shocked by the grisly message meant for him.

He was annoyed as all get-out.

The boldness of the blood writing, in the midst of

the buildup to the holiday season, infuriated Mitch. He didn't care about his Christmas, but if his students saw the message it'd scare the Santa Claus out of them.

Dropping his armload on the laboratory counter, he ignored the beaker of candy canes he'd knocked over and pulled his cell phone out of his back pocket to take a few snapshots of the message before he used speed dial to call his second place of employment.

The Trail Hikers was a clandestine government shadow agency that officially didn't exist, except for those who worked for it.

"This is Claudia." Claudia Michaels, the CEO of Trail Hikers and his sister-in-arms, answered, her voice strong and commanding over the connection. She, too, was a war veteran; a retired US Marine Corps General.

"Good morning, Claudia. Mitch here. Our Rainbow Hater's raised the ante. Now he's threatening to kill me." He told her about the fifth message from the entity they'd named the Rainbow Hater. So far there wasn't conclusive evidence linking the hate crimes to the cult that had formed in Silver Valley last year, but several law-enforcement agencies, to include the FBI and more locally, Silver Valley PD, believed the crimes and cult were connected. The cult, known as the True Believers and originally based in Upstate New York, had regrouped in Silver Valley after prison sentences had forced its leaders into hibernation for two decades. The threats at Mitch's school had a definite True Believers Cult "feel" to them. The cult had become a most unwelcome presence in otherwise serene Silver Valley, a quintessentially American town in South Central Pennsylvania.

As he sent Claudia the photos via text, he filled her in on his impressions. Since he was a Trail Hikers' agent, he had the training to handle it himself, which was what he wanted.

"Let me get involved, Claudia. Trail Hikers will solve this twice as fast as Silver Valley PD."

"We expected this, Mitch. Do as we've planned. Let SVPD collect the forensics. Don't touch it." Claudia was right—Silver Valley boasted one of the top local forensic teams in the state. It was all thanks to their police chief's insistence on thorough training and his ability to ensure their budget received the necessary allocation each fiscal year.

"Are you sure I can't help? Let me take care of this and we'll catch the bastard in no time. If I need assistance I want TH at my back, not local cops. Plus, you know word will get out and the last thing we need is a bunch of upset parents, especially right before the Silver Bells Ball holiday formal. We're only a few weeks from Christmas break."

"SVPD is the best, Mitch. And this is happening in their jurisdiction, their high school. What we suspect, *who* we suspect to be behind this, is irrelevant at the moment. We're months away from taking the True Believers down. The focus now has to be on the Rainbow Hater." Claudia's tone was crisp as she continued to spell out the Trail Hikers' involvement with monitoring and eventually eliminating the potentially deadly cult currently setting up shop on the outskirts of Silver Valley. "Remember, the highest

levels of law enforcement are on this, but they're staying hands-off as long as SVPD and TH can work it."

"They're probably putting one of my kids up to
this, Claudia. I don't take well to anyone bullying
a student."

"Which is why you're being targeted, and why
you're the best teacher they could be messing with,
for our sake. Inform Principal Essis and let her call
in SVPD. If you have any problems, you can go directly to Colt." Claudia referred to the formidable
SVPD chief of police, Colt Todd.

Mitch heard her sigh over the clear line and understood in that moment that she was as frustrated
as he. They should have caught the cult members by
now, but they were hardened criminals and had been
slippery, outsmarting the laws that had put them behind bars over twenty years ago.

"And, Mitch?"

"Yes, ma'am?"

"Stay the hell out of SVPD's way. They're going
to be sending in an undercover officer, according to
Colt. Work with whomever it is. But watch your six
in case whoever wrote those words turns out to be
crazy enough to follow through on his threats."

"I pray for the opportunity to face him."

Claudia chuckled. "I'm sure you do, but you know
our ground rules." She hung up.

Rules. Yeah, he knew them. All too well.

Mitch called Principal Essis and waited for her
to come, his fingers itching to take a sample of the
blood on the whiteboard. Claudia was right. He had
to always give the appearance of being only a chemistry teacher. His vocation was teaching and he didn't

want to risk losing the best job he'd ever had, besides serving as a Marine. Working under contract to the Trail Hikers during school breaks used the skill set he'd gained in Marine Recon and, while he enjoyed it, teaching was his first love.

Watching students' eyes light up when they got the meaning of a chemistry equation or solved a lab problem on their own was what he relished.

Which made him want to employ his other abilities in the most effective manner: to catch whoever wanted Silver Valley High School to stop supporting its teen LGBT club.

"I'm ready for whatever you need me to do. I haven't done any long-term undercover before, nothing more than a few weeks. But I know I can do this." Nika sat in a government-issue office chair at the Silver Valley Police Department and watched the team leader for the Rainbow Hater case at Silver Valley High School, Detective Bryce Campbell. "I have to ask, though, why me? Why not one of our younger officers?"

Bryce blew out a long breath. "There's more to it, Nika. We think the hate crimes against the Rainbows club and teacher Mitch Everlock are somehow connected to the True Believers."

"I saw the morning report. Leonard Wise is out and free to live here if he wants to." Wise had been the leader of the True Believers in Upstate New York two decades ago. His prison term was up, and several of his former cult members had been released from prison, too.

"Zora feels horrible about all of this." Bryce looked as miserable as Nika knew his fiancée was feeling.

"It has nothing to do with her. Wise is sick and would have set up somewhere again. He found her first, so he settled on Silver Valley."

"Yeah, but...you know."

Bryce didn't have to elaborate. Nika *did* know—when Bryce's fiancée had been only twelve she'd been a potential victim of the cult. She'd reported the cult, and Wise in particular, saving herself and many other girls. Zora had been moved to Silver Valley and started a new life with her adoptive family. But last year Wise had tracked her down and sent Zora's mother to Silver Valley to go after the daughter she'd betrayed. Bryce, Zora and SVPD had worked together last Christmas to stop a serial killer who'd targeted Silver Valley's female ministers. Nika wasn't privy to all of the details but Zora had somehow worked in disguise to catch the Female Preacher Killer. She'd drawn her biological mother out and was instrumental in having her committed to a mental hospital, where she should have been when Zora was a young girl—before the True Believers Cult had held Zora and her mother hostage.

"How is Zora? This Christmas is going to be a lot different for you two."

Bryce grunted. "We're doing the minimum for Christmas as it's the last week before our wedding. You have a date yet?" He shot her a collegial grin.

She grimaced. "No. Every time you ask, my answer will still be the same, Bryce."

"Right. Well, you've got a few weeks to find a date. So, back to the Silver Valley High case. We've got someone who's got a hard-on for the LGBT club and Mitch Everlock in particular. You go in there without your usual makeup, your hair plain, the right clothes, you'll pass for a high schooler. Have you seen some of those girls? They're like cover models. They all look twenty-five, whether they're freshmen or seniors."

"I doubt they all look that mature, but go on."

"There's a student whose mother is really into the meetings that the cult is holding, over in the trailer park." The trailer park on the edge of Silver Valley had been purchased by Leonard Wise last year and occupied by his fellow former True Believers founders. "This mother is the only one we have a concrete connection to."

"What's the student's name?"

"Rachel Boyle. You need to get in there and see what you can find out. I'm not saying become her best friend, because from what Mit—Mr. Everlock—has told us, she's pretty withdrawn. At least, over the past semester she's withdrawn."

"That doesn't mean she's the Rainbow Hater, Bryce." She didn't call him on the fact that he'd referred to Everlock by his first name. It was obvious he and the science teacher must know one another outside of the case. "We don't even know for sure if the Rainbow Hater is attached to the cult."

"No, we don't. But it's the best lead we've got right now, Nika."

Three days after having his life threatened by the latest bloody message, Mitch took a long look at his first-period class. He made sure he made eye contact with each of the twenty students. He hoped they each knew that he was here for them, whether it was about chemistry or personal matters. Especially if they were being coerced by the True Believers Cult members to commit a crime.

"Who can give me the resulting compound, given the variables we introduced into our lab experiment?" Mitch switched on the SMART Board, scrubbed clean of the tape goo from the hate message. As the digital whiteboard booted up he took another chance to peruse his smartest group of students. Period one, Monday through Friday: high school seniors, all but one or two destined for the top universities in the state. Many would go out of state, maybe one or two to an Ivy League. Acceptances hadn't been sent out yet, but he'd seen enough seniors to have a good feel for where each would end up. He felt so damned privileged to be teaching the best of the best.

The thought of any of them being involved in the hate crimes left the taste of bile in his mouth.

"Anyone? What did you do this weekend that's making you so tired on this fine Monday morning, folks?"

A raised hand. Amy Donovan, the class favorite. Not a teacher's pet, but the class's go-to girl on how to keep the labs safe and accurate. She was also the senior class president and a cheerleader. Silver Valley High's all-American girl.

"Amy."

"It'd be ammonia."

"That's right. Anyone else want to add your observations from last week's lab? Neel, I remember you had several questions about the Bunsen burner." The roll of laughter didn't embarrass the first-generation Indian American who sat straighter and flashed a bright white smile.

"Jeffrey helped me with that just fine, Mr. Everlock."

More laughter. Neel had accidentally singed his eyebrows with a Bunsen burner at the beginning of his junior year.

Had it been almost two years with this group already? They'd been the best Mitch had ever taught.

"I'm going to miss you losers over the holiday break. But we've still got three more units to get through in our textbook. Let's keep the discussion going." They all grumbled over their laughter at his teasing. They knew they were cherished, he suspected.

Mitch never got enough of the youthful energy. This class more than the others was special to him because they all wanted to be here, to go wherever their brains could take them. Which, for a good portion of them, would be very, very far.

Hopefully not as far as a war in Iraq or Afghanistan, where he'd been.

Using the techniques he'd learned through therapy sessions with his counselor, Zora, he took a deep breath and let go of the images of smoke and blood that filled his head as he was transported back to his time in the Middle East. The harrowing memories wanted all his attention—but he had a class to teach.

I'm in Silver Valley, Pennsylvania. I am safe. Today is Monday and it's a B day on the school schedule.

The practiced reminder of reality settled him.

"Mr. Everlock?" Bright blue eyes reflected no notice of Mitch's brief return to what had been his hell on earth.

"Shoot, Gabi." Gabriella Boland had that line between her carefully shaped eyebrows, the line that meant he'd better pay attention. The straight-A student and senior class homecoming queen was as formidable in chemistry class as she was on the basketball court, where she hoped to lead her team to the state championships as she had last season.

"When are we going to get into how we can use chemistry to help the environment instead of making compounds that harm it?" Her face was innocent enough, her question valid, but could Gabi be the teen who'd written the message earlier? The one who'd left notes last semester, leading up to the last few weeks of school before summer break?

Keep your cool.

He hated how the threats were making him suspicious of every one of his students. It was like being back in the war—he couldn't trust anyone.

"That's something you can explore in your environmental studies at college, Gabi. For now, we'll focus on getting our study guides in shape to tackle the final exams in six months. Mine and the IB's."

A collective groan rose at the mention of the International Baccalaureate exams that had, for this class, replaced the Advance Placement—AP—exams. Mitch held up a hand. "It's the end of the first semester for me, too, folks. You're not the only ones with a full load. You think I wouldn't rather be getting my Christmas shopping done?"

Immediately wisecracks flew across the room, the students snickering as though they were back in middle school. Mitch ignored it. This was Mitch's sixth class of seniors since he'd left the Corps, gone back to college and started his teaching career.

The bell rang and the classroom emptied. Mitch had two periods without class in front of him, almost two full hours. Instead of using the valuable time to grade homework or to prepare his lessons for the chemistry review, he had to go to SVPD and put in a full report of what had happened in his classroom since when the notes started last March. He'd given the responding officer his take and then been asked to leave the classroom while a forensics team did their work. It had chapped his ass to be cut out but he'd complied. As far as the SVPD was concerned, he was a normal high school teacher.

"Are the Rainbows still having their holiday celebration, Mr. Everlock?" Rachel Boyle had hung back when the other students had rushed out. Now she stood in front of Mitch's desk, her close-shaven head a stark contrast to her large brown eyes and expertly made-up face.

"Of course. Why wouldn't we?"

Please, please don't let it be Rachel. Or Gabi. Or any of my students...

She shifted on her feet. "I heard that some parents were stirring up the pot again."

"Which parents would that be?"

She shrugged. "I don't know. They didn't say."

"Who's 'they,' Rachel?"

"Just some of the kids at lunch. The hot gossip is that you've been getting warnings from the principal to cancel the Rainbows." Her stance remained neutral but he couldn't discount the concern in her eyes. The Rainbows had taken Rachel in as a sullen, shy freshman and helped her build her confidence to become the strong young woman who stood before him. A bright student who'd been dropping in her scores, showing less and less interest in her academics. Lately the Rainbows seemed to be all she cared about.

Mitch sighed. "You know I'll never let them cut the Rainbows or any of its programming from the schedule. And Principal Essis is never going to let anything happen to the club, either. Silver Valley High is about inclusion, period. You know that and enforce it better than I do, Rachel."

"I know you're behind us, and most of the teachers are, but some of the parents are crazy, you know? They think the Rainbows turned their children gay, lesbian, bi or trans, and they'll do anything they can to shut it down."

"I can assure you, Rachel, that Silver Valley High will keep the Rainbows going as long as I'm here. And Principal Essis is supporting us, too." He looked at Rachel. She dated boys but had shared at one of the Rainbows meetings that she'd joined because she understood what it felt like to not fit in, and wanted to support all students at SVHS. She wanted to support the group.

"Excuse me? Mr. Everlock?" A girl Mitch didn't recognize had walked into the classroom via the back lab entrance behind him. He hadn't heard her approach and it rattled him.

Where was his training?

"Hi. I'm Nika Collins." The girl held out her hand to Rachel. "I'm new, my family just transferred."

Mitch's instincts went on alert. A midyear transfer? In senior year? This had to be the undercover officer Claudia had mentioned.

"Hi." Rachel gave her a little wave and started talking to her. Mitch used the moment to check out the new "student."

"I've already completed my credits to graduate but since we moved here before the end of the year the district wants me to attend class until graduation. We moved from Iowa."

She was good, *really* good. With no makeup and flawless skin, her face easily passed for a teenager's. Her clothes were adolescent typical, too, from her form-hugging polo shirt to her low-slung skinny jeans and Sherpa-lined suede boots. But those biceps and the overall athletic build that accentuated her feminine curves, her most definitely *adult woman* curves, confirmed his suspicion. As a civilian teacher, he wasn't supposed to know about it; Claudia had informed him as a Trail Hiker. He had to play dumb, but he also had to be prepared in case the True Believers started to pull their crap again. Principal Essis had been notified, too, and he knew that many of the faculty would expect nothing less with such serious threats.

Claudia wouldn't have had to tell him this gal was undercover, though. The new "student's" appearance, along with his gut instinct, which was rarely wrong, clued him in. He had to give the undercover operative kudos—the kids wouldn't think twice of her except as a new classmate.

He hoped like hell his instinct wasn't letting him down now, because this woman was hotter than hell and he hadn't ever glanced at one of his students and felt a physical attraction before.

"Mr. Everlock, Nika's going to come to our Rainbows meeting this afternoon." Rachel's voice brought Mitch back to the classroom.

"Glad to have you, Nika."

"Sure thing."

Rachel checked her phone. "I've got to go or I'm going to be late for French. Madame Kramer is doing a big finals review today. I'll see you later, Nika."

"See you." Nika wiggled her fingers just as Rachel had done, looking every bit the new, slightly awkward student who wanted to fit in.

Once they were alone in the classroom, he waited for her to speak. He had to. To make sure.

"I think you know who I am, Mr. Everlock."

"Do I?"

She looked carefully around the classroom before she held out her hand. "Nika Pasczenko, SVPD."

Mitch Everlock was going to get his due. It was only a matter of time. They were still holding the Rainbows meetings.

As he watched the students head to their next classes from his spot in the school parking lot, some leaving early, some skipping, his blood boiled. He'd been warned that it might not be so easy to sway Mitch Everlock. What the stupid teacher didn't realize was that the messages telling him to end the Rainbows weren't a joke. This was about the truth, what was best and right and true for everyone in Silver Valley. Whether they wanted to believe it or not.

No officals had been out to the farms to test the

blood, not yet. He knew they were slow, but it was taking them a long time. He fully understood, though, that the SVPD would eventually show up asking for samples of their most recent slaughter.

He was already ahead of them. The blood he'd used was from last year. He'd frozen it after he'd met Mr. Wise at the New Thought meetings, just in case he'd be able to use it for a future escapade. And he had.

"Do you have time to talk to the folks from Agriculture today?" His assistant's voice came over the car's hands-free speaker. He hated distractions but had to pay his bills for the time being.

"Of course. Anytime. Let me know what works for them."

"Will do."

The government oversight was constant. The state and federal governments didn't trust him to run his own damn farms any longer. Before long, it wouldn't matter.

When he'd found out about the Rainbows at his very own dinner table he knew that his support of the New Thought planned community hadn't been in vain. All of the meetings he had attended were going to pay off. He missed the meetings but trusted Leonard Wise. It was better for him to study at home now, while he helped Mr. Wise prepare Silver Valley for what was coming.

Leonard Wise was always right. He was a brilliant man who had come to save Silver Valley. It all made sense. Silver Valley High School was a nest of lies, the way the innocent children of their community were being indoctrinated into society's evil ways. The Rainbows club's existence only cemented it.

He'd done what he had to: sent adequate warning that the likes of their sick morals wouldn't be tolerated. That stupid chemistry teacher thought he was so smart, so savvy, helping the kids get into faraway colleges where their sinful lives could be lived out without their parents watching over them. And there was another problem. Most of the parents in Silver Valley were just as stupid and blind as their children.

But he saw what was happening. Leonard Wise and his brave teachings had enlightened him, given him a reason, a purpose. He was going to bring down the Rainbows and all the students in the group. Mr. Wise would be so pleased, because it would help bring more members to their effort. Once the Rainbows were gone, and the school wasn't able to function, the parents would be forced to see that their children were running wild. That they needed discipline. That their girls needed to be dedicated to New Thought and to bring new members into the fold in the best, most pure way. Through perfect births.

But first he had to take out the man at the center of the Rainbows. The idiot teacher who was poisoning the children with the same sick lies that were plastered across all the newspapers and internet.

Mr. Mitch Everlock.

Chapter 2

"Isn't it risky to talk here?" Mitch Everlock placed a hand on the dark counter at the front of the classroom. "And you didn't have to tell me who you are, Nika. I knew the minute you walked in."

Nika wondered if he'd felt the same zing of attraction she had. His eyes were a deep holly green, sparkling like her favorite emerald earrings. Nika had left them on her dresser this morning as she'd prepared to come into Silver Valley High undercover. Her relief at Rachel's acceptance of her as a student was derailed by the disapproving expression on Mitch Everlock's face.

"You saw me check out the classroom for any students. I'm not here to play games, Mr. Everlock. As far as anyone is concerned, we're just a student and teacher, right?" She shrugged, hoping the move she'd practiced looked like a typical adolescent gesture. He wasn't what she'd expected and he made her nervous. The dowdy chemistry teacher she'd imagined was instead a hot stud. The kind of man she'd normally love to have a night or two with. Before she let him go. Because she always let them go.

"How old are you, Nika?"

"Let's just say I graduated college while most of my 'classmates' were still in middle school. These kids were being born when I went through this same school at their age." She made air quotation marks.

"Huh." He stood back from the counter and stretched, affording her a nice view of his broad chest and lean hips. He started arranging beakers and scales on the laboratory surface, ignoring her. He didn't fool her—his movements were meant to distract her, throw her off her game. "Why weren't you at the station when I filed my report three days ago? I would have remembered you." His voice was like a sexy caress and she hated herself for the cli-chéd comparison, damn it.

"Three days ago? I was on a domestic call. I didn't know I'd be working the Rainbow Hater case with you until last night." She hadn't asked to be assigned to babysit a teacher who couldn't keep control of enough of his classroom and students to already have cornered whoever had left the threats. But no one had asked for her opinion.

"Whoa, Nika. We're not 'working' on anything together, not officially. I'm a Marine vet, no longer working any kind of cases or missions. I'm simply a chemistry teacher. If you have orders to be here, okay, but I'm fine on my own. I can handle whoever this idiot is. You called him the Rainbow Hater?"

"Yes."

He was not going to make this any easier and Nika was tired of working with egos. She'd survived the ugliest breakup of her life last year and, in retrospect, saw that her ex had been egocentric. Sometimes she wished she could break up with people she worked with. Like this Everlock dude. For once couldn't someone she had to deal with be reasonable, the yin to her yang? His tone made her want to scream. Instead she remained silent, waiting for him to speak.

"That's fitting, because whoever it is has a lot of hate issues for the Rainbows. And while I appreciate you've been sent here to do your job, you have to understand that I'm the one who knows these kids. I'll figure out who it is."

"Are you really fine on your own? The messages have gotten more personal, aimed at you. If the kook who left the most recent message decides to come in here with a weapon, you think you can handle it? Keep all your students safe?"

"You bet your…bottom dollar I can, Nika. I don't believe it'll come to that, though. Do you, really?" As he asked she saw him check her out again. His gaze lingered on her breasts before he made an assessing sweep, pausing as he looked at her lower legs. Did he think she had a weapon holstered to her calf? She gripped her designer bag, courtesy of the local thrift shop frequented by teens, tightly over her shoulder, ready to retrieve her pistol if need be.

"I try to never underestimate a criminal, Mr. Everlock."

"Stop thinking *I'm* your enemy. As long as I'm in the classroom, my students are safe." His confidence didn't come across as boastful but matter-of-fact.

She forced her fingers to relax from the leather bag's handle, rested her hip on a student desk. Her face was hot and she damned her pale skin, which she knew had to be obviously red. "I don't think that at all. You were right. We should save our talk for later, either after hours or at the station."

"So Nika is your real name?" His eyes were closer to jade than emerald, she decided.

"Of course. It's much easier to keep up the ruse with my real first name. 'Collins' is not my surname, though. Fortunately most of the students I've met haven't asked for my last name."

"They're too busy studying for semester finals, dreaming about the holiday break and figuring out who to take to the Silver Bells Ball in a few weeks. At least, this crowd is. My other classes are mostly doing well, but the last class of the day, the General Science group, is struggling. I'm lucky if I get half the class to even attend."

"I'm sorry to hear that. Just so you know, I'll be coming in and out of your different classes if that's okay."

"How are you going to explain that to the students? Won't they expect you to attend a variety of subjects, just like they do?"

She shook her head. "I'm telling them what you heard here. I'm a transfer who only needs to clock classroom time for the state of Pennsylvania so that I can get my degree by May. Which class I do it in doesn't matter. And since I've received several scholarship offers, and want to major in chemistry, it makes perfect sense that I want to spend my time here."

"I don't suppose you ever took chemistry?"

"In high school, and one semester in college. I wasn't a big fan of it, though. I do know my way around a meth lab, unfortunately." If her chemistry teacher had looked as good as Mitch Everlock she might have considered becoming a pharmacist. Not that she'd tell him that.

"Is there anything we need to go over? Do you have any questions about what I've been dealing with?"

"That's best left for outside class hours, don't you think? Is there any way you can meet me at SVPD headquarters after school today?"

"I was going to head over there now to file my final report about this last threat, but I suppose I can kill two birds with one visit later. What time?"

His dark hair and brows were the perfect contrast to his eyes and she was intrigued by the lines that fanned out across his forehead, his deep smile lines, the sexy cleft in his chin.

"Um, five okay with you?"

She'd never been the kind of student who was hot for her teachers, but Mitch Everlock might be her first illicit crush. Not that she'd do anything about it. Not yet, anyway.

"Is there something on my face, Nika?" His voice was stern but there was a glint of humor in his eyes.

"No, of course not. I was admiring your tie." She nodded at the pattern of dancing laboratory Santas holding beakers and test tubes.

He grinned and opened his mouth to reply but the words she leaned in to hear were cut off by a loud crash and then a thump on the classroom floor.

"Down!" he shouted. She went to grab him but his reflexes were quicker and she found herself facedown on the linoleum floor, the weight of an extremely fit man on top of her. Out of the corner of her eye she saw a large rock with a piece of paper wrapped around it. The silence was broken only by two distinct plinks of broken glass as they dislodged from the window frame and fell to the floor. The student desk she'd been leaning on had toppled over, covering her legs.

Mitch lifted himself slightly, giving her room to breathe while still protecting her. "You okay?"

"I'm fine. Was it only the rock? No explosive?"

"Yeah. Stay down while I investigate."

As soon as he was up and on his feet she jumped to hers. He gave her a scowl but didn't stop her from running to the broken window, scanning the parking lot below.

"No one. The son of a bitch is fast, and has a very good throwing arm." Mitch looked poised to jump through his second-story classroom window.

She looked at the rock. "Do you have latex gloves in here?"

He turned to reply. "On the back counter, in the purple boxes." She met his eyes and gave him one quick nod. Not in response to his directions but as an acknowledgment from one LEA to another. Because there was no way Mitch Everlock was only a chemistry teacher. His reflexes, his calm demeanor in the face of danger, weren't natural. He'd been trained, and had kept up his training—this couldn't all be leftover Marine Corps skills.

"Maybe it's my turn to ask you who you are, Mr. Everlock."

"Save it for after school, Nika."

"Fair enough." With the gloves on, she unwrapped the rock. She could feel Mitch's body heat as he leaned in to read the message with her.

Ragged red letters spelled out "End the Rainbows or Die with Regret."

"They're focused, I'll grant them that." She turned the paper over and saw that the ink had soaked through the ubiquitous copy paper. She brought it to her nose and sniffed. And immediately bit back a gag. "This doesn't smell like paint."

"We're waiting on analysis of the ink that was on my whiteboard. But my bet's on pig's blood. There are plenty of pork farms in the area that it could be from."

"Who's doing the analysis? Who's 'we'?" She hadn't read about the lab orders when she'd been briefed by Bryce about coming in undercover.

Mitch looked momentarily stymied. If she hadn't been staring at him she would have missed it. Within a heartbeat his expression was back to neutral.

"SVPD, of course. They told me they were going to send out the samples they took."

"Did they? I'm not always copied on lab request emails." She took photos of the paper with her phone and quickly put her cell back into her purse. Since she couldn't be seen at the school before going undercover she hadn't been part of the initial SVPD response this past week. "If this had hit you in the head, you wouldn't be standing right now."

"No, and I usually stand over there when I'm lecturing." He pointed to the spot the rock had arced over. "He missed me by an hour." Mitch grinned. "Not the smartest bad guy. But he's got a decent throwing arm, I'll give him that."

He'd missed him when he'd thrown the rock. When Everlock's face appeared at the broken window, looking for the thrower, the disappointment had been keen. His belly, full from lunch, had threatened to spew.

It wasn't nerves. It was his disgust that the sinful teacher hadn't been hit by the rock. He'd tried to time it better but work had kept him from getting there earlier. More government inspections. His assistant was upset, so worried that they could lose the entire business, every single farm, all of their income. The government suits wanted to know where his profits had gone. Today, they were from the IRS. Tomorrow, it would be another agency that had figured out he'd embezzled from the agricultural corporation he'd been hired to protect.

Yeah, his assistant was concerned. Frantic. She knew her job wasn't secure. She didn't understand that he'd been giving his money to the only cause that mattered. The only thing that was going to give them all the security mankind needed. The True Believers and their new mission, New Thought.

His wife was on board but the children didn't know the riches they were about to enjoy when they moved into the New Thought community. He wished he'd been able to join the group years ago, when they'd been known as the True Believers. The government had shot Leonard Wise down then. But, Wise, the group, the purpose, was greater than any court of this world's law. The True Law was with New Thought and Mr. Wise.

His biggest challenge would be getting his family to move without a fuss. The younger ones weren't a problem but he had to make sure his eldest stayed on the straight and narrow. When he'd heard there was a new student in the school, in the chemistry classroom, he knew it was divine timing at its best. A new student was the perfect target to send home the message that things were going to change in this town. The native Silver Valley families wouldn't get hurt, not if they heeded the message. It would be worth whatever it took to hurt the new student, as a warning.

God had come to Silver Valley and chosen him to help Leonard Wise fulfill what he'd started a long time ago in Upstate New York. He was glad Wise had picked Silver Valley because, really, it meant that they were *all* chosen. If they wanted to be.

Chapter 3

"How goes it as a high schooler, Nika?" Bryce Campbell didn't look up from his computer as he entered case notes. Nika took his query as a cue to enter his office.

"You were wrong, Detective." She dropped into the chair next to his desk. "The chemistry teacher is definitely not gay."

This caused the ever-busy Bryce to look at her. "I never said he was gay."

"No, but you implied that he probably was, being the teacher in charge of the LGBT club."

"No, I said he was a teacher who had his own reasons to be supportive of the Rainbows. What difference does it make? You have a job to do." Bryce went back to entering his handwritten notes into the SVPD case database.

"He's a little difficult, is all. His ego is a mile wide."

At this Bryce took his hands off his keyboard and gave her his full attention. "SVPD is full of male egos—you've not been fazed by them before. Why, Officer Pasczenko, you're not hot for teacher, are you?"

"Give me a break. It's a case." *Oh, God, please don't let him see how close he is.*

Bryce grinned. "You know, I told myself I didn't have feelings for someone I had to work with, and look where it got me." His smile might melt his fiancée's heart but it only annoyed Nika.

"It's not like that, Bryce. I've never gotten personally involved in a case. I'm not starting now. And you knew Zora from before. You had a history. I don't know Mitch Everlock from Adam. How is Zora doing? How goes the wedding plans?"

Bryce scratched the back of his neck and to her relief he accepted the change of topic. "Zora has turned into the redheaded bridezilla of Silver Valley. She wants everything to be perfect, and if it wasn't for her best friend, Kayla, being a florist and also heavily invested in the event, I'd have eloped with Zora to Atlantic City by now."

"Atlantic City? Surely you'd have the class to at least take her to Vegas?"

"Yeah, well, you know what I mean. It's hard to believe New Year's Eve is only a few weeks away. How goes your date search?" He might be up to his ass with police work, since he was in charge of SVPD's overall operation against the True Believers, but Nika could see Bryce was just as invested in his future wife's wedding dreams. She wondered, not for the first time, if she'd ever meet a man who'd be willing to cater to her needs, her career. Not that she was looking, or even wanted to have more than a very short-term relationship with any man. Her heart was still too sore from her breakup with Ron.

"Stop asking. I told you I don't need a date. If you insist, to make the dinner tables even, I'll bring my mother." Except then her mother would start the "when are you going to stop being a policewoman and marry a nice man?" routine.

"I know several young police studs I can fix you up with if you need me to, Nika. And none of them are Pennsylvania state troopers." Compassion shone in his eyes and she wanted to spit.

"Now you're just being gross, Campbell. And I'm over that jackass. I already told you that months ago." Nika leaned over her seat and put her elbows on Bryce's desk.

"I'll believe you're over him when you let your guard down enough to admit you could use some love in your life. We all need it."

It'd be a long time before she'd be willing to do that, but she kept her thoughts to herself. "If we can drop the silliness, I have something to report. We had an incident while I was at the school today. Right before I left."

"I saw the initial call come in." Bryce whistled. "What happened?"

"A rock crashed through the class window, aimed at the exact point where Mitch Everlock usually stands when he's lecturing." She detailed the event, giving Bryce time to type it up into his computer.

"Don't think for one minute I'm your secretary, Nika." He grinned. "But I'll send a copy of this to you when we're done."

"Thanks."

"So, Everlock saw the rock coming before you did?"

"Neither of us saw it. The sound of it hitting the window alerted us."

"I would have loved to see your face when Everlock shoved you to the floor." Bryce teased her as well as her brothers did at family gatherings.

"There wasn't anything to see since I was eating the floor." She wasn't about to admit that she'd been too aware of Mitch's hard shape on top of hers.

There was a quick rap on the door frame.

"There she is, our brightest high school student. Tell me, Nika, have you tried out for the cheerleading squad yet?" Rio Ortego, another SVPD detective, leaned his head into Bryce's tiny office.

"Screw you, Ortego."

Rio laughed at her quick response.

"Is there a problem, officers?"

Rio straightened, as did Nika and Bryce. Chief of Police Colt Todd entered the space, his fit body and youthful good looks belying the twenty or more years he had on all of them.

"No, sir." They spoke in unison, which made Chief Todd grin. His brows rose as he took in Nika's civilian, teenaged appearance. "How goes it?"

"Fine, sir."

"Officer Pasczenko was just telling me how hard she's crushing on her new chemistry teacher, sir."

Nika wanted to reach over the desk and give Bryce

a quick sharp jab to the ribs. She loved her brothers-
and sisters-in-arms but, just like a biological family,
they had their days.

"Campbell, is that all you have to worry about,
Nika's love life? I guess that means you've figured
out how we'll take down the True Believers?" Colt
Todd had a stern expression on his face and Nika almost felt sorry for Bryce. Almost.

"Actually, sir, Nika's our best bet to find out who
the families are that are most involved with the cult
to date. Forensics yielded that the blood was indeed
pig's, and we're taking samples from a couple of local
butchers. We might get it down to the actual farm by
the end of the week."

"That's great," Nika said. "There are several kids
in my classes who are involved in 4-H, and more that
live on farms. It might all come together."

Chief Todd nodded. "It *will* come together. We're
going to get this bastard. But I need all of you up to
the task. Instead of busting each other's balls—sorry,
Nika—use that energy to bring this loser or losers in.
I want every single one of those cult nuts back behind bars in short order. No one left on the outside
to perpetuate their hate agenda."

"Yes, sir," they answered in unison again, and
Chief Todd walked out. Rio waited a full ten sec-
onds until he stage-whispered to Nika, "It's okay if
you have a hard-on for your teacher, Nika. It happens to the best of us." Bryce harrumphed a laugh
and Nika gave Rio a lovely hand gesture.

"Why don't you keep your focus on your girlfriend, Rio? Don't worry about me. I'm not going

to try to jump the chemistry teacher any time soon, trust me."

Rio winked at her as he left. The door was immediately filled by the SVPD receptionist. "Detective Campbell, Mr. Everlock is here to complete his report."

Mitch Everlock stepped into the space and filled it with an aura of humor. Was his chest puffed out with more than just muscles? He nodded at Bryce and then shot Nika a shit-eating grin that left no doubt about how long he'd been waiting in the passageway to enter Bryce's den of teasing.

Mitch had heard enough, enough to think Nika might indeed have the hots for her teacher.

"Mitch, have a seat." Bryce motioned at the seat in front of his desk. Nika ignored the heat in her cheeks and sat straighter, trying to appear more professional as Mitch sat next to her. A waft of his unique scent immediately reminded her of the long moments she'd spent underneath him in the science classroom.

"Thanks, Bryce."

Interesting. Bryce and Mitch had met, and Nika would bet it wasn't just since the harassment against Mitch started. An air of camaraderie existed between them that she'd only ever experienced with the SVPD. As if they were law-enforcement colleagues.

"You two met earlier today." Bryce pulled up a file on his screen as he spoke. Mitch's eyes found hers and she had the ridiculous urge to look away. As if she were some kind of freaking shy schoolgirl.

"Nice to see you again, Nika. Now can you tell

me where you keep your weapon while you're in the school?"

"I could, but you don't really need to know, do you?" She forced herself to continue to meet those beautiful eyes of his without wavering. Crap, this case was not going to be the piece of cake she'd hoped. Finding the perpetrator of the ugly written threats was only the surface of a much bigger problem. She felt it in her bones. Add her unwelcome and most inconvenient attraction to Mitch and it wasn't looking pretty.

"Fine. Don't tell me. I'll figure out where you keep it." Mitch's smug smile didn't have the effect she thought he'd want, as it made her stomach tighten, her awareness of him on overdrive.

"Nika, you know that Mitch is a former Marine, right? Spec Ops, wasn't it, Mitch?"

"Something like that." He clammed up.

That's why he'd responded to the rock so instinctively. He had specialized military training—he wouldn't have reacted so quickly, so professionally, so damned correctly, when the rock crashed through the window if he hadn't. He hadn't mentioned Spec Ops when he'd said he was a Marine veteran.

Nika chewed on her lip, trying to ignore the swell of annoyance that these two men weren't going to let her in on their shared history. She was certain she'd never been in the station at the same time as he had been—he'd be impossible to miss. He was an attractive single male. Not a lot of them on SVPD, as most of the officers were married, about to be married or at least in a committed relationship.

"Nika, you with us?" Bryce was staring at her.

Oh, God, she'd let her mind wander back to the feel of Mitch's body on top of hers.

"Yeah, I'm here."

Again, she'd let her attraction to Mitch distract her. It wasn't like her. Not at all.

Bryce nodded. "Thank you. So, Mitch, do you have anything beyond what you already told me the other day? When you got the message written in blood on your fancy chalkboard?"

Mitch shook his head. "No, unfortunately I'm afraid I've given you all I remember from that morning. But I did have a hunch today. It's nothing solid."

"Go on." Nika jumped in, ignoring Bryce's surprised glance. Usually she was the quiet one in the station, the SVPD officer no one expected to ever test boundaries or regulations. Bryce was a detective and technically she was reporting to him for this case. But she was the one in the trenches with Mitch.

"It's about one of my students. You met her, Nika. Rachel."

"Yes, the one in your morning class, the one who's also in the Rainbows?"

"Yeah, that's her. I can't pinpoint what she's said or done in particular, but something about her is making me think that she's involved. On top of that she's let her grades drop, and she's looking worse each day. She's been downright hostile, less interested in her grades and where she's going for college. As far as I know she's not planning to even apply anywhere challenging. She's playing it safe by saying she's going to Silver Valley Community College for her first two years, then transferring. That's a great plan for most students, but she's always been way above average."

"Did she say anything to you about either incident, the blood writing or the rock?"

Mitch shook his head. "No, no, of course not. In the first place, there's no reason the kids will know about the rock, and we've kept the written threats as quiet as possible. Only the faculty has been told about them. In the second place, I'm not the teacher the kids come to for touchy-feely things. I'd never expect Rachel or any other student to confide in me. I just see her drift off at times, and then she got a bit belligerent over a lab procedure."

"How can you say the kids don't come to you when you're the teacher sponsor of the Rainbows?" Nika wasn't going to let him off so easily. She didn't think he was playing a false modesty card but his comment didn't make sense to her.

"Sure, the LGBT community and their supporters have found a safe place in my classroom to hold their meetings. They know they can trust me—I won't repeat anything I hear in their meetings, unless I think someone is in danger or needs professional help. But I'm not their go-to-guy for pep talks, if that makes sense."

"That's probably wise, too, given today's climate. You said yourself you're not a professional counselor. You're at heart a caring teacher with an interest in seeing the students have the support they need." Bryce spoke as if he might know why Mitch had volunteered to be the teacher sponsor for the Rainbows.

Nika made a mental note to ask Bryce about it at a later time.

"Nika, it'd be helpful if you can become friends with Rachel. Find out what's behind the change in her behavior." As Bryce spoke, Mitch looked intently at her. While she heard Bryce's suggestion she couldn't look away from the silent message in Mitch's eyes. Did he feel the chemistry bubbling beneath the surface, too? And not the laboratory kind?

"Nika?"

"Sorry, Bryce." She turned back to him. "Sure, I can do that. But we need more to go on than a hunch. I'll try to find out what her friends know about her." She turned back toward Mitch. "Have you known her for more than this year?"

"She's been in my class since sophomore year. It worked out that I was teaching honors chemistry her sophomore year, and then I was promoted to instruct IB chemistry, a two-year course. Rachel, along with the other seniors you've met, has been in my class for IB chem since last year. She's been in my classroom for three grades now, but these past few months she's been squirrelly. She used to be more happy-go-lucky."

"Do you think she's doing drugs or alcohol?"

Mitch sighed. "I sure as hell hope not. But I know we can't rule it out. There hasn't been one class I've taught since I arrived here six years ago that hasn't had at least one or two students take the wrong path. The honors kids aren't immune to addiction any more than the rest of us."

Bryce looked at Nika. He didn't have to say anything; she understood the grim expression on his face.

"I've got it, Bryce." She stood. "Mitch, I'll see you tomorrow."

Chapter 4

Nika waited for the sun to set and changed into her regular clothes. She laughed to herself—her usual taste in clothes was far less hip than what she was wearing as a student. As a high schooler she made sure she'd picked the brand names favored by teens, as well as the colors. Her normal look was jeans and either T-shirts, long-sleeved T-shirts or turtlenecks, depending upon the season, all in muted, more natural shades.

As long as she was working undercover at Silver Valley High School she had to be very careful about being seen too much in public in her regular adult clothes. She was fairly confident that her demeanor as a student didn't come close to resembling how she looked in everyday life, but she didn't want to take any chances.

The thing was that if any of the students discovered she was a cop, they'd assume she was there to bust a drug ring. Prescription painkillers were traded frequently in the high school. SVPD had discovered the sellers were using their earnings to buy heroin. There were other officers working that case, however.

Her mission was to help bring down the True Believers, aka New Thought. To do that, she had to find out which students and families were undermining the open, accepting atmosphere of SVHS. The threats against the Rainbows was typical of the kind of bigoted sentiment the True Believers had fostered decades ago as they'd recruited vulnerable citizens into their evil fold.

Nika considered it fortunate that she lived in a town-home neighborhood just outside the Silver Valley school district, so she had little chance of running into any of the teens in her neighborhood.

She made use of her automatic garage-door opener as she pulled her mother's small SUV into the cleared space, grateful for the ease with which she was in her kitchen and eating dinner after her first full day as a "senior" in high school.

Her doorbell rang and she checked the peephole before she let in her best friend and neighbor, Ivy Shaw.

"Hey. I just sat down to eat. Want some leftover shepherd's pie?"

Ivy's dimples accented her scheming grin. "I wouldn't want to look like I came by to eat and not spend time with you…"

"Get in here." Nika walked back to the kitchen

table and Ivy followed. "Help yourself. There's Chardonnay in the fridge if you want it."

Ivy looked at Nika's glass of water. "Aren't you having any?"

"Nope. I'm on a case and I have to be supersharp in the morning."

"Anything you can talk about?"

"Nope."

"Oo-oh, that means it's a good one. Will I hear about it at some point?"

"I hope so, once we get the bastards."

They both laughed. Nika appreciated that Ivy understood her need to keep a lot of her work *at* work until her cases were solved.

"How was work for you today, Ivy?"

"The usual. The little ones are so excited about the holidays. I have a display of all of our winter and holiday-themed books and the kids love sitting in the cozy corner and reading." Ivy was the Silver Valley Elementary School librarian. "Of course, we had a few parents complain that we were being bigoted by including nontraditional Christmas and holiday stories, along with the more traditional, expected fare."

"You can't please everyone."

"The fact is that we have such a diverse community and the kids are so much more accepting of the different cultural celebrations than the parents are."

"Are there any parents in particular who have been giving you a hard time?" Nika tried to not look too obvious. She ignored the twinge of guilt that she was pumping her best friend for information that might lead to an arrest. Ivy would understand.

Ivy pulled her plate from the microwave and sat

across from Nika. Her supercurly blond hair accentuated her sparkling blue eyes and she was pursing her lips the same way she did when she pondered the ins and outs of a romantic comedy.

"There is one mother who has been the most vocal this year. She stirred up some trouble last year when we acquired a children's book about how boys and girls could have the same jobs. She came into the library yesterday again, all fired up. Her youngest is in second grade, and she has a daughter who's a high school senior. I had her when she was little, too.

"The family was normal then, and Megan used to volunteer in the library, stacking books. She was fun to be around, always joking. I couldn't believe she was the same woman who stomped in yesterday, wearing a drudge dress down to her ankles. It was as if she's completely let herself go. Her hair is long and straggly, and she acted like she was on drugs or something. It was scary."

"What was her chief complaint?"

"That we had taken the real meaning out of the story of Christmas. That we were unaccepting of people who lived a true belief."

True belief. True Believers!

"What did you say her last name was, Ivy?"

"I didn't. It's Donovan, Megan Donovan. Why?"

Donovan. Could this be Amy Donovan's mother?

"Just wondering."

"Sure you are."

Ivy grinned but knew not to ask for more. She respected Nika's work and knew Nika would share what she could when she could.

Nika sipped her water. "Ivy, for once I wish I could

tell you about my job while it's happening. Please know you may have just helped me work out something that otherwise would have gone unnoticed until it's too late."

"Are you sure you're not in any danger with your current case? I mean, I know you're in danger all the time. But are you doing something more scary than usual? Whatever Megan Donovan is involved with, it's pretty frightening to make her go from a gal you and I would hang with, to some kind of religious wing nut."

Nika grinned. "I love the scary, and no, this isn't that interesting in terms of dangerous. Although, nowadays we have to be prepared for everything to turn dangerous, right?"

"Yes." Ivy sighed. "It used to be a lot simpler when I started teaching." She ate some more. "These plates are so cute. I love snowmen."

"I can't help myself at Christmastime." She'd set the table with snowman placemats and a snowman lamp glowed from the far kitchen counter.

"It's always so festive at your place. I love it. But, more importantly, what's with the big grin, Nika? Is there a handsome man involved in this secret case of yours who you haven't mentioned? Another guy you're going to love and leave?"

"Maybe. But he's way too high maintenance—he's brilliant, hot and probably has his share of women kissing his feet. And why would he go out with someone he had to see at work the next day? Besides, you know what happened the last time I got involved with someone I was also working with."

"You can't judge them all by one state trooper,

Nika." Ivy's expression bordered on pity and Nika cringed.

"It's not the job. It's the kind of guy. I don't need another alpha type in my life. I'm alpha enough!"

They both laughed and clinked their glasses.

The next day Nika made it a point to sit with several of the chemistry gang at lunchtime.

"Why are you coming to school if you don't have to?" Neel ate his sandwich as he asked her, his mouth full of wheat bread and lettuce. Nika hadn't missed the lack of manners with teenagers in her adult life.

"Yeah, if I were you, I'd stay home and goof off for the year. Or at least get a fun job until college starts next fall." Jeffrey spoke over a pile of nachos he'd topped with jalapeños.

The girls from the class stared at her, waiting for her to dish.

"First off, where I went to school before wasn't as competitive as here. We didn't have IB classes, and Mr. Everlock's letting me get caught up to where you are from last year. Besides." She did the shrug she'd practiced countless times for a moment just like this. "I, um, get lonely. I'm not a gamer and I'm not much into TV. Plus, my parents would kill me if I didn't come to school. They think there's always more to learn." Nika rolled her eyes and the girls laughed. *Phew!*

"They're right. There always is more." Ted, a tall, gangly boy with oily skin, pushed his glasses up his impossibly long nose. "They say that once we're in college we're going to realize how stupid we are." Nika watched the young man as he sat straighter and a slight blush ran up his neck and cheeks. "I think you're smart to keep coming to school."

"Dude, can you be any more obvious?" Donald Mather, the only student in the class who knew where he was going to college already thanks to early decision, slapped Ted on the back. He leaned in toward Nika. "What Ted's trying to say is that he wants to take you to the Silver Bells Ball. You know, he wants to ring your bell." The boys hooted and hollered while the girls at the table groaned. Ted turned several shades of coral.

Shit. She hadn't thought about the ramifications of looking the part of a student so well.

"This is kind of embarrassing, but where I was before, in Iowa, I went to all of our dances with a group of friends. My parents won't let me single date yet. They're old-fashioned." Geez, she wanted to roll her eyes again, but at herself. As if being a teenager once in a lifetime wasn't enough, she felt confused and unsure of her next step, just like she had ten years ago when she'd *really* been a senior. "Why don't we all go as a group? I mean, unless you all already have dates. Or is that how they do it here? Everyone has to have a date?"

Their response was immediate and positive. The girls blushed with excitement and the guys looked like they wanted to cheer at the suggestion.

"We'd rather go as a group. It's too intense when everyone pairs up. And this way we don't have to go matchy-matchy." Gabi spoke up. "It's such a pain in the ass to find the right color cummerbund to match a dress. Besides, we all wear black, right?"

"Yeah, who wants to get matching flowers?" Nika hoped she sounded logical.

"But we can still have wrist corsages and boutonnieres, right?" Rachel spoke quietly. "I like flowers."

Nika cleared her throat. "There's a great florist over on Main Street." The conversation stopped and the table grew very, very quiet as all eyes went to Nika.

Oh, boy.

She shrugged again, hoping she wasn't overplaying her signature teenager move. "My mother had to order flowers for a friend and we went into this shop. It's cool, kind of retro." Nika made a mental note to tell Rio to let his girlfriend and town florist, Kayla, know that Nika was the one responsible for an influx of last-minute dance orders.

At least she'd managed to get out of taking an underage boy to the dance. That's all she needed to report back to Bryce and Chief Todd.

Which brought her back to the legal but most inappropriate candidate for a relationship. The man she couldn't stop thinking about.

Mitch Everlock.

The following Monday, Nika decided to touch base with Mitch. They weren't officially working this case together as he wasn't in law enforcement. But she wanted him to know that she hadn't discounted him as a valuable resource in solving the case. It would take everyone they had to bring the Rainbow Hater down, especially if he turned out to be linked to the cult.

"That smells wonderful." Nika sniffed the delectable aroma of Mitch's coffee as she spoke with him in his small office in an annex off the lab. "I hope you don't mind that I'm stopping by. It's important to me that we connect."

"I don't disagree with that. And you're welcome to some." His eyes sparkled with interest as he nodded at the coffee. "I don't picture you as the black-coffee type."

"I am, but I do enjoy some real cream in it, too. I'd better not. I doubt a lot of students drink it that way. All I've seen them drink are very fancy, expensive lattes and other sugar concoctions."

"You're right, although I've had an odd one here or there who joined me in a mug of black. Go ahead, have some. We have a good half hour before any students show up." He leaned back in his chair and Nika absorbed the sight. Button-down shirt, khaki slacks and upscale comfortable shoes. She helped herself as directed.

"Thanks for not kicking me out of here this morning. I do need some extra help with my homework." They'd agreed that their "cover" whenever they had to get together to discuss the case would be that Nika needed some extra assignments, and perhaps some guidance as to where she should apply for college since she wanted to stay in Pennsylvania.

"What's up?"

"First, I want to apologize for assuming you didn't know what you were doing when the rock came through the window. You obviously have extensive training for dangerous situations."

"I do. But so do you, Nika. You would have been fine if I hadn't been around."

"But you were there, and you saved me from what could have been several nasty cuts or bruises." Maybe even a concussion.

"Apology accepted." He leaned forward, his elbows on his knees. "Nika, I owe you an apology, too. I assumed you weren't going to be able to pull this off. To me, you look like a grown woman, in the best way. But the students seem to have taken to you. They accept you as one of them."

"Have any of them said anything to you?" Her gut tightened. From concern over how well her undercover disguise was working, not any reaction to Mitch's compliment. She had to succeed at this op.

"Only Rachel." He lowered his voice. "She hasn't come in to see me outside of class since she started behaving differently. But she stopped by after class last week and said she's not sure having you in class is a good idea."

"Did she say why?"

"Only something vague about letting in new students who didn't even need the class. Said her mother had the concern, not her. But since then, I've noticed she's spending more time with you in and after class. Is this true?"

Nika nodded. "Have you met her parents?"

"Yes, last year at open house, but I barely remember them. Since Rachel's always been a good student, there was no need to see them since. They didn't come in this year, though." He looked thoughtful.

"What are you thinking, Mitch?"

"I could be way off, but I've had students here and there who are from very strict families, who aren't allowed to be real teenagers. I worry most about them, actually. Because no matter how well they do academically, there are certain rites of passage that need to happen in high school to help the kids go on to survive in college, or wherever they go next."

"And you think Rachel's from one of these families?"

"Hard to tell. She has older siblings, but they're in college or living away. It's just her and her parents, as far as I know."

"Do you have any reason to think she's in danger?"

"No, but if her family's fallen in with that crazy cult, it would explain her sudden lack of enthusiasm about schoolwork and extracurriculars. She used to be a more active part of the Rainbows but hasn't participated much since the end of last semester, last spring."

"What cult are you talking about?" Nika thought that while the general public might know a bit about the former True Believers Cult members showing up in Silver Valley, the SVPD was working closely with the media to make sure the most important details of the case against the True Believers were kept out of the spotlight.

Was Mitch blushing? Not for the first time she had to wonder if he was *only* a chemistry teacher.

"The one that they think might have been partially responsible for the church fire last Christmas, and the huge takedown that happened at Mayor Charbonneau's daughter's wedding." He looked directly at her as he spoke.

He was telling her the truth, per se, but her gut never proved incorrect. Mitch knew more than he was telling.

She'd let it go, for now.

"Yes, well, that's a scary thought. That a girl you knew as a bright, confident student is suddenly under the thumb of controlling parents, who might be connected to a dangerous group. Do we know if her parents have actually had contact with the cult?" She didn't want to reveal anything she knew to Mitch. Not yet. Even with his military background, he was still a civilian and didn't need to know everything.

"Again, no. I have no idea about her family."

He leaned back and touched the holiday lights strung around his desk. "Tell me something, Nika. I appreciate that you're dedicated to your job, and that you no doubt always get your man. But you seem really, really intense about this. As if it's personal. Is there something you haven't told me about this case? Have you been affected by this group of wackos?"

She shook her head. "No, no. It's not that." She looked into her coffee before she faced him squarely. "The deal is that I'm first-generation Polish American. My mother and father came over right after the Berlin Wall came down. They had nothing, just the clothes on their backs. They were political refugees. They'd fought against tyrants and an oppressive system that essentially brainwashed its citizens to believe its lies. Granted, the True Believers Cult is much smaller, but if we can save one child, one family, from suffering, and help get those bastards, it's worth it, right?"

"Getting the bad guy is always worth it, yes."

He had a pained expression on his face but again she didn't feel she knew him well enough to push it.

But she wanted to. She wanted to know more about Mitch than she had any business to.

"Hey, Mr. Everlock!" Neel faltered when he spotted Nika sitting in the office, his bright red sweatshirt emblazoned with the face of a red-nosed reindeer.

"Good morning, Neel. What can I do you for?"

Nika smiled at Neel. "Um, we're done here, Neel. Mr. Everlock just gave me a list of universities a mile long. I had no idea there were so many places I could major in chemistry just in Pennsylvania! See you in class." She bolted for the door. And prayed that it was what any other high school student would do, and that her being in Mitch's office so early wouldn't draw attention to her.

Chapter 5

The next several days were like any other school day, save for Nika trying to comprehend all that had changed since she'd wandered these same halls over a decade ago. Gone were the blatant Christmas decorations, replaced by generic wintery lights and garland. One hallway of the large school had tables and bulletin boards dedicated to the several different holidays celebrated by students this time of year, including Hanukkah, Kwanza and Christmas. What hadn't changed was the fun air of expectation—a long school break was near, and the big dance would put an exclamation point on the anticipation.

When the bell rang after each class, Nika did her best to look like all of the other kids fighting to get to their lockers, change out books and report in to their next class. All in four minutes. With a high school as large as SVHS she wondered how any of the students ever made it to class on time. How had she done it?

Since she was only interested in Mitch's class for the case, and the other kids thought she was doing special assignments for Mitch, she was spared the genuine worry of making it to class on time. It would have been a nightmare, because if she were late she'd bring attention to herself. Every extra bit of attention was a risk at being discovered.

Each time a kid or teacher looked at her funny, she worried they were going to shout out, "Hey, aren't you a cop?" or "Didn't you give me a parking ticket last month?"

Her second Thursday at Silver Valley High she was on her way to Mitch's classroom when she realized she needed to use the restroom. She ducked into the nearest bathroom and smacked into a woman dressed in yoga pants, a polo shirt with the school's mascot emblazoned above her left breast, and a referee whistle.

Kristine Rattner, one of the high school's four physical education teachers. Kristine had graduated with Nika. *Please don't let her recognize me.* Kristine had been the girl Nika had wished she could be back in school. A cheerleader, her classmate had always been perfectly made-up, and a cute-boy magnet.

"Excuse me, young lady. Don't be late for class." The leggy blonde crossed her arms in front of her and Nika looked away. *Crap.* This was too close for comfort.

Recognize her? She'd never even noticed her all those years ago.

"No, ma'am. I have a pass." She held up the pass

she'd obtained from the principal when she'd started to prepare to go undercover. Other than Mitch, Principal Essis was the only person in SVHS who knew Nika was an SVPD officer.

"What grade are you in?"

"I'm a new transfer senior."

"I thought so. I don't recognize you. I've had all of the senior class at least once since they were freshmen. Where are you from?"

"My family just moved here from Iowa."

"Huh. You look familiar. Do you have cousins who went here?" Kristine stared at her and Nika did her best impression of a distracted teen, refusing to meet her eyes.

"No." She made a show of shaking her leg. "I have to go really bad."

"Very well."

Nika locked herself in a stall, grateful for the small but significant barrier.

Apparently she'd done a good job of reassimilating into a teenaged population. Maybe too good. Did Mitch think she looked like the mousy teen she'd been?

Get over it.

The bathroom was empty as she washed her hands and checked the makeup she'd carefully applied this morning. No, there was no reason Kristine would remember her from ten years ago. She'd never worn makeup as a student, and she'd been much meeker around teachers back in the day.

Heading back into the hall she hoped this last class period would go more quickly than the last seven. Being a high school student again was exhausting.

* * *

"You really like the Rainbows, huh?" Nika hoped she kept her expression as neutral as possible. Rachel was the smartest kid in the senior class, according to Mitch. Which made Nika all the more determined to get to the source of Rachel's misery and discontent.

"Yeah." Rachel didn't bat an eye as they sat across from one another in the back corner of Mitch's classroom, where he'd set up a sofa and two easy chairs. She'd noticed that during the chemistry classes he allowed some of the students to sit here if they preferred, as long as they continued to actively participate in class. It made a great place for students to hang out after school.

The last bell had rung and other Rainbows members were straggling into the room, many of them with heavy backpacks.

Mitch had told her that while not all of the Rainbows identified as LGBT, many of the members were interested in showing support for their friends or family members who were. So she figured she could join the club without it raising any suspicion. So far no one had questioned her about her attendance at the meetings.

"Hey, everyone. Shane and Erika should be here shortly—they have the funds to get pizza and sodas from the cafeteria. Jon, do you want to go ahead and open the meeting for us?"

"Sure, Mr. Everlock." Jon, a tall boy with a crew cut and Philadelphia Eagles sweatshirt slid into a desk positioned to face the group of approximately twenty-two kids. Nika had counted. She figured in a school of almost two thousand kids, this was a good turnout.

"Last month we voted to use our treasury to host a welcome party for any transfer students in January. We have a month left to plan but first we have a new item that we need to take care of. As you know, all the Silver Valley clubs and sports teams are eligible to host a table at the Silver Bells Ball, to help raise money for charity. Like last year, the school has voted to raise money for the US Marine Corps Toys for Tots campaign. It's a good cause. But we have to raise the money to pay for the table rental. Does anyone have any ideas on how we can raise this money, and is anyone willing to be on the committee for it? Any volunteers?" Jon spoke like he'd been leading groups his whole life. Nika didn't think she'd ever been so together in high school.

"I'll take care of the decorations." A girl with hair dyed black with purple tips raised her hand.

"Okay, thanks Trish, that's great. But first we need to know what we'll sell, and when. Anyone else?"

"I can pick up supplies. I need someone to give me a list, though." The boy who hardly spoke in chemistry class smiled.

Nika watched as students who'd shuffled into the room perked up as the hour went by and they planned for the Silver Bells Ball. Mitch stayed in the background, sitting on a stool at the lab counter. He had his shirtsleeves rolled up, exposing well-defined forearms. She forced herself to look away, only to meet Rachel's astute gaze.

"Do you have a thing for Mr. Everlock?" Rachel's

query sounded more like an accusation and alarm bells jangled in Nika's mind.

"No, of course not. That's just wrong." She affected the disgusted posture she'd practiced.

"Then stop staring at him." Rachel's voice was quiet so the rest of the group wouldn't hear her, but it had a steely tone Nika hadn't noticed before.

"What's wrong, Rachel?"

The girl stared at Nika, her eyes flat and disconnected. A chill went down Nika's spine. Had Rachel been tested for mental illness?

"Nothing you'd understand."

"Try me."

They proved to be the smartest two words Nika had used so far in her stint as a teenager.

"I used to be nicer, you know. I was involved in more things, and I looked forward to school every day."

"And now?"

"Now all I do is dread when I have to go back home and deal with my dipshit mother again." Rachel sucked water out of her refillable sports bottle. "She's lost her mind. Church was always important to her, but since she started doing these book studies with the New Thoughts she's been like a crazy woman." Rachel made air quotes around New Thoughts. "Yesterday she actually told me that she believes if we don't listen to some old guy she met, we're all going to end up in hell. She's fixated on doing whatever he says, reading whatever he tells her to."

"What about your dad?"

"He left us, and town, months ago. I have an older sister and brother, too, but they've left home. Everyone thinks I'm having a great time, being spoiled by my mother."

"And you're not."

"Not at all. She's changed too much for that."

"Why don't you two ladies pay attention and help us out? Want to share what you're talking about?" Mitch spoke up from his seat and Nika wanted to tell him to shut the hell up. Of course, he had no idea that Rachel had all but given Nika what she'd been looking for.

A connection to the True Believers and the hate crimes against the Rainbows.

Mitch could only ignore Rachel and Nika's low murmurs for so long. He had to play along and treat Nika as any other student. They couldn't risk blowing her cover under any circumstances. Nika's angry eyes looked like the flame when germanium was burned. The palest blue, but bright enough to resemble the silver-white heat from aluminum's flame. He'd prefer to see her eyes lit with heat that he caused, but right now her glare was glacial.

"We were figuring out when to meet to make cookies for the newcomer event." Rachel saved them both. Interesting.

"In my old school we did bake sales all the time to fund-raise. Can we do it here at SVHS? To raise money for the table rental at the Silver Bells Ball?" Nika smiled, her student persona perfected.

"You only have a week to do it. What do you say, everybody?" While Mitch was the teacher representative for the club, he didn't run it. That was up to the kids.

"The other clubs hold all kinds of fund-raisers. Anybody got a better idea?" Jon took the reins back.

"Sounds good to me."

"Good idea."

"I'll go to Costco and bring in some muffins to sell. You know, those huge, ginormous chocolate ones?"

"We can sell as soon as we get permission from the school administration, in the lobby during lunch, and before school." So many club members spoke at once that Jon had to tell them to repeat their statements for the group secretary, whose fingers were flying over her tablet computer's portable keyboard.

The club went on to decide the details for the bake sales and then, thinking optimistically, what they'd want to give away at the dance with any extra money earned. Mitch avoided staring at Nika, but just barely. She was sending off vibes she had to be aware of, even if the kids didn't notice. Didn't she realize how hot she was in that tight T-shirt and those smokin' leggings? She'd obviously checked out the school dress code, because nothing was outside of the fairly strict rules. But, like any other teen girl, she was playing very close to the lines. As if she wasn't aware of the power of her sexuality yet.

But Nika knew damned well the effect she could have. So did Mitch's dick.

As soon as the group cleared, he watched Nika walk out with Rachel and felt a pang of disappointment.

It's a case, jarhead. Let her do her job.

He hadn't been this hot for a woman since…since he couldn't even remember when.

* * *

Nika dialed Bryce's number as she prepared to head to Rachel's house after school.

"I'm going over to her house in ten minutes." Nika spoke to Bryce from her mother's car.

"Be careful. Are you sure she's not on to you?"

"Not at all. At least, I don't think so. We're going to bake cookies for the Rainbows bake sale, to raise money for the Silver Bells Ball. She says her mother's into cooking and baking, and they have lots of ingredients on hand."

"Won't her mother take issue with you baking cookies for the club that supports LGBT kids?"

"No, Rachel supposedly told her that it was for the school dance and Toys for Tots, never saying anything about the Rainbows."

"Okay, well, check back as soon as you leave her house."

"Will do."

She put the small SUV into gear and drove. As she made her way through Silver Valley toward its outskirts she thought about how surprised Mitch had looked when she'd glared at him. That was too funny. Of course, she'd almost blown it by laughing at him. That would have made it harder for their cover story that she was interested in a career in chemistry and Mitch was her mentor of sorts.

In reality she'd never allow a man like Mitch be a mentor, or more, to her. Her inherent mistrust of military men, from her parents' lifelong issues with military authority, was one reason. The other reason was that she'd learned early in her career to not get involved during a case. Those relationships often ended once the fuel of the threat of danger was depleted. And made future work together incredibly uncomfortable.

There's more. You don't trust him.

She couldn't trust him, not yet. She didn't know him well enough to gauge his trustworthiness. He was honorable and had proved it by protecting her from the thrown rock. But the way he and Bryce had conversed, she'd felt shut out. Exactly how her parents described living in Soviet times. As if there was a big secret and she wasn't part of it. It only added to her deeply imbedded mistrust of men in positions of power, and how easy it was to cut women out of important decision making, intentional or not. And, in all truth, it reminded her of how deeply she'd fallen for Ron, believing he'd accept her career as something she needed and wanted, not something she'd throw away once they were married.

Mitch's job as a teacher didn't intimidate her, but his past left her feeling less certain. He'd been a US Marine during wartime. Special Forces. That was heavy duty. There was more to Mitch than met the eye, and Nika had enough work keeping herself on track and happy. Adding a man to the equation, especially one as complex as Mitch, was overwhelming.

Nika was sick of the men she hooked up with being threatened by her job. For once she wanted a relationship with someone who wouldn't compete with her. She wanted a man who wouldn't require huge amounts of work and energy when she was at the end of a long shift. Was that too selfish?

"In eight hundred feet, turn left." Her GPS jolted

her back to reality and she looked for the name of the road Rachel had given her.

Turning onto the blacktopped street, she was dismayed when it turned into a gravel road. At least it hadn't snowed, so her mother's practical SUV traversed it okay. She pulled up at the end of the "street," where a modern-looking ranch house with a steep roof and round attic windows perched on a slight ridge.

It looked menacing in the fading December light. No porch or indoor lights appeared to be on, but it was definitely the address Rachel had given her. Single electric candles were visible in each front window, a typical decoration in many homes in central Pennsylvania. The window candles were a sign of welcome, a holdover from a century ago when Pennsylvania Dutch culture had thrived in the area. But, like the rest of the lights surrounding the property, they weren't lit, either.

"So much for Pennsylvania Dutch hospitality," she muttered to herself as she got out and slammed the car's door. She almost jumped when she saw the lace curtain of the far right window move to the side a few inches. She couldn't make out a person but she knew she was being watched.

Nika walked up the middle path to the front door and before she rang the bell the door popped open.

"You found it. Welcome to purgatory." Rachel stood in stockinged feet as she deadpanned her quiet greeting.

"Yeah, the drive up here was a little crazy, especially in my mom's car." Staying as close to the truth as possible in her story kept being undercover much simpler.

Rachel craned her neck to see the vehicle. "You don't have your own?"

Nika shook her head. "With the move from Iowa and all, it was too expensive to get a car, especially since we don't know for sure where I'm going to college. If I go to Temple or Drexel, I won't need a car, you know? In Philadelphia?" She hated speaking in questions but it was how the kids did it.

"Rachel, who's at the door?" A woman's voice called out from the darkness behind Rachel.

"Just a friend, Mom." Rachel turned back to Nika. "Come on in, and remember, my mother is bat-shit cray-cray."

Nika entered a polished wood-floored hallway and immediately sensed the lack of warmth. It felt colder than outside. "Is your heater on?"

Rachel shook her head. "We haven't used it since Mom decided we should only use our woodstove. She hasn't ordered the cord of wood we need for the winter yet. She says I should be out collecting twigs to make sure we can always get a fire going in the woodstove. It's all her nutso-survivalist crap." She lowered her voice to a whisper as she motioned for Nika to follow her into the kitchen.

"Hello." A tall, skinny woman sat at a round table in a nook in the far corner, her eyes huge and buglike behind rimless glasses.

"Hi. I'm Nika." She gave Rachel's mother the typical teen mini wave.

"I'm Belinda Boyle. I'm sure Rachel's complained to you about me." Dry skin that flaked on her nose and around her lips stretched across what Nika thought had once been a pretty face. Beautiful, even. The flatness in her eyes and stilted manner in which she spoke was unnerving. No question, this was a woman who'd lost touch with herself and maybe even reality. Nika had seen it with compulsive shoplifters, gamblers, drug addicts and alcoholics. Rachel might be right—her mother might very well be addicted to the sick liturgy of Leonard Wise and his cult.

"Drop it, Mother."

"Don't speak to me with such disrespect, Rachel."

Nika knew a teen would be uncomfortable in such a situation so she tried to look pained when in reality she was eager to find out what was causing the friction between the two. And it wouldn't be so awful if Belinda Boyle came a little unhinged and revealed some of the cult tactics.

"We're baking cookies, Mom. Would you like to join us? We're going to talk about boys."

"Very funny." Still, Rachel got her way as Mrs. Boyle stood and gathered the books and notebook in front of her. "I'm going up to my room to continue my studies. Dinner will be at six." With that, the spindly woman was gone, her back stiff as she exited the room.

Nika waited until she heard footsteps above them. "Wow, is she always that formal?"

Rachel huffed. "'Formal' isn't the word I'd use. 'Zombified' is more like it."

"Is it since your dad and she divorced?"

"I didn't say they divorced, although they're headed there. Dad left for Pittsburgh last summer and hasn't been back. He invites me to dinner when he's in town on business, wants to spend time together."

"But?"

Rachel waved her hands. "Whatever's he's doing with work in Pittsburgh is more important than checking in on me. Except when it's convenient for him." Rachel shrugged. "It's not a big deal. I'm used to being on my own since my brothers and sisters are so much older and have families of their own."

"But he left you here knowing that your mother was losing it?"

Nika watched as pride warred with bare need in Rachel's expression.

In that moment Nika knew she'd do whatever she could to make Rachel's life easier.

Chapter 6

Rachel slammed down a cookie pan. "I don't want to have anything to do with my father. He left me here with her and, yes, she's nuts. Probably even certifiable. He wanted to take her to some kind of psycho intervention. You know, to make her see that she's lost it, that she's being brainwashed by these crazy people. But she wouldn't go to any kind of counseling, so he left. I could have gone with him but it's my senior year and I didn't want to have to change schools. I don't know how you did it, Nika. Plus, I don't want to leave her alone. Mom drives me crazy but she's so, so vulnerable, you know?"

Nika fought to not embrace Rachel in a reassuring hug. It wasn't something a teen would necessarily do, and she didn't know how much Rachel knew about the True Believers. How they'd reformed as the

New Thought ministry. Only SVPD and a handful of federal agencies like the FBI knew how deadly the True Believers were.

"You're a good daughter."

"Or a very stupid one."

"What about when you go to college? You're going to go to college, right?"

Rachel pulled out flour and chocolate chips. "I wanted to apply to Johns Hopkins. I have the grades and SAT scores, and I wanted premed. But with mom so sick, and now that my father left, I can't just leave her, you know?"

"Why not? Maybe if you leave she'll figure out that what she's doing is crazy. You know, like letting an addict hit their bottom."

Rachel shook her head so hard Nika thought she'd sprain her neck. "No. She's under their spell and until she breaks free of it, she has no one but me. She's cut off her sisters, her whole family. No one wants to talk to her after this summer, anyhow."

"What happened this summer?"

"She made a big speech at our family's—her family's—Fourth of July picnic. We all get together and go up to a lake in the Poconos, where we have a cabin. She told everyone that they were going to burn in hell if they didn't start learning about the New Thought process and change their ways. Said we all need to start stockpiling and preparing for a long drought of food and living supplies."

Rachel rolled her eyes. "That's why she won't run the gas heat. The woodstove is all we can use. She lets us use the kitchen stove and oven only because she thinks it's close enough to how the woodstove works." Rachel stopped pulling supplies out of cabinets and stared at Nika. "Do you see why I'm so tired all the time? I've got a lot going on here."

"Do you have aunts or uncles who could help you?"

"Sure, but they all have their own kids to raise, and they're too far away. I know it's selfish but I want to finish high school in the same place I started it." Rachel's eyes shone with a determination that Nika knew would serve her well through life. It was heartbreaking that she'd had to channel it so soon, though.

"Why don't you ask someone at school for help, Rachel? One of the counselors, Principal Essis or even Mr. Everlock?"

"Are you kidding? The last thing I need is for the authorities to come up here and haul my mom away. It will only convince her that she's right—she thinks the police are the faces of the devil. I'm eighteen, so legally I can live on my own, but my father would insist I come live with him, and like I said, he's four hours away in Pittsburgh. I don't want the hassle of moving."

"I get it." Well, Nika didn't get the "police being evil" part. But she understood something about Rachel that Rachel didn't even comprehend. Rachel scarily reminded Nika of herself. She cared too much, to the point of making herself suffer from the bad choices others made.

"No offense, Nika, but I don't think you could get it at all. Your parents are together and they're not being brainwashed by some scary group, are they?" Rachel smiled, showing a sense of humor that made Nika again want to hug her.

"You're right, but my family did survive the Soviets. My grandparents and parents came over here right after the Berlin Wall came down. I've been told all my life to never trust the government." This was all true. As was the fact she was now a part of the government. But that wasn't something she'd tell Rachel, at least not now.

Nika vowed to help Rachel after this case was solved. No teen should have to suffer because of this damned cult. If she could put Leonard Wise behind bars right this minute, she would. But it wouldn't be enough.

The entire cult had to be brought down.

"Where's the bathroom? I drank a latte on the way here." The kids were all drinking specialty drinks in the high school, so Nika thought it was a plausible excuse to get out of Rachel's kitchen.

"Down the hall, to the left." Rachel was focused on not burning the batch of Christmas cutout cookies they'd put in the oven. They'd stamped out dozens of snowmen and snowflakes.

Nika walked down the hall, turned on the bathroom light and vent, and then kept walking. In the living room she found piles of brochures and cheaply printed books. The books were printed on bright white paper, not unlike copy paper, and sported glaringly glossy covers with titles like *What the Government Won't Tell You*, *How to Live Off-Grid and On Your Own* and *Survival Basics in the Apocalypse*. All authored by Leonard Wise. They were awful and inflammatory but there was nothing that indicated criminal wrongdoing. She put the pile the way she'd found it, needing to get back to the kitchen. Her gaze landed on a book she'd initially missed and she froze.

New Thought Basics: The Best Years for Family. Skimming the table of contents, her gut twisted as she read the beginnings of the first chapter.

"'It's preferable to have girls live in community with the entire family after their menses has started. This keeps them intact until they are able to serve the highest purpose.'"

The twisted rhetoric was the same that the True Believers had spouted twenty years ago. When Zora Krasny had been a brave little twelve-year-old and broken free of the cult.

Nika felt immediate revulsion and elation. Repulsed by the words and the psychologically ill person who wrote them; sickened by the evil the words lent themselves to. Elated that she was holding proof of the sick bastard's plan.

Leonard Wise was planning again to start his own "nation" of perfect children, this time in Silver Valley. She pulled out her phone and took as many photos of the leaflets and books that she could, especially of any pages that would prove Wise was planning criminal activity. Or worse, already involved in it. If she thought she could take the books and not be noticed, she would, but it wasn't doable, not if she wanted to remain undercover for the next few weeks.

Putting her phone away, she reached for the book with the most incriminating title: *Why New Thought Survives Hostile Law Enforcement.*

"Nika?" Rachel stood at the edge of the living room, staring at her.

* * *

Nika wasn't sure how she'd done it but she'd managed to convince Rachel that she'd been interested in the Silver Valley weekly paper that had caught her eye as she'd peeked into the living room.

"I saw the Beauty Is Us ad and wanted to see if there's a coupon. My mom threw ours out before I had a chance to cut it out."

"You shop at Beauty Is Us?" Rachel's sweeping, dismissive assessment of Nika's appearance could be interpreted as hurtful but Nika wasn't feeling anything more than relief that she'd wiggled out of a tight spot. She'd narrowly missed blowing her cover.

"For mascara and skin cream." It was obvious she wasn't wearing any other cosmetics. She'd toned down her everyday makeup to look more like a teen than a twenty-eight-year-old.

"We used to go there, mom and I." Rachel turned and went into the kitchen, and Nika followed. "But since she's gone hard-core on this group, and dad left, there isn't any extra money for things like makeup." Or clothes, or shoes, judging from how threadbare Rachel's outfits were at school. Today she wore an old, faded sweatshirt with tired leggings and ratty slippers. Nika made a mental note to get Rachel a gift certificate to the consignment store favored by the teens. The one with all of the latest fashions and brand names, gently used and more affordable.

But it would have to be after the case was closed, when hopefully Rachel had a semblance of a normal life back. Nika wasn't sure how she'd help make it all happen but she would. Rachel deserved more than this.

Nika worked alongside Rachel for the next hour, until they had several dozen cookies baked, cooled and sealed into storage bags. "Do you want me to put these in your freezer?"

Rachel scowled. "No, I'll do it. No telling what kind of crap you'd have to dig through in either of the chest freezers to make room for these." She didn't elaborate and Nika left it alone. She'd gotten more than she'd expected from her time in Rachel's house.

"Okay, well, I've got to head out now. My mom needs the car back for her book group tonight." The lie came easily off her lips for the sake of the case. What concerned Nika was afterward—she wanted Rachel to be able to trust her, to rely on her for what promised to be a difficult adjustment once the cult was apprehended and her mother sent to a mental hospital.

"Thanks for coming over. I'll see you at school."

As Nika drove away from Rachel's she took note of her surroundings, and not just in the usual manner dictated by her police training. The dark night was ominous and suffocating under the tall trees that lined the driveway. She'd seen most of Silver Valley, or so she'd thought, on her many patrols over the years. What was frightening about the Boyle home was that it had been purposefully let go; it was run-down from choice. This was the effect of a different kind of addiction than Nika was used to seeing: a dependence on a sick message from a twisted mind.

She wasn't a psychoanalyst but Nika knew one thing for sure: the sooner Rachel was away from her mother and the New Thought's cunning tactics, the better.

* * *

"I know you said to keep this in the hands of SVPD, and no offense to you, Colt, but I think we'd all benefit if you'd let me handle this from a Trail Hikers' perspective. We'd certainly wrap it up more quickly." Mitch addressed the SVPD Chief of Police Colt Todd and their Trail Hikers' boss, Claudia, as they sat in Colt's office. Mitch could tell that he wasn't getting anywhere with Todd or Claudia, but he had to keep pressing his point. The safety of his students depended on it.

Bullshit. You're worried about Nika, too.

"Can I have a little more hot water, Colt?" Claudia stretched her arm out to hand him her mug.

"Sure. Here you go." The police chief reached for the carafe of water and leaned over his desk to meet Claudia halfway, filling her cup. "You like my new tea?" Colt and Claudia's eyes met and Mitch bit back the urge to tell them to get a room.

Hell.

Sitting cross-legged with his foot on his knee, Mitch stretched his neck and tried to stop shaking his foot. They'd decided to meet at the station as it was a good cover for Mitch. No one would bat an eye at the chemistry teacher showing up after he'd had a rock thrown through his classroom window. Claudia was in and out of the station on an almost daily basis and had been given the cover job of SVPD Social Media Director, or as Colt referred to it, Facebook guru. SVPD had its own Facebook and Twitter accounts, and now Claudia was working with local community college students she'd recruited for internships to establish a Snapchat account. Anything to keep abreast of the modern world and tap into the word on the street.

More like the word in the cloud.

Claudia was dressed down for Claudia, which meant she was in a spotless business suit complete with four-inch heels. Mitch watched how she sat back down, how the blush in her cheeks contrasted prettily with her silver hair. Mitch knew the chief was more than interested in his TH boss, and while he didn't blame him, he really didn't want to know the details, either.

"'Your' tea, Colt? Did you pick the leaves yourself?"

Colt grinned. "It's a special blend of jasmine, lavender and green. I added some cinnamon for a Christmas taste."

Mitch couldn't stand it.

"Look, can we get to the bottom of our issues? I'm convinced there's a lot more than a disgruntled student harassing me. Do you think it's possible that the cult somehow knows about TH?"

"No." Colt and Claudia spoke in unison.

"Has something got you worked up, son?" Colt Todd's eyes were on him.

"Nika was going over to Rachel's—the student from class—house after school today. To bake cookies for the LGBT club fund-raiser. Rachel's the one with the mother who's gone a bit overboard with the cult. She could be our way in." He looked at his watch. "I thought we'd hear back from her by now. Or that Bryce would hear back." He looked at Claudia, hoping she'd finally see a way to let him into this as more than an observer.

"You're concerned about Nika Pasczenko." Claudia didn't miss a damn thing.

Neither did Colt. "I can vouch for Nika, Mitch. She's one of the finest officers on SVPD, and she knows how to run an undercover op better than most."

"Yeah, but she's all there is to this undercover op. No backup. You don't even have her wired, am I right?"

Colt held up his hands, palms up. "Whoa. This isn't high risk, not yet. Nika will call in the minute anything hints of an escalation or potential for danger."

"I call a rock smashing through a classroom window dangerous. Definitely escalation after the previous threats being notes. How do we know the thrower wasn't aiming for Nika? That someone knows she's working undercover?" He tried to keep a lid on his angst but was finding it increasingly difficult as all he got from Colt and Claudia was nonreaction. Didn't they see how quickly a situation with the cult could become volatile?

"You know yourself how careful we are with our specific roles, Mitch. I'm sure no one suspects Nika of being undercover—yet." Claudia clucked as if she were his mother and not a Marine who'd had the same training he had.

"Trust me, Mitch, Nika's taking every precaution to stay safe. Look around you. Everyone in this station thinks you're here about the message in blood on your classroom SMART Board and the rock. They have no clue that you're anything but a Silver Valley High chemistry teacher. Hell, do you even tell anyone about your Marine Corps experience?"

Mitch grimaced. "No. Although I told Nika."

He saw Claudia's eyes narrow and inwardly groaned.

"Mitch, have you been having more of your PTSD symptoms?" Only Claudia could be so direct.

"To be honest, yeah, I had a little one right after the last blood message."

"The rock didn't trigger anything?"

"No, not at all." As he said it he realized that no, he hadn't had any reaction to the shattering window. His only instinct had been to protect Nika.

"It sounds like you're doing much, much better. Except for maybe being a bit overly concerned about Officer Pasczenko." Claudia sipped her tea, trying to hide her grin. Her casual posture didn't fool him.

"I am doing better. Much."

"Several of my officers have dealt with the same thing, as so many of them are vets like you, Mitch." Colt leaned forward. "If you'd like to talk to any of them, I'm happy to put you in touch."

"I'm okay for now. It's not pleasant, as you know, but it's manageable at this point." He was so damned grateful Claudia had still taken him on for TH, despite his lingering symptoms. She'd sought him out shortly after he'd settled in Silver Valley.

"You misunderstand me, Mitch. I mean that I'd like you to talk to my officers who aren't as far along in their healing as you."

Mitch grimaced. "You caught me, thinking it was all about me. Of course I'll talk to them, anytime. Please pass along my number." God, he'd been so focused on Nika and the case that he'd missed Colt's backhanded compliment.

He straightened and cleared his throat. "Since you two don't want to entertain TH coming into the school op, let me ask you—does Nika know anything about TH?"

Colt shook his head. "The only officers who know about TH are the ones who are TH agents. They have to be read into the program to have a clue about it." Colt shrugged. "That said, SVPD isn't *that* large and our team is close-knit. I'm sure several of the officers have thoughts on some of what they see, but they're law-enforcement pros. They know that each op in Silver Valley is need to know. Hell, when our cases involve FBI, ATF or Homeland Security we only inform the officers working on the case, not the whole department."

A quick rap on Todd's door was followed by it opening. Nika's head appeared. "Oh, sorry, Chief. I'll come back later."

"No, no, come on in, Nika." Colt shot Mitch a glance that said "See, she won't ask about TH. She doesn't even know about TH."

Claudia, for her part, remained the picture of poise. He was relieved neither of them mentioned his concern over Nika's welfare. Mitch had to shove down the inexplicable urge to pump his fist in the air, he was so relieved to see Nika.

"What can I do you for, Nika?"

"Hi, Mitch, Claudia." Nika nodded to each before she focused on Colt. "I'm getting ready to go home for the night but I wanted to let you know that I've made some headway on the high school case. Bryce isn't in his office—I thought he'd be here. I just left

Rachel Boyle's house and I've collected some evidence." She cast a quick look at Claudia, then Colt.

"Bryce cut out early to attend to some wedding issues. It's okay to talk about the case in front of all of us. Claudia's cut in on the high school case. She has to be—the kids are using social media more than anything else to communicate. We need her eyes on what they're posting on the school Facebook page."

Claudia grinned. "Actually it's Snapchat that we're following, but the concept's the same. Just a smaller window to see what's going on."

Nika nodded. "Okay." She gave Mitch a small smile as she slid onto the tiny leather sofa in the corner of the office. Her glance cut through Mitch as she met his and he had a hard time playing the platonic colleague. Her hair was in a straight, shoulder-skimming bob, not styled up in an easy, simple ponytail like it was when she was Nika the Student. She'd traded her teen clothes for dark jeans and a formfitting charcoal turtleneck that emphasized her most unteenaged figure. Her breasts were...holy cow. Mitch's fingers had itched to touch her hair, make her straight locks messy, but now all he could think about was holding those ample breasts. Sucking on her nipples...

Crap. He was in too deep. And they'd only met last week.

Chapter 7

The glint in Nika's eyes conveyed her similar response and the rueful twist to Nika's smile told Mitch she was on to him. She looked away and took a deep breath.

"Rachel's started to confide in me. Not as much as we need, but it's a start. She's not at all happy with her family. It seems her father is pretty absent since he left them last summer, and her mother is going off the rails with her religious fervor. I spent the last couple of hours at her house, and met her mother. That's one strange woman, let me tell you."

"Explain 'religious fervor.'" Colt spoke.

"It's not just Bible study or church services, or even a church youth group. A lot of teens fight their parents at some point about things like that. This is different. Her mother is involved in the New Thought

ministries. Have you heard of it? She's insisting that
Rachel study about natural herbs and medicinal rem-
edies. Says they need to prepare for the 'big change'
to come, that they're going to need a well-stocked
pantry."

"We've all learned to keep a stocked pantry after
the past several winters. What is she saying that's
concerning you, Nika?" Claudia spoke quietly, almost
casually, but Mitch knew Claudia missed nothing.

Nika leaned back on the sofa, her arms on the back
of it and her heel propped on her knee, mirroring his
posture. It accentuated her trim waist and sexy hips.
Mitch bit back a groan and forced his eyes to stay
steady on Nika's face. If he looked at her breasts or
hips again, he'd be hard-pressed to keep from acting
out his attraction to her the next time they were alone.

*Who are you kidding? You'd love to be alone with
her.*

If they weren't involved in a case together, sure.

"What's different is the amount of time that's being
spent on it. Rachel reports that her mother comes up
with these long lists of supplies they'll need. They
took care of the basic foodstuffs two months ago.
Now the focus is on preparing their basement for
habitation."

"She told you this, in those exact words?"

"She's been pretty open about having to follow
some kind of rule book that her mother is going by."
Nika air-quoted "rule."

How had he never noticed her long, graceful arms
before?

"Any chance you could get a copy of that from

her?" Claudia put her empty mug behind her on Colt's desk and pulled out her phone.

Nika grinned. "I couldn't lift a copy from their living room but I did the next best thing." She waved her phone at them. "If you open up the forensics file I emailed you, we can all look at the photos I took. I couldn't take the pamphlets—it would have been too obvious. They don't get a lot of visitors from what Rachel's said."

Colt wasted no time opening the correct files on the SVPD system. He turned his monitor around so that they could all see the photos.

"The book about young women—still minors— being the perfect age to bear children in the New Thought family is going to give me nightmares." Nika pointed to the exact places where Leonard Wise's dogma was printed.

"We'll get these bastards." Claudia's voice was steady but her knuckles were white as she clasped her hands together.

"Yes, we will." Colt spoke with conviction. "Nika, how is Rachel taking these demands from her mother? Does she seem to agree with any of it?"

Nika shook her head. "Not at all. If anything, she is biding her time until she can leave for college. Or, at least, she *was* planning for college. But now she's truly worried about her mother's emotional and mental state. Since her father took off she feels responsible for her mother's welfare, odd as it sounds." It wasn't odd to anyone who'd served on the force. Kids with alcoholic or heroin-addicted parents stepped up and took over adult roles as a matter of course. Rachel was no different; her mother's addiction was the cult.

Colt sighed deeply. "That's a damn heavy load for a kid to shoulder. It sounds like her mother needs to be in a psych facility. What about Rachel? Do you think you'll be able to get her to open up more, maybe even help us get to Wise and the cult?"

"I'm trying. I can't be too obvious, not yet. I can't risk scaring her. First, she has to trust me one hundred percent, and we're not there yet. If she found out I was a cop now, it'd be a mess. She's protecting her mother, remember. Rachel's beaten down and depressed, but she's not stupid."

Mitch's gut twisted. "By 'depressed,' is it something we need to worry about? Should we be pulling in the school counselor?"

Nika shook her head. "She's a typical teen in that she's totally unhappy with her parents and her house. She talks a lot about getting away, going somewhere else to find work, taking her mother with her. As if she were thirty instead of seventeen."

"This is a damn shame because she's one of my brightest students. Last year she was all set to apply to Penn State or Johns Hopkins. She wanted to be a pharmacist or work in pharmaceutical research. Said she wanted to make a difference. Help people live better lives."

"Do you still think she could be the one who's behind the blood writing?" Colt asked.

At Nika's silence Mitch continued, "I don't know. We can't rule her out, but she certainly doesn't seem enthused about the cult at all. And since she's a member of the Rainbows, I'd be hard-pressed to believe it's her. Although it would be a brilliant disguise—acting as a supporter of the Rainbows while secretly damning them." He didn't have to point out to his present company how intelligent many cult members were, no matter how awful the tenets of the cult.

"I don't think she's behind the blood writing or the rock, Mitch, but your hunch was right in that she's painfully close to the cult." Nika uncrossed her legs and leaned forward, her breasts pressed against her turtleneck. Her breasts were luscious, of course, but it was the intelligence and dedication with which Nika committed herself to this case that was the real turn-on. "She still does her chemistry homework, still wants to go to the holiday formal, even though she says she can't, it would be too much hassle from her mother. And it seems her father disappeared from the picture, more or less, right about when her mother started going to the 'fellowship' meetings in the trailer park."

"Trailer park?" Mitch thought he was pretty clever, pretending he had no idea what she was talking about. As a high school chemistry teacher he'd have no idea that the local LEA believed the True Believers Cult was regrouping and had made a previously abandoned trailer park neighborhood their center of operations in Silver Valley.

Nika's eyes swept over Claudia and landed on Colt. "Chief?"

Colt coughed. "Yeah, well, that's enough for now, Nika. Any idea how you'll get more information out of her?"

"She's invited me to come over again on Saturday. When her mother is expected to be gone."

"Sounds good. Just be careful out there, Nika."

Colt was the best kind of leader; he empowered his officers while still showing he cared about them.

"Will do." Nika looked at her watch and stood. "I've kept you long enough, Chief. Claudia." She nodded and turned her head toward Mitch. "Mitch, I'll see you on Monday morning."

"I'll walk you out." He stood, ignoring the smug glances he saw Colt and Claudia exchange.

Nika didn't respond as they left the office and went directly to the station's locker area. Mitch stood a respectable distance away as she gathered her personal belongings. After she'd shoved her arms into a puffy purple down coat, she faced him. "You don't need to follow me out, Everlock."

"We're back to last names? Wait, I don't even know how to spell your real last name." He hated lying to her by omission, playing an ignorant crime victim. But unless she was a Trail Hiker, he had taken an oath not to reveal his role or the Trail Hikers' involvement in the case against the True Believers.

She grinned. "I told you the day we met. P-a-s-c-z-e-n-k-o. But it's probably best for you to remember me as Nika Collins. You don't want to slip and call me my real last name in front of the kids, that's for sure."

"Do you think they'd notice?" He fell into step with her as she left the locker area and checked out of the station, going past the security guard, receptionist and metal detector. Everyone seemed eager to say his or her own farewell to Nika. She was certainly a bright spot in the otherwise sterile atmosphere of the station.

"Maybe. I just don't like to take any chances undercover." They were outside, gravel crunching under their feet as they traversed the large, stone-filled parking lot that was hidden from the road by high hedges on two sides and the long windowless side of the building on the other. It was isolated and he was glad he was with her. Not that she needed his protection, of course.

Nika walked across the tiny stones as though she were wearing hiking boots not fancy cowboy boots. He knew how precarious his balance was on the loose gravel; the fact that she was so even footed underscored her athletic prowess. A must for a capable police officer.

"What?" She caught his stare and stopped, her arms crossed against her chest.

"You look a lot different than you do at school." Older, sexier, *legal*.

"What do you mean?" She tilted her head and rested her hand on the roof of her car.

"You're dressed more…more…"

"Adult? Like I might have a real life outside of high school?"

"Something like that, yes."

"Should I be flattered, professor?"

"I'm not a professor—I still have a few years and a dissertation to go on my doctorate. Stop deflecting, it's beneath you. You know you're a beautiful woman, Nika." He couldn't keep the gruffness out of his voice if he tried.

"I'd be a liar if I tried to pretend that didn't mean something to me. Thank you." She leaned against her car, her back and hips resting against the driver's door. As they looked at each other in the dimming light, concerns about appearances, her undercover status, his giving away that he was a secret under-cover operative...all dissolved into the tangle of emotions that was his growing affection for Nika.

He reached to brush her cheek and stopped. Dropped his arm. "I'm overstepping here, aren't I?"

"Not at all." She straightened, putting them mere inches apart, their breaths mingling as an opaque puff in the December evening air. "I keep telling myself this instant kind of attraction has to be because we experienced a dangerous situation together. We both want the same thing—Rachel and your other students safe. But I've been in plenty of dangerous situations with other men and I didn't feel this heat, this pull." Her voice faltered and *pull* came out on a whisper.

"Nika..."

"Kiss me, Mitch."

His eyes were half lidded and his pupils dilated under the parking lot lamp. Light snow was swirling around them and she thought this would possibly be the most romantic kiss she'd ever had as she closed her eyes.

And...nothing.

A whoosh of cold air brushed her face and she opened her eyes to Mitch, who was a good foot away.

"Nika, not here, not now."

What the hell?

"There aren't any students around, Mitch."

"That's the problem."

It took her a heartbeat to absorb his meaning. "They'd force us to behave, is that what you're saying?" She closed their distance for the second time, but this time her hormones weren't driving her. "Let me be clear, Mitch. I'm a grown woman, probably not more than two years younger than you. I'm single, and clearly you are, too. We're consenting adults. We are both attracted to each other. The timing sucks, yes, but we can handle this if we want to. Apparently you don't want to and that's fine with me. Just do us both a favor and grow a pair. I'm not into the tiptoeing routine."

Before she finished her tirade she felt strong hands on her upper arms as Mitch practically lifted her to him and spun her around into a shadowed part of the lot, near the tall boxwood hedge that protected the parking lot from being seen from the highway.

His lips were on hers without warning and Nika had never welcomed such a surprise. This was no seduction or tentative first kiss. Mitch kissed her like a man kisses a woman he knows wants him just as much as he wants her. It was a kiss to start an equal relationship, not an alpha-male stamp of possession.

It was the best kiss of her life. Screw the romantic part of her that thought a sweet, tender first kiss under the softly falling snow would have been nice. *Screw nice.* This? This was what she wanted. An equal partner who took what he wanted while allowing her to take her share of the embrace, too.

Her hand went to his crotch as he cupped her breast under her coat. She groaned, their breathing short and sharp as it came out in small billows of white around them. He nipped along her jawline and then gently sucked on her neck. His kisses made clear thinking impossible.

And completely unnecessary.

"God, Nika, you're killing me." He thrust his pelvis against her exploring hand, his erection mirroring her want. Before she could start to stroke along his length he captured her hand, then her other, and held them to her sides. He lifted his head from her lips. She groaned in protest.

"Let me take you home."

She opened her eyes and looked at him. The stark need in his expression was her undoing. She was in free fall, a long, dangerous jump into the chaos that getting involved with Mitch would lead to. No question.

"I... I can't." She shook her head but the traitorous web of desire wouldn't shake loose. "I know I'm giving you mixed messages, Mitch, but as much as I want to be with you, you're right. It's too complicated. We're going to have to wait until this case is solved and I'm not undercover. And even then..." She wasn't sure how much to reveal to him.

"Even then what?"

"I was involved with someone for a long time. He's a state trooper stationed in Altoona. We had a long-distance relationship that turned out to be his opportunity to find someone else. It was awful, and I don't care to do that again. My heart still hurts."

"I'm sorry you went through that, Nika. But I'm not that guy."

"No, but I'm the girl who went through the worst kind of breakup." One she wasn't sure she'd come back through yet.

"It doesn't have to be a long-term commitment, Nika. We're consenting adults, remember?" He stared at her. "Meet me this weekend. Your place or mine?"

It was the cold splash of water her emotions needed. It was one thing when she'd been the pursuer; she'd felt in control. The men she'd dated since Ron took it better when it was time to end a brief relationship, because Nika made it clear from the get-go that she didn't do long-term.

"I can't do this now, Mitch. We're in too deep, too close to catching the bad guys. I'm going to Rachel's on Saturday, for God's sake. Your student's home."

She saw what *she* felt—desire, regret and frustration—war to claim his expression. He closed his eyes, his hands on his hips. "Aw, hell. You're right."

"I'm sorry, Mitch."

He opened his eyes and the current of lust that shot to her most intimate parts had her ready to jump him right there in the parking lot again.

The sound of the back door to the station opening doused her want. Shared laughter spilled out into the parking lot. In the shadows of the boxwoods, Nika and Mitch were invisible to the couple that walked to Chief Todd's personal vehicle. Silently they watched as he opened the passenger side of his SUV to allow Claudia to climb in. He walked around and slid into the driver's seat. As his car started and warmed up in the cold night, it became clear that his engine wasn't all that Colt Todd was heating up as his profile met and blended with Claudia's.

"The chief and our social media officer?" Nika whispered, stifling a giggle.

"Gee, who woulda thunk it? The SVPD parking lot is the new Skyline Scenic View highway pullout." Mitch referred to the scenic viewing area along the highway that coursed through the hills surrounding

Silver Valley. For generations it had been known as the place for couples to find some quiet and privacy away from the prying eyes of Silver Valley's more inquisitive residents.

"Please don't use 'pull out,' when talking about the chief and Claudia." She giggled while she shivered as the cold damp reached under her coat. Without Mitch's scorching touch, the night's frigid temperature was catching up to her.

Mitch's arm was around her shoulders and she felt the kiss he planted on top of her head as he drew her to his side. "That's a fair request. And it's time for both of us to go home. We're going to have to wait for them to leave first, though."

"I know. Let's hope it's quick. It's getting pretty chilly out here."

As if he'd heard, Chief Todd's vehicle's brake lights lit up as he backed the car out of its spot and drove out of the lot. Instead of relief, Nika felt the raw edge of envy. The chief and Claudia looked like they were very happy together, and she was certain it wouldn't be a temporary hookup. Neither had the personality for anything but long-term commitment. Would she have to wait decades for the same?

"Looks safe enough now." She stepped away from Mitch, needing to be alone to process what had just happened between them. She wasn't stupid enough to think it was only a kiss. Or a kiss that would blend into her memories of all the kisses that had come before. Kisses that didn't seem to matter much anymore, if they ever had. "I'll see you on Monday, Mitch."

"If not sooner." He walked away and she fought against her instinct to ask him what the hell he'd meant by that, but Nika knew when she was at her limit. It was imperative that she get into her car and drive away, quickly, or she was going to run up to Mitch and beg him to go with her.

To make love to her.

Neither of them needed that kind of distraction.

Chapter 8

Nika went to Rachel's as planned on Saturday morning. Unlike before, Rachel was more talkative and less gloomy about her home situation. They worked on their chemistry homework and Nika prayed the whole time that her lack of accomplishment wouldn't give her away. She'd barely made it through two problems.

"Thanks for having me over again. Are you sure your mother isn't upset that I'm back?"

Rachel rolled her eyes from where she sat on her twin bed. "Do you have to ask? She's tuned out. And today's meeting day. She'll be leaving to see her New Thought weirdos anytime now."

"Do you ever go?"

"Sometimes. I went in the beginning, when she was more normal and I thought it was going to just be a group of people trying to start a new church. I had no idea they were as far from a church as you can imagine."

"And she doesn't get mad that you don't go with her? My parents get upset if I don't do stuff with them." Thankfully Nika hadn't had to explain much about her own family as the students accepted that she was there with her father, living in a temporary apartment, while her mother and siblings had stayed behind in Iowa until their old home sold. Plus, it would be easier for her made-up family to leave their Iowa school at the end of the semester.

"Nah. She used to care more, when Dad was still here." Rachel punched molecular weights into the calculator on her phone. She looked up, a small smile on her face. "Done! We've made it through all of the weekend homework."

"Thanks so much for helping me. I took a lot of chemistry at my old school, but Mr. Everlock really teaches at a higher level."

"Yeah, he can be intense."

"But you like him well enough, right? I mean, you joined the club he reps. You never told me why you're in the Rainbows, by the way. Not that you have to, it's truly none of my business, but if you want to tell me, I'm listening."

Rachel shook her head. "No worry. I'm not hiding a secret or anything. I used to be friends with someone who wanted to come to the meetings but her parents forbade it. I'd already been going for a few weeks, and liked the kids. I don't fit in all the time because I'm not LGBT, but I support anyone who is, so the group doesn't have a problem with me participating. Do you think it's lame or something?"

Nika made it a point to keep filling in her workbook with the answers to their chemistry equations. "Not at all. I'm joining it to support it, too. We all have friends who join because of who they are, and I want to be supportive, too. I've noticed that the students out east are way more accepting."

Rachel's eyes widened. "You're kidding, right? I think it's pretty conservative here. We're in the middle of nowhere."

Nika shrugged. "Some of the grown-ups are total bigots, sure, but you're closer to big cities. I don't get a vibe from the students here that anyone thinks they're better than anyone else."

Rachel snorted. "Stick around a little longer. You'll see."

Nika left Rachel's just after noon, after which she and Ivy went shopping together at Costco as planned for their quarterly stock up. They split the cost of things to make it economical and practical for each of them, since neither had room to store entire case loads of anything. And of course the extra Christmas and holiday gift packages of cosmetics and jewelry were an added bonus.

As Nika drove them home the snow started to fall and she spotted a familiar vehicle in her rearview mirror. The same pickup that had been in the SVPD parking lot the previous evening, and the same one she'd noticed parked to the side of the main road right before the turnoff to Rachel's country drive.

Mitch Everlock was following her. Damn it. That man needed to leave things be. She wasn't afraid as she knew that he was doing this to protect her, but

the next time they spoke she'd remind him that his
Marine days were over and she wasn't on his squad.

She played it cool. Instead of stopping her vehicle and forcing him to drive past, she drove as if she
didn't know he was there. There was no reason to
mention it to Ivy. It'd probably only freak her friend
out. When she turned into the driveway she and Ivy
shared, Mitch drove on to the next cul-de-sac, where
he turned around and headed out toward the development exit.

She ignored the tingle in her stomach that his near-
ness triggered. She also ignored the fantasy of Mitch
pulling into her driveway to spend time with her.

Ivy was like a dog with a bone and the bone was
Mitch Everlock.

"Stop being a cop 24/7, Nika. I know it's your job,
but you deserve to have a personal life, too. So what
if you're working in the high school? We don't have
any high school students living in our development.
We're on the outermost edge of the school district.
There's nothing keeping you from going on a date
with this teacher, as long as no one finds out. What
did you say his name was?"

"Mitch." They were unloading the back of her car
after the trip to the grocery warehouse store. Nika
had explained to Ivy that she was doing some work at
Silver Valley High and had fallen hard in lust for the
chemistry teacher. She didn't mention she was undercover or that Mitch was a former Special Forces type.
Ivy knew about Nika's mistrust of men in authority.
She'd even called Nika on it one time, explaining why
she thought Nika had chosen to be a police officer.

Ivy's theory was that one of the driving factors in Nika seeking a law-enforcement career was to control what had been so uncontrollable for her family during Soviet times.

Nika didn't disagree with Ivy's assessment but she'd also picked law enforcement because she'd always believed in justice.

"I know you, Nika. You say you're not ready to date anyone steady, and while I have never seen a guy last more than a couple of days with you since Ron, this sounds different. Care to explain?" Ivy handed her a huge plastic-wrapped case of toilet paper and grabbed an equally large package of paper towels they'd divvy up once inside.

"I don't know how long I'll be working near him, so it would be awkward to date a few times and then stop seeing each other, which we would, while I have to still see him during my workday. I like a clean break."

Ivy heaved her paper towels across Nika's entryway. "You are the only person I know who plans the breakup before you even make it to first base with a man."

Nika stopped in the kitchen, her arms hugging the toilet paper to her as if for protection. Truly she prayed Ivy couldn't see too much of her face behind the plastic and paper.

"Oh. My. God. Is Nika Pasczenko blushing?" Ivy's eyes were round, her brows raised and hands on her hips. "Dish. Did you have him here last night?"

"No, no, nothing like that. It was a quick…kiss."

Ivy studied her before she bent to the paper towels and ripped them open, placing roll after roll atop

Nika's empty kitchen island. "It was more than a kiss, judging by your beet-red cheeks." Three more rolls of toilet paper stacked up. "It's none of my business, Nika, but I've seen you do so much for everyone else. Ron was an ass and never deserved you. There are other men out there in positions of power who aren't anything like him or the men from your parents' Eastern European days. And you've been on the SVPD long enough to know that there are men in power who are still great guys, right? And Mitch isn't even a police officer, he's a dang high school chemistry teacher. I would think you'd jump on him—he's perfect for you, and you obviously share your own chemistry together." Ivy giggled at her pun. "Get it?"

"Yeah, I get it." She placed the few remaining paper towel rolls that were her share on the island and held up the half-full bag that belonged to Ivy. "Your half."

They continued to talk as they meandered back and forth from Ivy's car to each of their town houses. Nika knew that Ivy was her biggest supporter but being unable to share the exact sensitivity of the op at the school and its possible ties to the True Believers Cult left her with no means to convey just how complicated her whole attraction to Mitch was. How impossible any kind of relationship with him would be, at least during this op. And after...well, Nika was still too raw from the disastrous relationship and breakup she'd suffered with Ron. The last she'd heard he was happily engaged to a woman he'd fallen in love with before their breakup. No, her heart wasn't ready to be tossed around again, even if Mitch was available, even if the case wrapped up soon.

* * *

After Ivy went to her town house to prepare for a date she had that night, Nika tried to use the rest of her afternoon to relax. She puttered around the town house, not wanting to go back out. Maybe she'd rent a movie and open a bottle of one of her favorite reds tonight. The case was only going to get more intense as they neared the Silver Bells Ball and she needed to enjoy quiet time to herself while she could.

At six thirty she paused the TV series she was binge watching and decided to order takeout. Did she want Chinese, Thai or sushi?

As she walked to the kitchen to grab one of the many menus from the drawer under the phone, her doorbell chimed. Ivy wasn't due back until much later and rarely stopped by after a date. They waited to rehash their dates over coffee on Sunday, or the following week if either opted to spend the night with a man.

The doorbell sounded again as she crossed the foyer. Her instincts were on high alert and her fingers itched for her weapon, stored in her gun safe.

She looked through the peephole and immediately threw the door open.

"Mitch."

"Is this a good time?" He wore a knit cap that covered a good amount of his short-cropped hair. The tweedy black wool brought out the green in his eyes.

"Depends." She heard the bitchy tone in her voice and relented. "Come on in."

"I wasn't sure if you were a flower kind of woman." As he stepped into her home he handed her a bouquet that had a riot of color splashed against the holiday-themed tissue paper. White and red roses, ferns, red berries and decorative picks with candy canes and snowmen fought for her attention in the festive arrangement.

"I am, and these are gorgeous. Thank you." She motioned for him to follow her into the kitchen, where she set about getting the flowers into a vase. "First, how did you find my address?"

"I looked you up."

"You 'looked me up.' That's interesting, since my number is unlisted and I'm on Facebook with a different name—and I don't put my address on anything that I don't have to." She could let him off the hook, tell him she saw him behind her on Silver Valley Pike after she left Rachel's, but she waited him out.

He held out his hands, open palmed. "You saw me, didn't you? You caught me. I was worried about you at Rachel's. No one saw me there, don't worry, but I was on the street by her drive the whole time you were there."

"Some people call that stalking, Mitch. I'm a trained police officer, and I'm up for promotion to detective any day now. Still, you thought that you could help me by staking me out? While I was undercover?"

He had the humility to look chastised. "I'm not doubting your capability at all, Nika. It's the cult, the kind of people behind it, that have me worried."

"Mitch, since we're being honest here, when are you going to tell me what you really do?"

His face froze and she knew she'd hit a mark. But what mark, she couldn't be certain.

"I'm a high school teacher, Nika. I've done some

investigative work when I was in the Marine Corps. That's all."

She didn't buy it but wasn't going to push it. Not tonight.

"For the record, I knew you were there today. I saw you follow me afterward, and you turned around in the cul-de-sac at the end of my street."

He put his hands in his pockets. "I'm sorry, Nika. I owe you more than staking you out like you're a rookie."

"Yes, you do. I was about to order takeout. Why don't you pay, to make up for your transgression? Interested?"

He looked at the array of menus on the kitchen counter and grinned. "Most certainly."

"Is this what an SVPD officer usually does on a Saturday night? When you're not on duty?" Mitch ate his dim sum expertly with wooden chopsticks. She watched the play of the television's lighting against his face and wondered how such a sexy, attractive guy was free on a Saturday night.

"My best friend happens to be my neighbor, and we watch a lot of movies on the weekend. We spent the afternoon shopping after I got back from work. Rachel's. You know, where you—"

"Where I was following you. Again, I am sorry."

They'd forgone plates to enjoy the meal straight from the cartons on the floor in front of her television. She looked up from her General Tsao's shrimp to find Mitch thoroughly enjoying his meal.

"This is fun."

He tilted his head. "Explain."

"You, me, eating Chinese."

"As you said yesterday, Nika, 'you're single, I'm single.' Remind me again why we can't do more of this?"

"Mitch…" Did she have to tell him again that she wasn't the woman for him to get too comfortable with? Maybe she should tell him that a man who'd had the kind of power he'd had in the Marine Corps overwhelmed her. No, he'd never believe it.

"Tell me." Her small Christmas tree winked with multicolored lights, making the atmosphere cozy and…familiar. Warm. With Mitch's gaze on her, his body relaxed against the bottom of her sofa as they sat on the rug her parents had brought back from the Grand Bazaar in Istanbul last summer, she wanted to melt into him. Trust him.

"It's silly."

"Try me."

"I'm not up for anything more serious than what we're doing right now, Mitch."

"Eating Chinese takeout on your floor, under your Christmas tree? Damn, you're easy to please."

She set her chopsticks down. "I've never dated anyone longer than six months, except Ron, who lasted a year. Since him, it's been more like six *days*. My job is everything to me, Mitch. Keeping people safe from the bad stuff out there. From the more simple stuff like shoplifting and speeding and underage drinking, right up to the harder stuff, like trying to crack the heroin epidemic. Do you know that last month, before I started this case, I saved two different addicts right here in Silver Valley? One shot of Narcan to their thigh and they lived through an OD. I have no idea if they went to rehab, or are still alive, but in that moment, I made a difference."

"What about making a difference for *you*, Nika? Being a beat cop, any kind of cop, will get harder as you get older. Don't you want a family of your own to worry about someday?"

How could his words—plain everyday words— make her heart squeeze so tightly?

"As much as my mother would love to see me settle down and have a baby or two, no, I can't say the temptation has hit me. Besides, being a cop and a mother aren't mutually exclusive. If I ever had a family, kids, I don't plan to stop being a cop. You know that—you had to have served with women in the Marine Corps."

"Yes, I did, and many of them handled motherhood and their dedication to the Corps without a hiccup. As for deciding to have a family, in my experience the right person could change your mind about that." At her silence he laughed. "Chill out, Nika. I'm not auditioning to be that person for you. I've dated several women since I came to Silver Valley over five years ago. One got serious, but, well, she was like your Ron. It didn't work out. Like you, I'm still single, but it has started to cross my mind. The settling-down part. Give it a few years. I think I'm…what? Five years older than you?" They compared birth dates and found he was only two years older.

"Mitch, admit it. You didn't come here tonight to woo me. You're here because you didn't trust me to do what I needed to do at Rachel's. I'm impressed that you actually feel a little guilty about it. But not enough to stop you from doing it."

"Maybe. But all cards on the table? I want to get to know you better. Spend time like this." He motioned at their takeout picnic, the holiday decorations. "Where we aren't playing roles."

"It is a good idea to understand what makes each other tick, to a certain extent. Since we'll be dealing with each other for the foreseeable future and the situation is so high stakes."

Mitch stared at the fire. "How long do you think it's going to take?"

"To get to the bottom of the True Believers, or to find out who's leaving bloody messages in your classroom and throwing rocks through your windows?"

"All of the above."

"We'll figure out who wrote the threats in short order, I think. Maybe another week or so. I need more time with Rachel, and planning for the Silver Bells Ball is going to help with that. But taking down the True Believers?" She put her food down on the coffee table. "I'm not the lead on the case, Bryce is. And he's been working it for a year so far. We've made some great strides and it looked like we might have had them last spring, but then they got smart and laid low for a while. I'm sure you heard about the mess of a wedding at the mayor's house. If we're lucky, Wise is going to get cocky and slip up. The fact that I found all of that propaganda at Rachel's tells me that they're getting a little fast and loose, if not careless."

Mitch put his container on the table as she spoke and turned to face her, his expression intent. No one ever listened to her like this. Growing up, her parents had always been too busy making ends meet after arriving in the US with nothing but their clothing and passports. In college she'd put her nose in the books and graduated with honors, ensuring her entrance into the police academy. At SVPD, the officers were all busy with heavy caseloads. Finding out the most intimate details of each other's lives wasn't the objective. Even Ron, as much as he'd claimed otherwise, had never really listened to her except where it affected him.

As Mitch remained silent, she grinned.

"Sorry. You didn't ask for my entire life story." She leaned on her hands to get up. "How about some dessert?"

He put his hand on her thigh and his warmth seared through her yoga pants. She stilled, knowing where they were headed. And not only hoping for it but craving it with a ferocity that humbled her.

"Now, you don't expect me to let such a perfect setup go to waste, do you?" His eyes lit with what she knew she saw in hers. Want. Need.

"What I said before...it still holds." Her whispered words sounded futile, weak. Who was she kidding? She couldn't walk away from Mitch.

"One thing war and life has taught me is that all we have is right now. This moment."

"Yes."

She wanted him so badly she was even willing to find out how much it would hurt to let him go after they gave in to their desire. Because she *would* let him go, but only after she found out how good it could be. And then her heart would be in shambles again.

Her heart wasn't helping her now, as it pounded with anticipation, wiping out all logical thinking.

She waited for him to close the gap. She'd made her desire clear. Now it was Mitch's turn.

Awareness tingled all over her skin as if she were a teenager again. A teenager allowed to explore her deepest, most secret sexual fantasies with the man of her dreams.

Mitch drew out the anticipation as his fingers ran through her hair, cupping the back of her skull while his other hand caressed her cheek, her jawline, her throat. He watched her and she refused to close her eyes, refused to turn away from the intensity in his, refused to beg him to bring his mouth to hers. When his fingers tried to dip into her cleavage, her breath caught.

"What do you want, Nika? Tell me."

"I want you."

"How?"

"Oh, God, you know how." She was breathless, one thread away from completely losing it.

"Tell me." His insistence forced a red-hot blush onto her face and she knew he saw her vulnerable need.

"I want you inside me, Mitch."

In what felt like one move Mitch reached under her shirt and cupped her breast as he crushed his lips against hers.

Chapter 9

Mitch wasn't a man who usually let his need for sex affect his judgment, but with Nika he was entirely focused on her and the want she stirred in him, especially when she had her hand over his erection and was stroking him through his jeans.

Her tongue was as bold as she was. She kissed him with a thoroughness he'd only fantasized about and it threatened to get him off before they'd even started. He was barely beginning to do what he wanted to do to Nika.

"Slow down." He pulled back from their kiss and grasped her hand before she reached into his jeans. Damn it, she already had his belt unbuckled. He wanted her, but this woman was different. Their shared connection was inexplicable. Her eyes slowly opened and he saw the same urgency that he felt.

"Why?" She reached back up to kiss him and the pull of her was like a drug. A drug that smothered all of his anxieties, his worries about his PTSD coming back.

A drug.

"No." With what he thought was a superhuman effort, Mitch pulled back and sat up on the couch, putting badly needed distance between them.

Nika took a moment to register what he was doing before she scrambled to her feet. Her hair was wild around her flushed face, her nipples erect and pushing against her top, reminding him of what he was turning down.

He was a freaking fool.

"I'm sorry, Nika. Now I'm the one giving mixed messages. This isn't right. Not yet."

"Not yet?" Flames of desire turned to angry sparks in her pale blue eyes and he would have done anything to be back on the floor with her, to take her the way they both wanted.

"Please. Sit next to me for a minute."

She eyed him as if he'd sprouted horns and fangs. After what felt like an aeon, she sat on the chair opposite the sofa. Smart girl.

"Is this your usual come-on, Mitch? Bring a girl to...to her breaking point and then drop her?" She ran her fingers through her hair, deep lines between her eyebrows. "Hell, you're right. What on earth was I thinking?"

"Neither of us was thinking." He took a minute to will his erection away. "We've got something potent between us. It's beyond a physical connection and it deserves more than a one-nighter. But you know as well as I do that this is the kind of distraction that—"

"Gets people killed. I know." She buried her face in her hands for a moment before she rested her elbows on her knees and looked at him. "I'm the one who needs to apologize. You're not the one with a case to solve, I am. And I wasn't doing a good job of protecting you right now, was I?" Her rueful expression tugged at something deep in his chest that he refused to look at. Couldn't.

"You don't have to protect me, Nika. I do a good job of that, trust me."

"I couldn't even shield you from that stupid rock. You were the one who saved both of us." He saw the self-doubt on her face. Her core belief, that she could and did protect the community, was shaken in her.

"Nika, you're more than doing your job. What's going on between us at the personal level is just that—personal. It has nothing to do with the case and it won't keep you from bringing down the bad guys. I'll make sure of it."

"You're right." She let out a long sigh. "We both know what's best for the case—why this can't happen." She stood and started clearing their takeout boxes from the coffee table. "Would you like something else to drink?" Her hands shook and he wanted to grab them, comfort her.

He stood. "Hell, no, Nika. I don't want 'something else.' I want to know that we're cool, that you're not going to treat me like a pariah every time you see me from now on. We have a few weeks before the dance, and we'll be lucky if you solve the case by then." Shit, he'd said too much. He saw it immediately in how her body stiffened and her eyes narrowed. To her credit, she didn't call him out on it. Didn't ask him again what else he did besides teach high school chemistry.

"We're cool, Mitch." She stood looking at him, her arms full of their meal's leftovers, her expression weary. "I'm tired. Do you mind if we call it a night?"

He did mind—he minded a hell of a lot. But he couldn't tell her why. Hell, he didn't even know why.

"I'll let myself out."

Nika reported to the station at 0600 on Monday morning, a full hour before she had to be at Silver Valley High School. For once she was thankful that Bryce Campbell worked long hours. She didn't bother knocking on the frame of his open door.

"Bryce, I need some answers. About Mitch."

He looked up from his paper and took a long sip of coffee from a refillable gas station mug. "I'm surprised it took you this long, Nika. Shut the door and sit down."

Nika did as he asked and stared at him, hard. "Who the hell is he, Bryce? And don't tell me he's just a chemistry teacher, or that he's had Special Forces training in the Marine Corps. Or that he's a war hero or whatever. I already know all of that."

"You did an internet search, I take it?" Unspoken in Bryce's question was the fact that Mitch wasn't the kind of man who boasted about his military background, or what he'd seen in combat. He didn't need to—he was confident in his own skin.

"Yes. And I've worked next to him for the past two-and-a-half weeks, Bryce. He saved me from the rock, and he's obviously holding back on what he knows about the case. I feel like he knows more than I do. Tell me, Bryce. I swear I won't let him know that I know. He's a Fed, isn't he? FBI or DEA? No, wait—is he ATF? That makes sense, with the True Believers and their history of stockpiling firearms."

Bryce held up his palms. "Nika, stop. It's none of the above. I can't tell you directly what Mitch is all about."

"Well, someone had better because it's my job to keep him safe from whoever is threatening him. How the hell am I supposed to do my job if he's got some kind of secret role in all of this?"

"Are you through?"

"I haven't even started."

Bryce grinned. "I can't tell you about what Mitch is doing, but I know who can and I've already asked permission for you to be let in on the truth."

"Okay..."

"First, call in to SVHS. Tell them you'll be late today, that you have a dental appointment. Then go to this address. Don't tell anyone you're going and, when you get there, park in the big parking garage next to the building. Take the sky bridge to the offices on the third floor. They'll buzz you in." Bryce handed her an embossed business card with only an address on it.

"This is here, in Silver Valley." She recognized the location of one of the larger groups of office buildings off the main highway through town.

"Yes. But the building you're going to isn't what you think. Trust me on this, Nika. Just go."

"Does Chief Todd know about this?"

Bryce's eyes narrowed and he stood. Nika followed suit.

"You'll find out some of the answers to your questions once you get there. Go, Nika. Time's a wastin'."

Nika left Bryce's office with a clenched stomach—even his Johnny Cash reference couldn't soothe her nerves. She thought she'd feel validation when her suspicions about Mitch were confirmed. Instead she felt inexplicably betrayed by a man she'd known for less than a month. A man she'd kissed, whom she'd allowed to nearly make her come without even having sex.

A man who'd played her for a fool.

Nika didn't know what to make of the posh surroundings she was ushered into. A receptionist in a trim, no-nonsense business suit motioned toward the leather seats in a lounge area. A glass-topped table sported a humongous arrangement of red and white poinsettias with sparkly gold tree branches in an uncut crystal vase. "Wait over there and I'll come get you as soon as you're cleared."

Cleared? Nika looked around, stymied. Clearly whatever this place was, whoever these people were, they were all funded far better than a local police station like SVPD.

She didn't have long to mentally review her expanding list of questions as the receptionist was at her side within minutes. "Let's go."

Nika followed the young woman, whom she placed around twenty-five. A huge wooden door opened and as Nika walked past it she could see by the door's edge that it had a steel core that was several inches thick.

A familiar figure stood behind a large, polished desk in the most luxurious executive suite Nika had ever been in.

"Claudia!" She stopped in the center of the room.

"I'll leave you to it, ma'am. Do you need anything else?"

"No, Laurel, that's all. Thanks for escorting Nika in." Claudia's cool gaze turned to Nika. "Have a seat. Would you like something to drink?" She stood as Nika eased herself into a very comfortable conference chair. "I can make you an espresso, cappuccino, latte? I'm having one, so please don't be shy."

"A latte would be nice, thanks." Nika looked around, seeing Claudia in a different light. Claudia, the social media guru, was some kind of government agent?

"I know this is all a bit of a shock to you, Nika. Frankly I expected you to ask about us sooner."

Claudia's attention appeared to be on the frothy milk she was pouring into a mug, but Nika knew there was much more going on behind her beautiful demeanor than how to teach SVPD the ins and outs of social media.

"How could I ask about something I didn't know about? Son of a bitch, Claudia, I don't even know what 'us' is! I asked Bryce if you—I mean, Mitch, was FBI or DEA but he didn't answer me."

"That's because we're neither." Claudia handed her the warm latte. "Before I go any further, I need you to sign a couple of nondisclosure forms." Without any signal that Nika was aware of, Laurel the receptionist was back, a black leather portfolio in one hand, which she placed on Claudia's desk in front of Nika.

"Laurel will stay here to witness your signatures. Do you have a problem with any of this so far, Nika?"

"You're asking me to sign contracts about something I know nothing about?" Nika opened the portfolio and read the forms. Short and to the point, they stated that she'd never divulge what she was about to learn in the offices of "TH, Esq," the official name of the "unofficial" organization. Or risk imprisonment and government fines totaling more than she'd ever make in forty years of working for the SVPD.

She could walk away, stay away from whatever Claudia was about to divulge. Never know what Mitch Everlock was really about.

Nika signed both forms.

"Date them here and here." Laurel waited for her to finish her part before signing on the witness lines. As soon as they were done, Laurel closed the portfolio and left. The quiet click of Claudia's office door closing didn't reflect the solidness of the door that Nika had observed, another hint of the technology employed by TH, Esq.

In the usually quiet town of Silver Valley, in bucolic central Pennsylvania, she was locked in a vault with Claudia.

"What don't I know, Claudia? What, or who, is 'TH'?"

Chapter 10

"Trail Hikers—TH—is a relatively new agency that officially is not affiliated with any government entity, foreign or domestic. We have 'esquire' on the business card to keep it more difficult to identify." Claudia sat next to Nika on a matching leather upholstered office chair, her elegant cream suit contrasting smartly against the dark furniture.

"But you're at SVPD headquarters so much and— Let me guess. Bryce is part of it, too? And Mitch Everlock? And Chief Todd?" Nika didn't think this would be a good time to mention she'd seen Claudia sucking face with Colt Todd.

Claudia smiled and her posture remained relaxed. Her eyes, however, were steely. "What we do here is highly classified, Nika. Chief Todd praises your capabilities and it's clear you're an intelligent woman. So you'd understand the danger in revealing the smallest aspect of any case and, most especially, who's working it. Do I have to spell it out for you, Nika?"

"No, ma'am." Nika got it. And this was Claudia's territory, Claudia's circus. She wasn't about to question her. "It's just a bit of an adjustment for me. I mean, before I walked in here today I thought of you as SVPD's social media expert. A retired Marine on a pension bringing in a little more cash. Now I find out you're the CEO of an elite group of operatives. And I've been 'read in.' Am I going to become a Trail Hiker?"

"Not unless you truly want to. Since you're one of SVPD's top officers it's a good idea to cut you in on what we do, as the department has found itself in the middle of several high-profile cases. A handful of police officers are on the TH payroll, too. It's only natural that you've wondered about what some of your fellow officers are doing on their off-hours."

It all made sense now. Snippets of overheard conversations, the chief calling in a select few for private briefings from time to time—much of it had to be Trail Hikers' related.

"What exactly does Trail Hikers do? Do you help with all of SVPD's cases?"

"Absolutely not. We're independent of any law-enforcement agency, but you could say we're at the federal, even international, level if we're anything."

"You mean CIA?"

"No, not at all. But similar to them, we conduct operations globally, and our agents are prepared to travel to the farthest points of the planet with little to no notice."

"So why are you here, in central Pennsylvania? Silver Valley, of all places?"

Claudia shrugged. "The same reason every major distribution center is." She referred to the plethora of logistics headquarters that made Silver Valley home to many Fortune 100 companies. "We're virtually equidistant from Philly, Baltimore and DC. New York is only another hour out. Quick access to major hub airports, the rail systems and major highways. That's not to say we don't get involved with local situations as needed, but only if there's a national concern involved."

"Like the True Believers. They were a federal case twenty years ago."

"How much do you know about the cult, Nika?"

"I know that the ATF and FBI converged on a tiny town in Upstate New York thanks to a tip from a twelve-year-old girl living at the compound with her mother. The girl was brave enough to approach a police officer in a fabric store. That girl was given a new identity and placed in an adoptive home in Silver Valley. She grew up to be Zora Krasny, Bryce Campbell's fiancée. Most of Zora's story is public, but not all of it. As I'm talking to you, I realize she must be in Trail Hikers, too. How else would she have been able to work undercover last year to help bring down the Female Preacher Killer?"

"Right. So we're on the same page with the cult. But back to TH. Nika, we're not officially federal. We're not officially *anything*. As far as anyone who's not read into our program knows, we don't exist. And, trust me, this office and my entire staff could be wiped out in a blink because of any one of the many operations we're involved in. If any of the criminals we're fighting to put behind bars ever gets wind of what we're really doing here, they wouldn't hesitate to take us out. That's what we're prepared for."

"There have to be contingency headquarters planned?"

Claudia didn't answer. Nika decided to focus in on the matter at hand. "How much are you helping with the True Believers?"

"Not much, for now. We have our analysts on it and we're in direct comms with other LEA intelligence offices. If Leonard Wise or any of his scum-of-the-earth associates gets to be too much for the local resources, of course TH would come into play. We specialize in quick insertion and extraction. And we invest in training a number of local LEAs like the few SVPD who work here. Unfortunately we're expecting Wise to necessitate our involvement soon. His recent activities have been troubling."

"Do Trail Hikers' activities take precedence over everything else? If, for example, I worked for Trail Hikers, would I be expected to drop my current SVPD caseload?"

"Trail Hikers deals with life-and-death situations that usually involve large numbers of people. That doesn't mean we won't be in the midst of what look like smaller cases, but ultimately they have to be tied into a bigger case."

"Like True Believers and New Thought ministries."

"Right. We can't underestimate the True Believers' next move." Claudia's mouth was set in a grim line.

"More than being a crazy mind-washing type of cult? A cult of a personality named Leonard Wise?"

Claudia ran her fingers through her perfectly coifed silver bob, the first sign of frustration Nika had ever witnessed from the cool professional. "Far more. But that's not something any of us need to focus on at the moment. They won't get to their ultimate goal if we take them down beforehand."

"So, in reality, I'm not really undercover to only find out who's harassing the Rainbows?"

"I'm afraid not. On the surface, yes, but as the sordid propaganda you discovered at Rachel Boyle's house proves, we're up against the ugliest side of human nature."

Nika's mind was overrun with images of what the True Believers would want with a beautiful place like Silver Valley. Nestled next to the Appalachian Trail, the state capital of Harrisburg, the Susquehanna River—it was at the epicenter of an authentic slice of America. And with Three Mile Island, the infamous nuclear power plant nearby, the destructive possibilities were terrifying.

"I'm ready to do whatever you need me to do, Claudia."

"You're already doing it, Nika. Normally we'd give you some initial training at this point, but you've had all of the weapons and evasive-driving training we'd offer a new agent. As you've probably guessed, all TH agents are at least prior military or law enforcement. Many, like you, are still active-duty police officers or other local law enforcement."

"What about other government agents, like CIA or FBI?"

Claudia let a small smile surface. "I can't comment on the former, but as for the latter, yes, we have an FBI agent or two on our staff. We employ agents from all over the globe and deploy them everywhere. I can't emphasize this enough. I've found that some SVPD agents thought TH was here for local ops only. That couldn't be further from the truth."

"Thank you for trusting me with this information, Claudia."

"Of course. And don't think I brought you in here only to appease your curiosity. Please don't deny it and insult both of us. I've seen the looks you've shot at Bryce and Mitch. Now it all makes sense, doesn't it? How Mitch seemed to know more than a high school chemistry teacher should, and how Bryce and Mitch have a camaraderie that can't be explained?"

"Yes." Nika swallowed, trying to keep her mind from focusing on only Mitch and what his involvement in TH meant for her case. And for their relationship. They shared much more in common than she'd imagined. "I'm still a little confused on where SVPD and TH overlap. A Venn diagram is how I see it, with SVPD doing its own thing locally, bringing down the True Believers. Trail Hikers is working on a much higher level, handling anything interstate and internationally related to the True Believers wanting to come back to their twisted version of power. But where does it overlap?"

Claudia stood and resumed her position behind her desk before she answered.

Nika didn't want to hear Claudia say what she already dreaded.

"You, Nika. You're the overlap."

* * *

Mitch was grateful for Bryce's heads-up when Nika came storming into his classroom office Tuesday morning. It was early with no other students around and few teachers.

She shrugged out of her ridiculously overloaded backpack, typical of a straight-A senior's, and dropped it on his tiny sofa. Melting snow spattered over the cheap upholstery and over the linoleum floor. Nika glared at him as though he were the devil incarnate.

"Can I help you, Nika? Are you struggling with the organic chemistry chapter? And, if you don't mind, would you please put that dripping backpack on the floor?"

"You could have given me a clue that you were more involved than I knew."

"No, I couldn't. I'm sure Claudia made that clear to you yesterday. Coffee?"

Her glance flickered from him to the coffeepot. "Sure. Heavy on the cream." Since adapting to how the students liked their coffee, she'd rediscovered the luxury of cream in hers.

He reached into his mini fridge and pulled out the pint of local organic cream he'd picked up for her before pouring his fresh roast into a large mug.

"Do you always keep locally sourced dairy products on hand?"

"For you, yes. I saw this in your fridge the other night." He dropped a dollop into the steaming mug. "Enough?"

"Perfect." She held out her hands to take it and he brushed his hand against hers as he handed the mug over. As soon as their fingertips touched his mind flashed back to Nika's body pressed against his, her tongue tangling with his, her breath hot on his skin.

"What?" Her voice was barely a whisper.

"Tell me you don't feel this, too, Nika."

Nika pulled the mug into her chest and put her head down.

He hated not being able to see her eyes, her full lips, as she bit down on her bottom lip, pondering the same shit he was.

What the hell were they going to do about this attraction?

What are you not going to do about it?

She looked up again and had a brilliant smile on her face. "I do. But we're not doing anything. For now."

"For now." He lifted his mug in a salute and kept his feelings to himself. Because to act on them in any way required physical expression that would get him cuffed and hauled away by the school's assigned SVPD officer and ruin his career.

"Neither of us can afford the attention an inappropriate relationship would draw, Mr. Everlock." She ducked her head out of the small office before she continued. "No one's here yet, but it would only take one misstep and the whole reason I'm here gets blown."

"Correct. And it's not about us. Now you understand that I understand all of this, Nika." Painfully so. "That doesn't mean I might not try to tempt you every now and then." He waggled his brows in his best skeevy-dude impression.

Nika giggled. Like a schoolgirl. If anyone did

walk in, they'd see a teacher and rapt student, nothing more. A mentorship of sorts.

But if they picked up on the blatant chemistry between them...

"We should probably talk about Claudia at the station."

"Or at either one of our places." She had a huge smirk on her face and he bit back a startled laugh.

"You just said..."

"And you said you'd tempt me. If no one sees us go to either place, it's safe, right?" She took a large gulp of her coffee. "At least now I won't freak as much if I see you following me." Her voice was low, so quiet that he had a hard time hearing her.

"Are you still angry about Saturday?"

"No, not anymore. I've been trained in evasive maneuvers, too, you know."

He leaned back and returned her obstinate stare. "We're a perfect match, then."

The rest of Nika's day at school was anticlimactic after her confrontation with Mitch. She'd wanted to scream at Mitch when he'd acted so smug and contained in his office. As if her discovery that he was a TH agent didn't bother him in the least. As if he thought her unprofessional for letting it bother her.

She slammed the driver's door closed on her mother's car and watched as the snow that had accumulated all afternoon on the roof slide over the side of the SUV. Activating the wipers, she pressed the windshield fluid button to clear the glass of ice and snow. She missed her ancient but reliable economy sedan. She'd still be out in the cold, brushing the snow off and scraping the ice, but the clunker was a part of her life. It'd seen her through college and all the years after, not an easy feat for someone with a lead foot like hers. She was particularly rough on the brakes, which carried over to her reputation at SVPD. It was a known fact among her colleagues that her presence in the driver's seat of any of the department's vehicles meant new brake pads would be imminent.

The school parking lot was empty except for the cars of kids practicing for the spring musical or winter sports athletes. So far none of her hours in the building had yielded more than what she'd learned at Rachel's house. Nothing had surfaced since, as if the perpetrator knew she was there and was watching and waiting for her to disappear.

Nika swung out onto the main road that ran through Silver Valley, her mind on the report she'd file once she was back at her station desk.

She didn't notice the lone figure on the pedestrian bridge until after she saw the huge chunk of rock as it fell from the overpass, straight at her windshield. Thoughts of identifying the culprit vanished as she yanked the steering wheel to the right in an effort to avoid the danger. It was too late. She'd managed to put the car into a spin on the slick pavement, away from the object, but not before the loud snaps of splintering glass reached her ears.

Chapter 11

The SUV's air bags exploded and Nika no longer had control of her vehicle. She sat helpless as it spun out over the shoulder and into the ditch at the side of the road.

Just great. Now her mother's car was toast, at least until the windshield was repaired and air bags replaced. Mentally going through her memorized checklist, Nika figured out that none of her bones were broken and that she didn't seem to have any other injuries. She was okay. The car was still on all four tires, only slightly tilted in the shallow ditch. As she prepared to exit the car the smell of gasoline turned on every alarm bell in her internalized warning system.

Gasoline. *Shit.*

She tried to open the door with no luck. Panic

tightened its icy fingers around her. Was this how her luck, her attention to detail, was going to run out? After the better part of a decade studying and training for this kind of situation, she was going to be outdone by a jammed door?

No. Freaking. Way.

Summoning every ounce of focus and strength she had, Nika moved the collapsed front and side air bags, getting them out of her way. Her left hand scrambled again for the door pull. Panic threatened at the edges of her awareness when her fingers pulled at the handle with no luck.

Lean.

She allowed her strength and gravity to use her body weight against the door. Finally the door moved a fraction of an inch. Metal against metal. Bracing herself, she shoved her shoulder against the door just as it was yanked open. She fell out of the car, knowing the ground was going to be hard and cold. Instead she was caught midair, the icy field a good foot below her face, her body secure.

"I've got you, Nika."

Mitch.

She'd fallen into Mitch's arms.

Nika blinked as she looked at him, her eyes an icy shade of blue from the way the sunlight touched them.

"You okay? Does anything hurt?" His voice was rough as his heart pounded in his throat. God Almighty. He'd watched her car spin out and hit the shoulder when they'd been going forty miles an hour. He'd thought she was a goner, depending on how her car reacted to the torque of the spinout.

"I'm good. I can wiggle my toes, promise. Just get me out of here. I smell gas."

Mitch did, too, and allowed his training to guide his motions, reflexive and instinctual. He heaved Nika's body from the SUV, hoisted her over his shoulder and ran across the farm field. His winter hiking boots were filling with snow, his socks growing wet and damp, threatening to freeze his feet. He had to get as far as possible from the vehicle. It was unlikely that it would—

A huge explosion rent the air and forced him to his knees. He managed to fall forward, at least, so that Nika landed on her butt. Her elbows kept her head from slamming on the frozen ground.

"Mitch!" She reached for him.

Mitch covered her with his body. Not so much to protect her from any flying debris—there wasn't any—but to reassure himself that she was alive. He was alive. They were both okay.

"Nika, I'm so sorry, baby. I've got you. You're going to be all right."

"Hell, I know that, Mitch." She pounded his shoulder with a gloved hand. Amazing how air bags could break bones but she was in one piece. Obviously her strong will hadn't taken a hit. "What about you? I'm no lightweight. Did you hurt your back carrying me? I could have run—"

He shut her up with his mouth. It didn't make sense, this incredible drive he had to feel her, touch her, know she was okay. *Nika*. Her warmth, her body, the reassurance they were both still here, alive on planet earth, was all he could think about.

She didn't hesitate to respond to his kiss and he wrapped his arms around her body as she wrapped hers around his neck. As quickly as the car's gas tank had exploded, their attraction blew up in a volatile mix of need, relief and potent desire.

Her lips pressed against him and her tongue fought with his before dipping and diving into every crevice of his mouth, making him harder than he ever thought he'd been. Especially after such a narrow escape. His usual reaction to near death wasn't an instant erection. But he'd never worked with Nika before, never known a woman like her. He pressed his hips into hers, allowing himself to revel in the contact, losing himself to the moment, the freaking hot need he had for Nika.

Nika's legs cradled his hips and she rocked against him, her little pants and gasps for air music to his ears. So much nicer than the wail of sirens.

Sirens.

"Shit, Nika, we can't—"

"We have to, Mitch. I was wrong the other night. I don't want to be a tease. Never, not with you."

He pulled back as huge, fat flakes of snow fell on her face. Her pupils were huge, widely dilated despite the brightness of the snow, her skin pale with a dangerous sheen of sweat.

"Goddamn it." Lifting himself off her, he pulled her into a sitting position. Normally he'd keep her down, elevate her feet, but hypothermia was a risk, too. "You're in shock, Nika."

"Am not." She started to tremble and her lips were turning purple.

Dismay and something much deeper, far more primal, rocked him.

Fear.

"Here." He whipped off his leather jacket and put it on her shoulders. At least she was in a winter coat so she wouldn't get too cold, but sitting on a wet pile of snow wouldn't help her warm up.

"Come on." He tugged until she stood and then he nestled her into his arms, doing his best to warm her until the EMTs arrived. Damn it he was still hard from kissing her. No wartime experience had prepared him for this.

They were visible to the road now that they weren't hidden in several inches of snow and dried branches. But they could be spotted by any trucker driving by, any traffic helicopter. What if one of the army choppers from Fort Indiantown Gap had flown over? In the midst of routine training the pilot and crew could have been treated to a most un-routine sight.

And his students. The seniors drove this stretch of highway as a matter of course. He didn't deserve their respect, not if they found him panting like a dog on top of a woman they thought was their classmate. If his colleagues witnessed their hot embrace, it would have been just as bad.

He tried not to hate himself as he held on to Nika and willed the EMTs to get to them as soon as possible. The way she was shaking scared him more than any overseas op ever had, more than the threat of losing his professional reputation.

Nika didn't think she was in shock, not really, but she couldn't control the shudders racking her body, so maybe Mitch was right.

It just felt so damned good here, wrapped next to Mitch, the snowfall quiet around them, keeping the reality of the sirens and chaos that promised at bay. She started to laugh and, just like the shudders, couldn't stop.

"What's so funny, sweetheart?"

Sweetheart? Mitch Everlock had called her *sweetheart?* The laughter turned hysterical. A tiny part of her brain that wasn't frozen told her it wasn't that funny but, like the chill stealing away her thoughts, she couldn't stop it.

"M-M-Mitch, y-y-you are r-r-right."

"Shh. Save your energy. You'll be back to yourself as soon as we get you warmed up."

And just like that, her peals of mirth turned to tears. They felt like splinters of ice falling from her eyes and all she could think of was chopping onions, her mother's homemade beef stew and sadness that she'd never get to make it for Mitch.

He was right; she was in shock. The tiny bit of her brain that remained detached and sane registered the fact and she tried to pull it together.

The shock symptoms didn't last that long, though. As soon as the EMTs arrived she was enveloped in a warming blanket and placed in the heated back of their emergency vehicle. Mitch wavered in and out of her peripheral vision.

"Sir, you need to stay back until we assess her."

"Okay, ma'am, how many fingers?" The EMT waved two fingers and Nika responded accurately. As soon as the warmth reached her fingers and toes she remembered she was supposed to be a student. Her car, no her *mother's* car, crap!

"Mitch—I mean, Mr. Everlock!"

"I'm right here." He grinned at the EMT who was

eyeing him as if he were a complete perv. "She's my student."

"Uh-huh."

"What's going on, folks?" Claudia was at their side, flashing an SVPD badge to the EMTs. "Is she okay?"

"Yeah. Just a little shock. We should probably run her to the hospital for a thorough checkup."

"That's not necessary." Nika was not going to go through having to explain to the attending doctor why she had a fake driver's license, that she was undercover at SVHS. The fewer people who knew, the better.

"I happen to also be her aunt. I'll take complete responsibility for her, folks." Claudia spoke with an easy authority that made so much sense now that Nika knew about Trail Hikers.

Something that had escaped her thoughts since the crash. Mitch was a Trail Hiker. They really were in this together.

"Hey, what's going on?"

He ignored the query and kept going as shouts and screams erupted around him in the school parking lot. He walked through the chaos, a hoodie covering his head, his face. He was dressed like a teenager and forced himself to walk slowly, to act as if he was unaware of the death he'd hopefully just helped bring about. His New Thought sister had texted him that she'd dropped the rock at the right time and it had hit the right car.

It was too bad, having to take out that new young girl. Her name was Nika and she was very bright, according to his source. She'd entered SVHS because her parents were relocating to the area. Her parents obviously didn't know that Silver Valley was a hell-hole, a place where the values that mattered were eroding more every day, every hour. He'd saved her from the evil to come and would be rewarded for it in the next life. That's what Mr. Wise said. Everyone who dies to achieve the spiritual cleansing needed for New Thought is another soul saved from this world's evils.

Sirens screeched through the winter air and he got into his car. He left the heater off. The cold kept his thoughts pure, his purpose singular. He left the parking lot the back way and turned toward the outskirts of town. Where he knew home really was—the trailer park development Mr. Wise had prepared for the True Believers, the ones who embraced New Thought. Mr. Wise had chosen him to be the sacred messenger for Silver Valley. He was so grateful, so humbled. He had to make sure he wasn't proud about it, but he saw no harm in being proud of his methods. Pig's blood on the Rainbows teacher's board; his threats to Mitch Everlock had been clever. But the rock through the window and now this rock, his killing rock dropped by another New Thought believer? That would make his message clear. Mr. Wise's message, the message that came from the One Who Mattered.

He had to make the people of Silver Valley see the truth. New Thought was the only way. If it meant he had to take all of Silver Valley High School out, he would. First, he'd started with the Rainbows. It might be enough, especially if the new girl wasn't an issue anymore.

He hoped she was dead, that the rock had done its job.

* * *

Mitch was relieved beyond measure when Claudia insisted she take Nika to the ER. He followed Claudia's vehicle in his own, and waited for them both as Nika was triaged and taken into an examination area. He wanted to lie, to tell the hospital staff that he was family, too. But why? To appease his worry? Was it his guilt over nearly making love to her in the open farm field, right after she'd almost lost her life?

Or was it more?

He flipped through one of the many worn women's magazines in the racks on the waiting area wall. He saw none of the words, none of the photographs, as he struggled to keep his deepest truth buried.

He was falling for Nika.

Nika's examination had taken all of an hour, as the West Shore had a new hospital and the sparkling facility was überefficient. Claudia had suggested they all rendezvous at Nika's within thirty minutes, and plan on eating there. She'd notified Colt and Bryce. Colt was to join them but Bryce had to stay behind in the station to process the evidence from the crash scene.

Mitch took in the gathering in Nika's living room as she sat wrapped in a thick faux-mink throw, her gas fireplace giving off a decent amount of heat in the small space. Her Christmas tree was lit and if it hadn't been for the ugly reason for their meeting, it could have been a pleasant holiday party.

"I had no idea the clam chowder at Silver Valley Grocer was so delicious." Claudia finished up a mug and placed it on the coffee table.

"As a single man I know where to get good, hot food at just about any time of day or night." Chief Todd practically preened as he passed around a box of chocolate brownie bites. "They also have the best bakery in town."

"Anyone need more coffee, tea or cocoa?" Mitch had appointed himself the beverage coordinator, but they all knew he was most concerned about Nika. She looked a lot better than she had right after the accident, but as much as her skin had regained its pinkish hue, the circles under her eyes told the real tale. She'd barely touched her food, and she was the one who'd requested the clam chowder as her favorite. It killed him to not sit next to her and wrap his arm around her to help keep her warm.

And reassure you, too.

"I'll have some."

"Me, too."

Colt and Claudia waited with Nika while he made the drinks in the kitchen. It would be a long night for the three of them while they got every last detail of what Nika remembered and then transcribed it for Bryce to add to the police report.

When Mitch came back into the living room Claudia was questioning Nika.

"Let's go back a bit, Nika. We've all read the initial report. You were getting into the car in the school parking lot."

Nika nodded as she stared into the fire. "Yes. It had started to snow and the polar vortex was dropping the temperature by the minute, it seemed. I made a mental note to take it slower going home. My mom's car is great in snow but not so much against high winds, and I knew they were predicted to come in at any point."

"Did you see any of the students, teachers, leaving at the same time as you?"

"No." She paused, her brow wrinkled. "Wait a minute—I did have a hard time making the left turn onto the pike. Once I did, I tried to get over into the left lane, for when I'd turn to head to the station. I couldn't get over—I was blocked in, right before I went under the pedestrian bridge. I thought I saw someone, a figure, on the bridge, but it was pretty dark and I only noticed him or her after I saw the rock already falling. To be honest, all I remember after that is seeing the rock smash against the windshield and hearing the crack. The air bags deployed before I saw anything else."

Mitch exchanged looks with Claudia and Colt. They all knew that other vehicles to her rear and left would have kept Nika right where the killer wanted her. In the right lane as she passed under the raised sidewalk.

"Can you remember anything about those vehicles? Their drivers?"

Nika shook her head. "No, it was already pretty dark and almost impossible to make out who was in any car."

"Do we have anything from forensics on Nika's car yet, Colt?" As Claudia deferred to the police chief, Mitch didn't miss the unspoken messages that went between them. There was a definite bond there that had nothing to do with Trail Hikers, SVPD or law enforcement at all.

None of my business. And if he wasn't so tuned

into Nika he might have been more interested in the sparks between the two officials.

Colt ran his hand over his face. "Nothing. It's only been a few hours." As he spoke, his phone vibrated in his hand. "Todd speaking."

They all sat straighter, hoping for an opening that would lead to the killer. Mitch used the opportunity to sit beside Nika on the sofa. He squeezed her knee. "You doing okay?"

She put her small hand over his. "I'm fine. Stop worrying." Her eyes went to Colt and Claudia before she looked at him. "Thank you."

He smiled and turned his hand over to hold hers. If they'd been alone he would have kissed her.

"Are you sure?" Colt's face remained impassive but Mitch saw his hands tighten on his mug to match the harshness of his tone.

Claudia took a sip of her coffee, obviously coming to her own conclusions. As did Mitch. He knew without a doubt that Nika had been targeted. The question was by whom. He knew why—she'd been attending the Rainbows meetings. As a 'new student' at SVHS she was an easy target.

Colt put his phone down. "That was Bryce. You two were correct. You smelled gasoline because your fuel line was cut very slightly to allow for a slow leak."

"Couldn't that have been from the impact of her spinout?" Claudia voiced what Mitch thought, but deep down he knew the answer.

"Highly unlikely. And if that were the case, the break would have been more rough, a tear. This was a clean cut with a tool of some sort."

"So that's why it exploded." Nika sounded as if she were still processing the event.

"There's more." Colt scratched the back of his neck with his huge hand. "There was a makeshift bomb, about the size of a large firecracker, under the carriage. The kind that detonates with a cell phone."

"Like a terrorist's?"

"Yes. But this was more primitive, similar to what we see from homegrown domestic terrorists."

"You think it's the True Believers, don't you?" Claudia spoke up.

Colt looked at her. "You're the expert in this, more than I am. The Feds are being called in. There are already two FBI agents on scene and one at the station. I expect ATF to file a report, too, due to the bomb."

"Did the bomb have the capability of harming more than just me?" Nika asked what the rest of them knew. Self-recrimination made Mitch want to hang his head in shame. Nika had been in shock when he'd kissed her. He behaved like a lust-struck animal.

"No." Colt and Claudia answered in unison.

"If it had, the explosion we witnessed would have been far worse." Mitch spoke up. He hated admitting it to her. "I don't think we'd have gotten away soon enough."

"Mitch is correct. The bomb could have been loaded with enough shrapnel to take out dozens of victims. Goddamned nails from the local hardware store." Colt looked shaken, but Mitch knew his frustration would turn to anger against the perpetrators.

Claudia was already there. "These bastards are going to pay."

As she spoke, Nika's phone lit up. Her eyes were

round, her brows in a determined line as she read the Caller ID. "It's Rachel Boyle. She's calling my student number." They all knew this meant the call had been routed through the station and would be recorded.

Claudia nodded at her. "Pick it up. We'll wait."

Chapter 12

Nika placed her phone on the coffee table and put it on speaker.

"Hey, Rachel. I put you on speaker because I'm trying to chill out on my bed." She knew everyone in her living room would stay quiet but didn't want Rachel to suspect anything if the connection wasn't as clear.

"Nika? Is this really you?" A broken, sad voice filled the room.

"Of course it's me, silly. Who else would it be?" She offered a quick grin to Claudia, Colt and Mitch as they listened in. Their expressions were rapt, as if she were receiving the codes to a nuclear weapon instead of trying to gain information from an emotionally abused teenager.

"Oh, my God. Are you sure you're okay?"

"Yes, I'm fine. Why wouldn't I be?"

"Thank God! I was so worried, Nika. I thought, I thought... I heard you were in an accident today."

"I was, but it was just a small fender bender."

"Nika, how can you say 'small' when I heard that your damned car exploded?"

"It wasn't my car, it was my mom's. And how do you know it exploded?"

"It was on the news." Rachel grew silent. "I heard there was a rock thrown at it or something?"

Nika's heartbeat felt heavy with dread. She'd really hoped Rachel had nothing to do with the rock-throwing incident, especially her crash. "Where did you hear that, Rachel?"

Silence.

"Rachel?"

A large sniffle, then louder sob broke through the phone connection. "Rachel, tell me what's wrong. I'm okay, really." Nika had to give herself credit; she had the wherewithal to still behave as a self-centered teen, as if everything was about her.

"I'm so glad, Nika. Because my mother told me you were probably dead and it was because you were in the same club as I am and that it was my fault because I encouraged you to join the Rainbows."

Could Belinda Boyle be the one behind all the crimes? Nika watched Claudia take notes and knew the thought wasn't hers alone.

"Rachel, listen to me. I've already told you once. I joined the Rainbows because I support the LGBT cause. I was in the same kind of club back in my old school. You didn't have to convince me to go to it. I did it all on my own, and would have whether I ever met you or not. The best part of the Rainbows is that I've gotten to know you, and Mr. Everlock is helping me to figure out where to go to college next year, too. And why would your mother think someone wanted to hurt me just because I'm in the Rainbows?"

"You know about what's going on with Mr. Everlock, right?" Rachel's voice wobbled. "That he's been getting harassed since he started the club?"

Nika looked at Mitch and he nodded. "Yes, I've heard a few things, but I thought it was just some creep. Not someone who would do anything to break the law."

"Nika, I think you're in big danger. I can't explain it, really. It's my gut feeling. There are a lot of people who don't like the Rainbows and think it shouldn't be allowed in Silver Valley High. They think it's immoral."

"That doesn't make sense, Rachel. A lot of parents support it and make all kinds of treats for us to sell at the bake sales. You said your mom is a little out of it. Maybe she misheard something?"

"No, she didn't. I was there."

"Where?"

Silence.

"Where, Rachel?"

"At the New Thought book study last weekend. I had to go and work in the kitchen, since I won't agree to joining any of the sessions my mother and the rest of those crazies are part of. They were having a spaghetti dinner. I boiled twenty-five pounds of pasta. While I was cooking I overheard them talking. Well, the loser guy who runs the whole thing, anyway. Mr. Wise. He said they were going to put a stop to anything that encouraged 'immorality' in the schools and the Rainbows came up. One of the parents of a Rainbows member was there and asked about it. Said her kid didn't agree with the group, either."

"Which parent, Rachel? Is the kid someone in our class?"

Silence. Nika looked at everyone else for a signal. No one moved. Like her, they were afraid to spook Rachel. Rachel's answer might finally give them what they needed.

A suspect.

"Rachel?"

Muffled voices came over the line.

"Sorry, I've got to go." Rachel spoke quickly before the line was disconnected.

Nika collapsed back against the sofa. "We were this close, damn it!" She reached for her phone to throw it but Mitch grabbed her wrist.

"Hey. You did good. We've learned a lot."

"If nothing else we know the rock from the bridge, the threatening notes, the rock through the window—they are all connected to the True Believers." Claudia spoke. "We all suspected it but now we know."

"But without a name, what good is that? How many people do we think are going to these New Thought gatherings?" Nika looked at Colt.

He sighed. "Last count, it's up to fifty, and that means there are at least four times that many in total that have been sucked into its grips. Wise is charismatic and smart. He knows that he won't get everyone he needs to show up for his brainwashing sermons, but his reach is out there."

"So we need a name, to figure out who exactly is

doing his dirty work for him." Nika shook her head. "Damn it, if I'd only made it past the bridge—"

"Your car would have been blown up underneath you and we'd be planning your funeral instead of our next move. Whoever this ass is, he wants to show off and he did, using a rock again. But he covered his bases, too, with the bomb." Mitch's interruption was full of anger, the gravity of their situation, and, dare she hope, a little fear? Did Mitch care for her?

She shoved the thought down. Even if he did care, she wasn't going to be able to have more than one of her usual, short-term relationships with Mitch. She couldn't—it would be too risky. Losing someone as wonderful as him would be more than she could take. "Mitch is right. As much as I hate to keep you in the crosshairs of these nut jobs, Nika, you're our best hope." Colt looked at her for a long moment before moving his gaze to Claudia. "I think we need to call in some backup here. SVPD has it, and we have FBI coming in, but Nika's our only deep undercover at this point."

"I'm far from 'deep' undercover. Let's face it, someone might have figured out where I live and that I'm not a student." She berated herself for not being more careful.

"I don't think so, Nika. Colt's right. If the cult knew you were a cop, or where you lived, they'd have paid you a visit here. They'd hit you where you live, even go after your family. Instead they're targeting what they think is a transfer student." Claudia's gaze was steady, her eyes expressive. "You do need Trail Hikers' backup at this point. I'm glad we pulled you in when we did. Mitch, you know what's coming. And I don't have to ask if you're ready for it."

Nika looked from Claudia to Mitch and back. "No. Absolutely not. I don't need Mitch's help in this. He needs to focus on being a chemistry teacher. I'll handle Rachel and the rest of it."

"That's the problem, Nika. 'The rest of it' involves a cult that we've recently found may have connections to international terrorists. It's no longer a simple high school undercover bust."

"It never was, Claudia. I knew that going in. We all know about the cult, and it was on my radar when I got called in to figure out who was leaving the messages in blood on Mitch's SMART Board."

"Nika, I'm not going to usurp your authority. And I promise I won't get in the way of what you're accomplishing with Rachel and any other students."

"You can't promise that, Mitch. You'll think you need to protect me. You can't help yourself."

"Hey, give me some credit. Are we developing a friendship here? Yes. But have I worked with women in lethal ops before, treated them like any other colleague? Yes. I'm a trained Marine, Nika. I've worked alongside men and women and never gave favor to either. Just had their six as they had mine." Mitch's declaration made her blush and she wanted to bury her face in the velvety throw over her lap.

"I can vouch for that. Here's the deal, you two." Claudia spoke as the Trail Hikers CEO, not as her acquaintance. It was in the sharpness of her glance, the way Colt looked at her with total acceptance of her authority. "You have to infiltrate New Thought. We can't afford to set off any of Wise's alarm bells.

We're taking him down for the last time and he'll spend the rest of his life behind bars. Colt and I are going to work out how SVPD will keep Silver Valley High safe, and how to block any other plans the bastards have to get into the school. You two work on Rachel and her mother. That's our in."

Mitch wasn't sure how he managed it, but he stayed in Nika's guest room all night. He checked in on her a few times to see if she was resting comfortably and had a full glass of water on her nightstand.

Awake early the next Saturday morning, he made them a huge breakfast. She never stirred as he worked in her small kitchen, poaching eggs for the eggs Benedict, his specialty. The Canadian bacon was almost done while he whisked the hollandaise sauce in a pan that was too big for it, but Nika didn't have enough pots for him to fashion a double boiler.

Shuffling steps sounded behind him.

"I can't stop what I'm doing or your breakfast, make that *feast*, will be ruined."

"Please, carry on." She patted his back before she poured herself a cup of coffee from the pot he'd programmed to brew as he cooked. "I had no idea I had the ingredients for anything as fancy as eggs Benedict."

"You had eggs, English muffins and the right kind of bacon. What else do you use your Canadian bacon for?" The sauce was perfect. He turned and poured it over the plump eggs, trying to keep his eyes on his task. He blew it when he caught a whiff of Nika's shampoo. Her skin was fresh scrubbed, her lips full and inviting. *Hell.* "You look a lot better this morning. How are you feeling?"

"Good. Not as if I'd been carried from a car about to explode—hey, watch it. You're spilling."

"Damn it." He put the pot on the stove and handed her the least messed-up plate. "Let's sit at your dining room table. I've already set it."

"I could get used to this, Everlock."

"Call me Mitch." Although she could call him dog poop if she ever looked at him like she was looking at her food.

"Chef Mitch." She slid into her wooden chair and without preamble dug into her food. He followed and they ate in companionable silence for several minutes.

"You were here all night, and now you're feeding me. It really isn't necessary, Mitch."

"Until we figure out who put a bomb under your car, yeah, it *is* necessary." He saw the defiance in her eyes and held up his hands, palms out. "I hear you. I know you're capable of taking care of yourself. But you'd just come out of shock, no matter how brief it was. I couldn't in good conscience leave you alone when you weren't up to par. Besides, Colt and Claudia suggested it."

"They did? Figures." She dug in to her meal. "You heard what Bryce told Colt. It was rudimentary. Any kid could do it—slice a fuel line. And the explosive— no more than a firework—was there to make sure it did its job in igniting the fuel. You know better than I do that it doesn't take someone highly sophisticated to make that kind of explosive."

"We don't know it was a kid, or whether it was a

single perpetrator or a group, Nika. We really don't know a whole hell of a lot."

"You agree the cult is behind all of this?" Her mouth formed around the egg on her fork and he was hypnotized by her lips. A bit of runny yolk dribbled on her bottom lip and her tongue peeked out to lick it off.

Mitch didn't want to be her bodyguard, her protector. He wanted to be her lover.

"Mitch?" Her gaze leveled him with an intensity that made his erection strain against his sweatpants. If they weren't sitting she'd see the effect she was having, and he'd have her pulled up against him.

"Um, yeah. The cult." He took a gulp of orange juice. "They are connected to the Rainbows de facto since Rachel is a part of the group and her mother is involved with the New Thought ministries. Whether the cult itself is behind the petty crimes, like the rock through the window and the blood on the board, that's not so clear, I suppose. But a car bomb, no matter how amateurish, is no longer 'petty.' You've read the TH files on the cult?"

She shook her head. "Not all of them."

"Of course not, you haven't had time yet. So far the cult has been connected with the town—remember when the mayor was arrested? This second one? And Mayor Lemmon was acquitted? The cult helped fund Mayor Charbonneau's election, and was feeding the county's protection team false information. Right before that, we had Zora's mother show up. You know she'd been in the original cult, right? The Female Preacher Killer was a lone operator but we now have reasons to believe he was being fed by the cult's peripheral operators. The Leonard Wise wannabes. They picked up on the killer's resentment against the church he worked for as a janitor and attended—Silver Valley Community Church. The cult exploited him, made his inner crazies come to life. It took us a while, but we've put all the parts of that web together."

"So why wasn't the cult taken down after any of those events?"

Mitch shook his head. "We didn't have enough hard evidence. When we get them this time, we need to be able to put them behind bars for good. You heard what Claudia said last night."

"Isn't that what the FBI's for?"

"Normally yes, but Leonard Wise is a smart man. He'll sniff out a traditional Fed and run scared in a heartbeat."

Nika snorted. "Great. So you're allowing Silver Valley and its citizens to become victims in order to make sure the cult gets the justice you all think it should? What about the future victims? What if Wise gets a hold of any of our teen girls?"

"That's the bitch of all of it, Nika. As far as we know, he hasn't touched another child yet. Not since Upstate New York. We have to try to draw him into his own snare, catch him where he's most comfortable. I'm thinking the compound he's making the trailer park into is the best place to hit him."

"Let me get into the New Thought group, Mitch. They'll think I'm another recruit. I can say I found the literature at Rachel's and liked how it sounded. Liked her mother, and what she had to say about the New Thought."

"No freaking way, Nika. First, it will look too

suspicious as any friend of Rachel's would not be friendly toward the cult. And Rachel may damn well need you. Has it occurred to you that her mother might make her go to a meeting and she could be assaulted by Wise or one of his cronies?"

Nika nodded. "Actually it has. But if I were there, I would protect her." She shrugged. "The truth is Rachel will never do anything she doesn't really want to. Her mother doesn't have the control over her she thinks she does. Except that Rachel wants to protect her mother."

Mitch looked at her. "You heard what you said, didn't you? It's too dangerous to attend one of those meetings at the compound. And you need to keep her away from them, too."

"The problem is that I have no place to take her to hang out. I can't bring her here; it's obvious it's an adult woman's home. I can't take her to my parents', she'll wonder why they're so old for a teenager's family."

"She might believe they're your grandparents."

"That's a good idea except there is no way in hell I'm bringing my parents into an undercover op."

"There's something else, Nika. What is it?"

"I *like* Rachel, Mitch. I don't think she's behind these events, as much as I know you and Chief Todd suspect her. After this all breaks I'd like to be able to be a point of contact for her. She'll need it no matter what happens with her mother. The least amount of lying I do to her now, the better."

"You have the training of a fierce warrior, Nika, but you've got a heart of gold."

"Save it, Everlock—I mean, Mitch. Don't go reading any more into this than me doing my job."

"Keeping the planet safe for democracy?"

"No, just Silver Valley." She warmed up her coffee. "Want more?"

"No, thanks. I had two cups before you woke up."

"I can't thank you enough for taking care of me yesterday. And breakfast today. It was a relief to be able to let go of the constant-vigilance gig."

"I hear you."

They sat in silence, Nika looking out at her two bird feeders that hung from the large oak she shared with Ivy's town house. Mitch couldn't look at birds or nature or anything but Nika. When Nika was in a room he couldn't focus on much else. Claudia and Colt had noticed it last night, and probably before that, too.

He didn't expect any grief from them as it was clear the SVPD chief and Trail Hikers CEO had their own fireworks show going on.

"Why are you looking at me like that?" Her demand tugged at his affection for her. With a dash of Bunsen burner heat.

"You know why."

"I suppose I do, and it's pointless. This is only going to get us into trouble."

"It's not criminal." Hope flared when she didn't deny their chemistry, the bond that was becoming much more difficult to ignore because it wasn't just lust.

She looked at him and he saw the moment her eyes flickered from interest to white-hot need. Still hard from being next to her, he stood when she did, reached for her as she did him.

Their mouths connected with no finesse, no seduction. He made short work of her robe, letting it fall with the tie to the kitchen hardwood floor.

She grabbed the bottom of his T-shirt and yanked it over his abs, over the arms he lifted without hesitation. He grasped her wrists, needing to make sure this was what she wanted.

"Nika?"

Chapter 13

The light of desire in Mitch's eyes made the attraction she had for him explode into need—need she'd been denying since they'd first kissed in the SVPD parking lot.

"I want this, Mitch. I want you. No more stopping." She lifted her arms so that he could take her sleep shirt off. As soon as her breasts were free, she pressed them against his bare chest, liberally sprinkled with hair as dark as his brows. His hands cupped her breasts and their foreheads met, breaths mingling, chests rising and falling in their fervor.

"God, Nika, you're so freaking hot." He kissed her again until her moans turned to whimpers. When he pulled back, her relief that they were getting to the best parts was short-lived as Mitch had a more sweet torture in mind.

His tongue tasted every inch of her throat, her chest, her breasts, her stomach and back to her breasts. Large hands grasped her buttocks and pulled her flush against his erection at the same moment his mouth suckled her nipple. Nika had heard of nipple orgasms but thought they were limited to fantasy. She was wrong.

"Oh, my gosh, Mitch, don't stop." He grasped her bottom more tightly as he switched to her other breast, moving his pelvis into hers with no doubt of where they were headed. She came with a loud scream, grasping the counter to avoid collapsing to the floor.

He pulled away from her and she cried out again, hating the separation.

"Your pajama bottoms, Nika. Off."

"Yours, too." Where Mitch's voice was roughly commanding, hers was breathless, the tremors of her climax still moving through her.

As soon as they were both free of any clothing, his hands gripped her waist and he lifted her onto the counter. The toaster slammed against the wall to make room. Mitch wasted no time and spread her legs apart, his hands hot on her upper thighs.

"I don't know how we're going to do this, Mitch, but I'm game for anything."

Laughter rumbled from deep within him and she loved how she felt it through his shoulders, his chest. She couldn't keep her hands off him.

"Oh, babe. This isn't for both of us, not yet." He stuck his fingers into her with no warning and she bucked, crying out for him, gripping the counter.

"Mitch, don't, don't..."

"Don't what, babe?"

"Stop."

Again the belly-deep laughter that only stoked her need. She had to keep her grip on the counter or she'd fall off and this exquisite torture would end too soon.

He licked his way to her belly button and then dipped between her legs, making her forget about falling or whether Mitch was laughing or not. Her hands were in his hair when she screamed out his name, the back of her head knocking against the spice cupboard.

When her breathing calmed enough for conscious thought, she glanced down to see Mitch regarding her as if she were a queen. Something precious. Someone he cared about.

"Turnabout's fair play, Mitch. Come up here." She tugged on his hair and he stood.

Nika slid off the counter and dropped to her knees in front of him. His fingers were in her hair, his breath was hitched, and she made sure he thought of nothing but her tongue, her mouth.

"Nika, let's go to the sofa, your bedroom…"

"No, Mitch. Here. Now. For you."

She reveled in his gasps of pleasure as she used her tongue on him. She wanted to make him feel as good as he had made her feel and didn't hold back.

His groan was a deep prelude to the cry he let out when she brought him to climax. She loved that she had the ability to do this to him.

"Nika."

They spent the rest of the day hashing out various scenarios Nika anticipated if she indeed got Rachel to take her to one of her mother's New Thought meetings. Neither mentioned what had happened in the kitchen. As if they both knew it wasn't where their focus could remain, not with a case to solve.

Nika had stupidly thought that once she'd been with Mitch, it would take the edge off her constant awareness of him. Instead she found herself tuning in to his every movement.

"As much as it's not my favorite idea, I agree that our best bet might be you getting into the New Thought meeting, to look far enough behind the curtains to see what's going on. But as a TH you have to understand that the ultimate goal is to take them out in their entirety. We can't piecemeal it, and if you run into trouble or need to get Rachel out of there quickly, it could turn dicey. It might get discovered that you're undercover and that would be enough to spook Wise."

"You're right. Which is why I'll go in with Rachel, act like a gullible teen, and then get out. I won't go in wired or with any weapons." Although that gave her pause. Her weapon was part of her when she was on the job.

"No, you need to be carrying, Nika. If the worst happened and one of his cronies decided to start threatening anyone, or opened fire, you'd have to be able to take them out. We won't be far away, either."

"We? As in TH?" She didn't like this. "No, Mitch. SVPD will know enough and they can sit in unmarked cars while I'm in there. But TH is too much. Remember what Claudia said—we have to handle this at the lowest level possible. And I'm not taking a weapon—for all we know Wise has his thugs frisk people at the door."

"SVPD has the Silver Valley High case, but TH

is in the cult op, Nika, and you're a TH agent now. You have to do it our way. You don't go in unless you agree to our terms. TH agents always carry a weapon."

"You mean *your* terms."

They contemplated one another and she saw the total concentration Mitch was putting into their planning. He wasn't going to budge.

"My terms are TH terms, Nika." He covered her hand with his own. "The most important thing is that you get in and out safely."

She pulled her hand away. "No, no, no! This is exactly why we should have waited until we closed the case to give in to our basic needs."

"Basic? Excuse me, but I disagree. Combining sodium and chlorine to make table salt, that's basic, ordinary. Making salicylic acid takes a few more steps, but it's pretty routine, it gives us aspirin. What we did? What we *shared* in there? Pure combustion. Like when we allow lithium to hit ambient air. Bam! It's not something we could stave off like hunger or thirst, Nika. And we're adult enough to know what we've discovered with each other is separate from the case."

When he shouted "Bam!" and used his hands to demonstrate an explosion, Nika tried to keep her face straight. The man she couldn't stop thinking about was a nerd.

"Mitch, this is life-or-death for our town, for the school. For your students. We need to remember what we're doing, why we're here together in the first place."

"That's a given. The 'keeping everyone safe' part. But, Nika, what we just experienced today, we can't ignore it, pretend it's not there. Isn't that what we've been doing for the past couple of weeks? Trying to ignore it? It's been here between us since you walked into my classroom."

Pleasure washed over her. Still, she hung on to her professional bearing. "I was a student that day, Mitch. You didn't know I was older than seventeen or eighteen, not right away."

"I knew the minute I saw you. And not because Claudia had let me in that an undercover officer was assigned to the case."

"You saw through my undercover disguise that easily?" True, she didn't wear a wig or anything special for the role, but the thought that *anyone* saw through her that easily shook her professional esteem.

He didn't answer her and she let it go. They had bigger things to worry about. Like how they were going to manage Mitch playing protector while allowing her to do her job unencumbered.

"My mother is driving me cray-cray." Rachel sat next to Nika at the large folding table they'd spread with a rainbow-themed tablecloth. A plethora of baked goods and candy was piled high and they didn't have a lot of time to talk, their conversation in bits and bites as they sold the goodies to hungry schoolmates.

"How much for three cupcakes?" An impossibly thin cheerleader tossed her raven hair as she held the paper plate of sweets in one hand, her other full of bills.

"It's a voluntary donation." Nika spoke up before

Rachel could make a cutting remark, her specialty with the girls who seemed less than friendly.

"Is a dollar a piece okay?"

"Sure!" Rachel grabbed the dollars and Nika hid her grin. She wouldn't have thought this was so funny in high school but from the outside looking way back, the ridiculousness of the cliques and snubs was excruciatingly obvious.

"How much have we made so far?"

"Two hundred, plus thirty-five cents." Rachel never looked at the cash box they were putting the payments into.

"How do you do that?"

Rachel blinked. "What?"

"Know how much we've both put in there."

"I hear everything. You know how some kids have photographic memories? I remember everything I've ever heard. If I listen to a class lecture, I can recall it during an exam." Rachel's cheeks turned red as soon as she finished her declaration. "That sounds so lame, doesn't it?"

"Not at all. I mean, no, of course not." Shit! Nika knew she was sounding too much of an adult and not the eighteen-year-old she was supposed to be. "I wish I had that kind of superpower."

Rachel's eyes lit up. "It is a superpower, in a way." Dimples appeared and Nika realized she'd never seen a genuine, unguarded expression on Rachel before.

"Five cookies, a brownie and two of those mini apple pies, but on separate plates. I don't want them to touch. And I want the cookies that are more chewy." Gabi from chemistry class stood in front of them, her smile wide and...fake.

"Do you want a latte with that?" Nika couldn't help poking at the perfect student's demeanor.

Gabi's smile disappeared for a split second, her eyes narrowed on Nika. She recovered quickly, looking like the perky girl who was always raising her hand to the hardest chemistry problems Mitch threw out.

"Here you go." Rachel handed Gabi a cardboard box filled with the baked goods and accepted a twenty-dollar bill in return. Gabi turned on her heel and walked over to a group of students Nika didn't recognize.

"She's not one to be messed with, Nika. She can be a real bitch if she wants to."

"If she was a bitch she wouldn't have just bought twenty dollars' worth of sweets from the Rainbows, would she?"

Rachel tilted her head. "You're from another kind of world, you know that? At Silver Valley High, no one is who you think they are."

"Have you made any money with these lame treats yet?" Amy Donovan interrupted them as she stood in front of the table, her eyes hungrily assessing the goodie table.

"We're bringing in a lot, actually." Nika adopted the same pose she saw Rachel use. The kiss-my-butt-you-stuck-up-bitch pose.

"Do you want anything, Amy?" Rachel's tone clearly said she didn't expect Amy to lower herself to help their fund-raiser.

"I would, but I don't have time to stop now. I've got to meet with the student council. We're voting on the rules about fringe clubs." She sauntered off and Rachel's hand hit the table, making the tower of cupcakes quake.

"That girl is such a jerk. She has the perfect grades, is the perfect Goody Two-shoes. But I don't buy it."

"Why not?"

Rachel shrugged and didn't say more.

"What are you doing this weekend?" It was the last few weekends before the formal, and most of the girls were lying low, studying and pleasing their parents so that they'd be allowed to stay out later after the dance.

It was Nika's chance to get into a New Thought cult meeting.

Rachel shrugged. "Studying for the exams the week after formal. Writing two essays. Trying to convince my mother that no way in hell am I going to go to one of those crazy meetings with her."

"What kind of meeting?"

"You know. That stupid group she's in, that I told you about."

"What if you agreed to go with her and brought a friend with you? It might be fun, seeing how nuts they really are." Nika prayed Rachel would see it as a chance to get Belinda off her back for a while, which would be a ticket to paradise as far as Rachel was concerned.

"You'd do that for me? You know we can't sell cookies from the Rainbows there, right?"

Nika laughed. "Yeah, I get it. I promise, I'll be superquiet and look like I really give a crap."

Rachel stared at her long enough to make Nika worried she'd pushed too far, too quickly. But time was marching on and the sooner the cult was blown apart, the better.

"I'll ask her, but I can guaran-damn-tee you that she'll say it's okay. Hell, she'll probably buy us a nice dinner after it lets out. She'll get good-girl points from the team leader for bringing in a new 'member.'"

Nika shrugged. "Whatever. I'm all about the free food."

"Six of the snickerdoodles, please." A stringy-haired boy with glasses and a nerdy graphic tee stood at the table and several more students were lined up behind him. It was a certainty that the Rainbows were going to have enough funds to buy a table for the Silver Bells Ball. Nika wanted to be happy for the group but her cop's sixth sense told her that it only made them a bigger target.

Chapter 14

"You absolutely cannot be recognized anywhere near that compound, Mitch." Claudia pinned him with her Marine Corps General stare and he shifted in the seat across from her desk.

"You trained me, Claudia. I know what I'm doing." And he knew she knew that, too. They'd first met on the battlefields of Iraq, years before either of them had ever dreamed of being part of a government shadow agency.

Claudia didn't relent. "You've got personal feelings mixed in here. That's enough to make any of us miss a step. It's not a fault, just part of being a human being."

"I'm not having any more PTSD events, if that's what's concerning you."

"Actually I'm not at all worried about your PTSD. You've apparently come through the worst and you're one of the lucky ones who can manage it. Is that fair to say?"

"Yes." In fact, the brief flash he'd had right after the last blood message in his classroom had been so fleeting, so quickly dissipated by a couple of deep breaths, he had to agree with her.

"And it's also fair to say that since Nika has come into your life you're not even thinking about the war, are you?"

Goddamn it. Claudia, ever the professional, had hoodwinked him with a tried-and-true interrogation method.

"While I've certainly been more involved in the cult op, as you've let me, it's not fair to say that Nika is responsible for whether I have a PTSD flashback or not."

"Not Nika, Mitch. Your feelings toward her."

"You don't ever play for fun, do you, Claudia?"

She looked at him thoughtfully and he swore he saw a softening in her eyes. "Admittedly I've been a hard-ass my entire life, or at least since I reported for my Plebe summer at the academy so many moons ago." The heavy academy class ring she wore on her right hand was unmistakable. "Do you think people can change, Mitch?"

The turn of conversation would have shocked him if he and Nika hadn't witnessed Claudia locking lips with Chief Todd. He thought about telling her what they'd witnessed, but it was too personal. Even the CEO of the Trail Hikers had a heart, a woman's soul. Theoretically, anyway. She deserved her privacy.

"Yes, I do. Not our basic natures, maybe, but if we want to we can always take a different direction, learn how to behave differently. Otherwise, what's the point?"

She looked at some location over his shoulder and didn't reply. He took it as a signal to end their talk and get out of the TH office. The urgency that filled him, knowing Nika was on her way to a New Thought event tonight, was undeniable, and made him damned prickly. As did the touchy-feely nature of his conversation with Claudia.

"If we're finished, Claudia, I need to go. I have some work to do before I join the stakeout tonight."

"The *un*-stakeout, Mitch. Keep your cover, no matter what you think is going on in that building. If Nika gets in trouble, let SVPD handle it. Not that it will happen—Nika has proven she's a worthy Trail Hiker."

"Roger. I'll report in anything I observe after she's out of there, Claudia."

"I know you will."

"Will you be there?" He was on shaky ground. It wasn't his place, or any TH agent's, to query Claudia on her activities.

"Not that you have a need to know, but, yes, I think I'll ride along with Colt. Chief Todd." Her cheeks turned an uncharacteristic shade of pink and he smiled.

"Boss, it's okay. Like you said, we're all human."

"That's enough, Agent Everlock." CEO Claudia was back and not about to take any guff from one of her employees.

As Mitch walked out of the TH building he couldn't help pondering the juxtaposition of the relationships that were developing. In the midst of what he thought might turn into a life-or-death struggle against a warped sociopathic cult leader, at least three couples had found love. Bryce and Zora. Rio and Kayla. Colt and Claudia.

Are you sure it's not four?

"Sorry about this part." Rachel spoke under her breath, just loud enough for Nika to hear as they slid into the backseat of Mrs. Boyle's car. It was a huge, house-size SUV, typical for a family with several kids. But since Rachel was the only one left at home, it seemed like overkill.

"No worries." They situated themselves in the backseat and Mrs. Boyle easily maneuvered the vehicle out of their gravel drive and onto the main pike.

It was the only part of her plan that bothered Nika. She wouldn't have her own vehicle to come and go as she pleased from the trailer park on the outskirts of Silver Valley. But it was better for her cover to ride with Rachel and her mother. It was best that she didn't have her mother's car, even if it hadn't been totaled by the crash, and no way in hell would she use the new car her mother's insurance was paying for. As for using her own dilapidated sedan or an unmarked police car, they weren't the best options, either. She had to be seen solely as Rachel's friend, a tagalong to the meeting. No telling which Silver Valley citizens she'd ticketed over the last eighteen months who were now part of the cult. She couldn't risk being recognized as an officer. She'd policed both the huge fiasco of the mayor's daughter's wedding last spring and the Christmas blowout at Silver Valley Community Church a few months before that.

It seemed that just as SVPD eliminated one faction of the reassembling cult, another popped up.

Whack-a-cult. A giggle escaped her and Rachel gave her an *are-you-cray-cray?* look. Nika smiled and shook her head. "Later." She mouthed the response more than spoke it.

"Are you two girls hungry? I can't promise there will be a lot to choose from at the potluck." Mrs. Boyle met Nika's eyes in the rearview mirror and for a brief instant Nika thought she saw the woman Belinda Boyle used to be. The mother who'd raised children, loved a man, had a career. Before she'd sold her soul to a devil like Leonard Wise.

"We're fine, Mom. But you know I won't turn down some mac and cheese at the Silver Valley Diner. Apple pie à la mode on the side."

"We'll see what we can do." Belinda turned off into the trailer park. Leonard Wise had purchased the entire run-down facility almost two years ago, before his release from prison. He'd used a corporate front and a former minion who'd only served a minimal prison term for activities related to the Upstate New York True Believers Cult.

Nika had entered the spooky park a few times but only as part of routine patrol ops. There was no reason to think anyone here would recognize her as anyone but a high school friend of Rachel's.

And a potential New Thought recruit.

Belinda parked in front of a prefabricated building the size of approximately three double-wide trailers. Nika noted the wheelchair access ramp and kept her outrage silent. Of course the building and entire compound would be accessible to people Wise thought would be more vulnerable and needy, like the elderly and disabled. She seethed with the need to bring this op to closure, put Wise and his men behind bars.

Because his cohorts were almost all men. The women who became involved in his cults were almost exclusively subservient to him, victims of psychological manipulation. Brainwashing. His beliefs were misogynist at best, evilly criminal at their worst. Wise would never allow a woman in his inner circle. Nika hadn't fully understood his motives until she'd had access to the TH reports that included a personality analysis for Wise and several of his more dangerous staff members.

His mother had abused him from a young age but he'd escaped his home and gone on to college. Where he'd been assimilated into a crazy cult himself. Until he'd left and worked in corporate America for several years, after which he surfaced in Upstate New York as the charismatic leader of a new "church."

Nika shuddered as she thought of the innocent people who'd been attracted to the idea of a church, a community that would give them something they'd been missing. Home, purpose, a family, community. Then they'd faced horrors of having their young girls betrothed to Wise, forced to have sex with a man decades older than them to produce the "perfect" True Believers.

Looking at the warmly lit building from the chilly winter night, it was hard to believe such a nondescript place harbored such malevolence.

As soon as she walked through the open door and was assaulted with glaring fluorescent overhead lighting and the equally stark stares of dozens of people, all here willingly, Nika's resolve was strengthened.

This is what evil feels like.

"Hello, friends. This is my daughter Rachel, who many of you already know."

"Welcome back, Rachel." They all spoke in unison. Nika counted at least thirty on one side of the large room, standing in front of their folding metal chairs, facing the back entrance. All eyes were on them.

"And this is Rachel's best friend, Nika. Nika is new to Silver Valley." Belinda spoke as if she'd bagged a double winner; Nika was a new student, her daughter's "best" friend and new to Silver Valley.

Vulnerable.

"Welcome, Nika." The singsong greeting chilled her and she tried to not meet anyone's eyes directly, acting the part of the shy, new girl. More importantly, she couldn't risk identification by someone that she'd ticketed or met at an SVPD fund-raiser. Although she was certain she passed as a teen at Silver Valley High, she worried that these kooks might see right through her disguise.

Mitch. If Mitch were here she'd feel safer. *Ridiculous.* She'd never been afraid or fearful during any other op, even with a gun in her face or bullets flying around. The rock through her windshield and following explosion had shaken her but she'd never felt afraid, not really.

Facing this group of people who looked as if they all knew the same moves, the "right" responses, she felt fear. Was this how her parents had felt under Soviet rule?

"Come, have something to eat." A pale woman ushered Nika and Rachel over to a folding table set up with a huge urn for hot water and several plates of baked goods. Nika declined anything to eat but figured the hot water would be safe enough to try; she made herself a cup of tea. Rachel refused anything.

As more members arrived Nika was able to get Rachel off to the side and find out who was who.

"How many of these people do you know?"

Rachel made a pretense of looking at her nails. "See that woman over there? That's Amy Donovan's mother. She's just like my mother; over-the-top with her belief of this stuff."

"Do you talk to Amy about it?"

Rachel shook her head. "Oh, no, no way. Amy won't even admit her mother is doing this stuff."

"Is she a single parent, too?"

"No, Mr. Donovan used be around the school for events all the time, but not so much now. Since Amy has so many younger brothers and sisters, he's probably taking them to sports and lessons and stuff. Probably thinks his wife is nuts for doing this, too."

Rachel pointed out a few other parents that she said had seniors at Silver Valley High but none in the chemistry class. Then Nika spotted a familiar face.

"Do you see what I see? Is that one of the PE teachers over there?" Nika motioned with her eyes to Kristine Rattner, whom she hadn't run in to since their face-off in the girl's bathroom.

"Yeah, that's Ms. Rattner. She started coming this past summer."

"Isn't it weird that an educated woman would be sucked into this?"

Rachel shrugged. "They prey on the lonely."

Nika glanced at Kristine and hoped she didn't notice her with Rachel. Not yet, anyhow. The less opportunity Kristine had to place her face, the better.

"Do they talk about things like the Rainbows here?"

"No, not directly, but they sure hint around it. Now, stop talking. You think no one notices us, but trust me, they're all watching."

After Nika and Rachel were placed in seats next to Belinda, Nika kept her focus on Rachel, who was staring straight ahead, her face blank. *Oh, God, please don't let her fall for any of this*. As much as Rachel was her own person, Nika had read in the TH files how powerful a person Wise was. Convincing.

A hushed quiet fell as the silence stretched out. The echo of a door slamming and several heavy footsteps preceded a group of eight men, walking in pairs from behind old velvet curtains hung from the ceiling at the front of the room. The drapes reminded Nika of an old dilapidated funeral home, and the men looked like gestapo. They appeared to thrive on the attention their arrival caused. As everyone stood, also in unison, she wondered what the invisible signal had been. The men? When they passed a certain spot in the room? They marched by, their hands clasped in front of their waists as if in prayer, their heads bowed. *Gross.*

The man of the hour walked in and he looked much like his prison photos. Older, his salt-and-pepper hair now stark white. Nika damned his solid posture, his obvious robust health. Apparently the rot that spewed from Wise didn't affect his physical wellness.

He started speaking and, from word one, it was clear: he was a man of conviction. Conviction that he was right and anyone, any entity that disagreed with his gospel of hate was wrong.

He went on and on for nearly an hour and Nika thought more than once that he stared at her for too long a time; that he was going to point her out. But he didn't and she realized she wasn't relieved as much as disappointed not to have a reason to confront the sick son of a bitch.

"Belinda Boyle will read the paragraphs on proper womanly behavior for us. Belinda?"

Rachel's mother proudly stood and walked to the front of the room, her posture erect. She didn't take the podium Leonard Wise had spoken from, as if it weren't allowed. She didn't even look at Wise.

Nika's anger threatened to come out sideways.

She had to focus, to stay grounded. The eventual elimination of this cult depended upon it.

Chapter 15

Mitch hadn't suited up for such a deep-cover observation in months, not since Claudia had delivered an order for him to join three other TH agents in an op in a remote region in Africa. It felt strange to have to take such precautions in his own damned town, even if he was merely a forward lookout for the op, an extra observer. SVPD was running it, Bryce Campbell in charge, which meant Bryce handpicked who was on the detail. None of them would blink an eye at a new guy working with them. If Bryce said he was cool, he was good to go.

Of course none of the officers working the case had contact with him, or knew he was in a tree fifteen feet above the ground. They only knew what Bryce would relay to them as the night progressed.

Mitch focused his night-vision goggles on the compound's meeting building, and specifically the three figures that appeared to be keeping watch outside. Officially the trailer park was open to the public, but unofficially it was the new compound for the True Believers, the foundation of Leonard Wise's New Thought cult, the True Believer's rebirth.

In Silver Valley, Pennsylvania. He stifled a growl. No cult was going to take his birthplace down. Not on Mitch's watch.

And he wouldn't allow them within an inch of hurting Nika.

The rock through Nika's windshield and the following explosion on Silver Valley Pike made Mitch wish he was an SVPD officer tonight. That he was authorized to do whatever it took to knock the cult out. He carried a single pistol in his back holster and one knife tucked away under his right leg, above his hiking boot, but he'd never use them, not on the cult members. Not tonight.

Posted in a deer hunter's blind in the midst of the deep woods that surrounded the back of the trailer park, he'd never be able to make out anything if it wasn't for the bare winter branches and his night-vision goggles.

What the hell was going on in that dilapidated building that it required guards? Even if the guards were mere thugs. He hated not knowing what Nika was going through, but his loyalty to the Trail Hikers and Claudia's command was paramount.

"You read us, Mitch?" Bryce's voice came over the earpiece.

"Roger. Nothing here—just the three idiots guarding the place."

Bryce's chuckle made it over the connection. "Yeah, we can say that about all of the folks that believe in this wack job, right? Let me know if you see them do anything out of the ordinary."

"What's 'out of the ordinary' for these dudes?"

"If you see a weapon pulled or hear any shouting. We should pick it up before you do, but you're our extra set of eyes."

"Roger."

He settled in to what used to be incredibly familiar— the long, uneventful surveillance part of most ops. His three brothers were into guy flicks with lots of action and explosions. While he enjoyed spending time with them they'd long stopped asking him if war scenes were realistic. They knew that ninety-nine percent of the time his answer wasn't only "no" but "hell, no." Since he couldn't reveal his role as a Trail Hikers agent, he rarely commented on law-enforcement television or movies, but let his brothers think it was all the same to him. Which, in fact, it had been.

Until now. Until he sat, feeling rather helpless, watching a building where he knew Nika was witnessing firsthand one of the craziest parts of human nature.

Two hours into what Rachel had warned Nika might be a three-hour "show," Nika hadn't grown bored or tired of Wise's calculated rant. Instead she found herself relying on everything she'd ever read about cults and cult leaders. She'd taken a course in college on cults and it had been one of her favorites, along with criminal psychology.

Leonard Wise was a conglomeration of what she

remembered from both university classes. If she met him in a coffee shop he'd seem like any other older gentleman in Silver Valley. Quick with a smile, bright eyes, probably a firm handshake. For the men. If he treated her as he was preaching women needed to be handled—"with kid gloves to protect their child-bearing ability"—she'd chalk him up to a product of his generation or having some kind of dysfunctional upbringing.

But the man who stood in front of dozens of rapt Silver Valley citizens, getting them to nod in agreement to his rants against government and "the children of today," was empowered by the very hate he preached. Because he was still preaching the twisted hate gospel of himself: Leonard Wise. Identical to the crap he'd dished out to the True Believers almost three decades earlier. He'd shined it up, thrown in some new buzzwords more familiar to a new generation, but it was the same ugly attempt to brainwash vulnerable folks.

"Stand by for the worst part of the night," Rachel whispered to her, pretending to tie her high-top sneakers.

"What's gonna happen?" She wished she was wired—but unless the FBI or Trail Hikers became involved directly, all they'd have for a record of what she'd heard was her memory. The men at the entrance to the building had checked them for purses, bags and phones. Rachel had warned her ahead of time so Nika had left her phone in her car, back at Rachel's. Along with her weapon. She felt naked without it.

"You'll see. Whatever you do, stay still, keep your

eyes down. Do not go up to the front of the room no matter how much they stare at you."

"Okay." Nika fought the sense that instead of Silver Valley they were in some dystopian young-adult genre novel. How was this possible in the twenty-first century, in a free country?

Everyone makes his or her own choices.

Her mother's words came back to her. Her parents had left Warsaw to seek freedom, to get the chance to make their own way through life—and set the example for her.

"Before we wrap things up tonight and enjoy the goodies and treats that our women have prepared, let us all be quiet and see if what we've learned has spoken to any of us. I'm asking you to use what you've heard tonight, what you've read in our handouts, and ask yourself if you're being called to be a New Thought founder."

Nika repressed shudders of disgust at Wise's blatant recruitment technique. She risked a look around the room and while she was trained as a police officer and not a psychologist, it was easy to see that Wise had ensnared several people. The only ones who weren't smiling at him or nodding in agreement to his calls for hate were the few who, like Rachel, had been all but dragged to the meeting.

Nika had to maintain her air of troubled but obstinate teen. Troubled and searching but tough enough to resist Wise's requests.

Her blood boiled with the emotions she had to keep repressed, invisible to Wise. She couldn't take them all out tonight. *Not your monkeys, not your circus.* She blew out a breath and kept her gaze on the cheap linoleum floor. Her one monkey was to be here, observe and get Rachel to trust her enough to let her in on anything else she knew about the cult. In the future it was feasible that she'd need to ask Rachel to testify against the cult, recalling what had led her mother to their doors and convinced her to stay, even at risk of her own mental health.

A soft touch on her shoulder jolted her and she fought against her training to grasp the wrist of the nondescript man who stood next to her, his face forward, his eyes on Wise. It wasn't as if he were holding her in place, but the proprietary nature of his touch made her gut twist in repulsion.

"Excuse me?" She twisted, tried to get away from the man without giving away her capabilities. "Who are you?"

"Rachel, shut your girlfriend up!" Rachel's mother hissed as she leaned over and slapped Rachel's thigh. "No one speaks until Mr. Wise is done."

"Leave it, Mother." Rachel didn't have to act the insolent teen.

"Now hold on, hold on." Wise's hands were up in the air, his grin splitting his too-smooth skin. "Let's get to know your friend, Rachel. Introduce us."

"Screw you." Rachel was doing what Nika was afraid could get them both locked up in some room somewhere on this compound.

"It's okay, Rachel, let's just leave."

"Girls, girls, no need for the upset. We are all family. You're in a safe place. I remember being a teen and it's normal to think adults are a little strange, am I right?" Wise chuckled and on cue the audience laughed at his comment. A hollow, synchronized sound. Nika was getting more uncomfortable by the minute. Her cop instinct was screaming at her that she was in danger. That meant Rachel was, too.

"Rachel, let's go." She kept her voice low, speaking in Rachel's ear.

"Mr. Wise is calling you to be welcomed." Mr. Limp Grip spoke like a robot and his grip remained loose while his fingers had started to dig into her shoulder. The same shoulder she'd used to knock down a door last year.

"Watch me, old man." Keeping her voice low, she sneered at him as she gave the most subtle twist possible to get out of his grip, and used the turn of her body and head to check out the exit. Two large men were standing at the back of the room where they'd come in.

When she looked forward again she saw the edge of doors behind the heavy velvet drapes.

She turned to Rachel and spoke in a whisper. "Trust me." Nika looked back at Limp Grip and snarled. "I'll do this on my own, thank you." She managed a smile for Wise, wanting—*needing*—to make him think she wanted to be here, wanted to do what was right in his eyes. She ignored the rising bile that threatened to gag her.

Nika walked past the aisles of folding chairs with Rachel alongside her. When they reached Wise, they turned and faced the group. It was far scarier than any time she'd faced a weapon drawn on her, the possibility of an explosion, an angry, drunk crowd at a sporting venue. Because these people believed whatever Wise said. They chose to accept his words as truth. And they were completely sober.

Wise didn't touch her but when his eyes met hers she saw the gleam of fanaticism, the certitude that he was all that he thought he was. All that he programmed these "believers" into thinking he was. It was as creepy as if he'd physically touched her.

"Now, see, here are two of our prettiest young ladies, future mothers of what will be the saving family of this country." He swept his arm at the crowd.

"Introduce yourselves, girls. Let us know your intention with our community."

Nika wanted to let him know her "intention" was to lock him up for good this time, but kept her role-playing up and her eyes downcast as she spoke.

"Hi. My name is Nika. I'd like to thank Mrs. Boyle for inviting me and Rachel for being my friend. I'm not ready to commit to anything tonight, but I'd like to learn more about New Thought." She clenched her teeth.

Wise's smile disappeared and he raised his arm next to her as if to hit her, but instead he started into what seemed to be his version of a blessing on her and Rachel. As his voice boomed, his followers had their heads bowed and eyes closed. Nika sought Rachel's gaze. Rachel's eyes were damp, her resolve shaken, but she didn't look away from Nika. Nika nodded very slightly and mouthed the word "now."

They ran for the back of the room, behind the ugly drapes and past just out of reach of the two burly men who were standing guard on either side of the make-shift stage. They didn't stop as Nika burst the double doors open. Cold night air rushed her cheeks but she kept going, listening for Rachel's footsteps behind her. They ran until they were out of the light cast by the building, on the edge of the forest surrounding the entire trailer park.

Mitch saw two figures run from the building an instant before the sound of the doors springing open reached his ears. His night-vision goggles were temporarily blurred by the spill of light from the opened doors but it didn't take him more than a second to recognize Nika's silhouette. Rachel was the girl next to her, he was certain. The thugs stood around the women, their pathetic shapes still. If Wise was going to enlist "guards" he should have made sure they were fit and not boasting paunches like these idiots.

He fought his instinct to drop from the deer blind and go after the women, save them from the slimy bastards. But he couldn't. He had to trust and believe in Nika's capabilities. And he had to follow his orders from Claudia. He wasn't supposed to even be here tonight.

The realization that he totally trusted Nika to do this right warmed him deep in his chest. Nika knew her business.

He tapped his mike.

"What have you got?" Bryce's voice was clipped. The SVPD lookouts were telling him things, too, Mitch was certain.

"Nika and Rachel are running for the edge of the woods. I see two—no, make it three men closing in on them. But it's strange."

"Strange how?" Bryce sounded impatient.

"They're not running to catch them. It's like they're circling them."

"Keep an eye on them. And, Mitch—"

"Yeah?"

"Do not engage."

Bryce's voice cut out and Mitch keep his focus on the area where five figures stood. His hackles rose as the larger, definitely male figures closed their distance to the two women.

Screw Bryce and screw the Trail Hikers directives. He wouldn't give away his location or presence, and he wouldn't interfere. But he had to be closer to Nika; had to be there in case she ran into trouble too deep to get out of in time for SVPD to be there.

No one could fault him for this.

Late-afternoon dusk had turned to deepest night and Nika took a moment to get her bearings, placing her hand on Rachel's forearm to still her, keep her from running all out into the woods.

"Shh. We're okay. Let's wait a minute and then I'll decide what we can do."

"It's freezing out here, Nika!" Rachel had her arms wrapped around her chest. It *was* cold, bone-chilling. A major winter storm had been predicted for the past week and of course it had to roll in when they were most vulnerable. They'd been forced to hand over their purses and overcoats when they'd arrived. "And I don't have my mother's car keys—she put them in the basket at the front of the hall when we came in. How the hell are we going to get anywhere?"

"We can walk if we have to. We could even run—can you run?"

Rachel nodded. "Yes. That's the only way I get a break from my mother." Nika remembered that Rachel had mentioned she'd been on the school cross-country team before her mother had become a crazed cult follower and Rachel quit running to keep a better eye on her.

"Going somewhere, girls?"

Nika spun around and faced a man she hadn't seen before. Rachel turned with her and moved close to Nika's side.

"We're going home." Nika spoke without rancor.

"Why do you want to go home?" He took a step closer. "I know it can be overwhelming inside with all of the family together. But no one bites. I wanted to leave when I first came, too. I'm so glad I stayed when I did."

Nika stared at the man and heard the snap of twigs on either side of her and Rachel. She looked in the darkness for other men and made out two tall shapes. "We'll come back another time."

"It's so cold out here. You don't want to catch a chill. Abigail Landry's baked her apple crisp—nothing better to warm you up on a night like this. Let's go back in and get you both warm."

"Oooh, no, I need my mother!" Rachel bent over and clutched her stomach. "Please, get my mother, Belinda."

"What's wrong?" This voice was from Nika's right side and had the same singsong tone as the man who'd first spoken.

"Yeah, what's wrong?" Nika whispered at Rachel.

"Oooh, I'm having horrible cramps. I need my mother!"

"Don't worry, we'll get her for you." The leader of the three nodded and Nika made out a man running toward the building. Bright light lit the dark around the structure as his knock on the door was rewarded by one of the inside guards opening it. A murmur of voices, followed by a shout.

"Bring her back here, we'll take care of her."

"Oooh, I'm bleeding all over. I got my peeeeriod!" Rachel moaned and the man on the left ran to the building. It was only Nika, Rachel and the man who'd done the talking. Rachel gripped Nika's arm. "Follow me."

They took off, easily evading the remaining guard, and when they were clear of the building they kept running through the streets of the trailer park. So many of the trailers that had been empty only six months ago were lit up from inside, but Nika knew no one was home—they were all at the New Thought meeting.

"Where are we going?" Nika wasn't going to let Rachel take them to one of these trailers to hide out. They'd be sitting ducks.

Rachel barely spared her a glance as she continued along the graveled road. "Out of this freaking park. We could hide in some of the trailers—they used some of them as smaller meeting rooms. But it's not worth the risk of having to deal with any of them again." Rachel's voice gave little indication they'd just escaped the clutches of a very powerful cult. She stopped for a second and looked at Nika. "Are you okay?"

Nika laughed. "I'm great. Lead on." They ran into the night, reaching the trailer park entrance in less than five minutes, and continued onto the main highway that would take them back into Silver Valley proper.

* * *

Mitch wanted to take out the three men who'd threatened Nika and Rachel. It would have been so easy, *too* easy from his concealed location in the bushes. He gave Rachel kudos for coming up with the period cramps excuse. Nothing could make weak men scatter more quickly than the mention of a menstrual cycle.

Since he was well hidden in the woods he used his position to take several photos of the area and the men who stood around as if expecting the girls to come back of their own volition. He was about to hike out and back to his vehicle when he heard a sound of movement. Silently, and in step, adults began to exit the building, coming out into the same clearing Nika and Rachel had escaped. Mitch videoed with his phone as the people started to sing a song he recognized as a Bible hymn but with different lyrics.

"We are home, we are home. You have found your home, it is here. You will come back always to here. For this is home, this is home."

Mitch didn't wait to see what else they were going to do. SVPD was on it; if the cult did anything criminal tonight, they'd take care of it. At this point he'd accomplished what SVPD needed from him as an extra lookout. As a Trail Hiker he wasn't officially here. More important, he wanted to get out onto the main road and help Nika and Rachel. They had an awfully long walk back to Rachel's home and Nika's vehicle. He needed to know they were safe. At this point he didn't think Nika would be offended if he offered them a lift.

Chapter 16

As they trudged along the main road from the trailer park into downtown Silver Valley, Nika made sure she and Rachel kept to the farthest part of the shoulder so that they'd be invisible to most vehicles. She'd expected the cult to come after them and said as much to Rachel.

"Oh, no, that's not their way. They want you to believe that it's *your* choice that you stayed. It's a sick game, let me tell you. Didn't you see how they got so close to us but never touched us? They want to be able to blame us for not doing what's right, not make it look like they forced us."

Nika stayed silent as her knowledge of the cult was far beyond what a teenager's would be and she couldn't risk exposing her undercover role. Yet she felt a sense of pride in how Rachel had behaved. "You know how to deal with these losers, don't you?"

Rachel grinned. "I have to. The bastards want my mother to move in to that trailer park. Can you imagine living there for the rest of senior year? I know you're new here, but trust me, I'd never be able to do anything with school again. They'd suck me in to their twisted life and take away my mother's car. Once that happens I'm screwed."

"Can't you call your father, Rachel? No matter what a jerk he is for leaving you with her, he has to be better than this cult shit."

"My father is dead to me. He left us when we needed him most."

"That's fair." Bright lights came upon them and Nika halted. "Quick, against the guardrail. We don't know who this is."

The car slowed and only after it came up alongside them did Nika let out her relief in a burst of frosty breath.

Mitch.

The driver's window slid down, revealing a familiar form.

"Hey, is that Mr. Everlock?" Rachel asked from behind the guardrail where they'd hid.

"You two sure don't look like deer. You ladies need a ride?" Mitch's teeth flashed white under the single streetlight he'd pulled up next to.

Nika looked at Rachel. "You okay with it?"

"Are you kidding? A warm car? Let's go!"

"Hop in, girls." Mitch's voice rushed over Nika, reminding her of how husky it'd sounded when they'd made love in her kitchen.

Definitely not a high school student's thoughts.

She and Rachel scrambled into the backseat of his pickup, the plush interior and leather upholstery incongruous with what she'd normally think of as a hunting vehicle. She hoped Rachel didn't notice.

By the way Rachel shivered in her seat, she was busy trying to get warm.

"I've been deer spotting as my brothers and I are supposed to go hunting tomorrow. It's my turn to spot and find where we'll set up our deer blinds."

Mitch focused on the road, his profile dark and only emphasized by his dark outdoor clothing. Nika knew he'd been doing more than deer spotting but said nothing.

"I'm so glad you saw us, Mr. Everlock. It would have been a long walk for us." Rachel's teeth had stopped chattering and she was unusually talkative.

"Are you two okay? What the heck were you thinking, walking this road in this weather without your coats?" Mitch's query was for Rachel's benefit, Nika knew.

"My mother's wrapped up with a group of weirdos. They meet on the weekends and I dragged Nika along with me to see how nuts it is."

"Are you safe, Rachel?" In the darkness of the car Nika stayed silent, marveling over how even though Mitch was a trained Trail Hiker his teacher instinct was stronger.

Rachel shifted in the seat beside Nika. "Yeah, as long as my mother stays in our house."

"Has anyone threatened you?"

"Not *that* way." Rachel looked out her side window and clammed up.

"Rachel just saved both of us from some really creepy dudes, Mr. Everlock. We were at this community meeting of weirdos and they wanted us to step forward and say we believed their bull—"

"What happened?" Nika was impressed how curious Mitch sounded as "Mr. Everlock."

"It's the crazy cult group. My mother believes their crap and Nika agreed to go with me, to make it easier for me. Nika and I decided we wanted to leave but some of the guys gave us a hard time."

"Guys?"

"Yeah, they always have some of the men act like they're bodyguards and keep people in their seats while the leader jackass is speaking." Rachel became more animated as she warmed up. "I went once or twice before with my mother and it's like torture. You have to sit in these uncomfortable seats for hours and listen to the most bizarre stories that make absolutely no sense. There weren't many other kids our age there tonight but sometimes the parents drag their kids and they try to convince them it'll be a lot of fun to join. When I was there the last time they said that any kid who signed up would get a year's pass to Insanity." Rachel mentioned the local amusement park where the teenagers like to hang out. "That's rich, isn't it? I mean, they meant the amusement park but being involved with New Thought is a sure ticket to insanity." Rachel giggled at her own joke.

"Do many of the kids take the group up on their offers?" Mitch made it seem like he was an interested schoolteacher, nothing more.

"Some, I suppose. I don't hang out there enough to know. Although there are some kids whose parents go that would surprise you."

"Really?"

Nika held her breath. She'd been waiting for Rachel to mention other names since they'd started hanging out together.

"Yes."

"Rachel, do you think anyone is in personal danger from this group?" Mitch turned onto the main pike through Silver Valley. Nika saw the pedestrian overpass and suppressed a shudder. Rachel didn't react to it, only confirming Nika's suspicions that Rachel wasn't involved in the rock-throwing incidents.

"No. Let's be real—if they're stupid enough to believe what that dope is saying, they deserve what they get." Harsh words typical of a girl Rachel's age. Nika agreed with her, to a point, but the people Leonard Wise preyed upon were also deserving of compassion and needed a helping hand from whatever their struggles were. Just not a one-way ticket to a controlled community.

"What about you, Rachel? Do you want me to drop you at home or do you feel safer elsewhere?" Mitch's tone was detached but Nika saw the way his hands gripped his wheel. He was holding back his protective nature, for her sake, but at the moment more for Rachel. He wanted Rachel to maintain her dignity in what was truly a crisis situation for her.

Nika felt her heart open and make more room for Mitch.

"No, take me home. I'm safe. Like I told you, they never make anyone go to them with physical force.

My mother might decide to go live in the trailer park, but I never have to. I'm eighteen and I'd drop out of school and get a job to live on my own before I'd ever go with her to that psycho place."

Nika wished she could invite Rachel to come home with her but that was impossible, until Rachel knew who she really was: a police officer.

"I wish you could come live with my family, Rachel, but we're not going to be in our new place until next spring. We're all going to be crammed into the business suite hotel on Silver Valley Pike. When it's just me and my dad, I have my own room, kind of. I have to sleep in the living room on the pull-out sofa."

"I'm fine, really. You know that—you saw my house. There's nothing to worry about."

After seeing how strong Rachel had been with her tormentors tonight, Nika had to agree, she had nothing to worry about as far as Rachel was concerned.

"We have to go to Rachel's anyway, as my car is there, Mr. Everlock." Mitch's gaze caught hers in the rearview mirror and she caught the meaning.

He was going to meet her at her place. Afterward.

Nika filed her report about the New Thought meeting as quickly as her fingers could enter her impressions into the SVPD digital file system. As she was finishing up, Bryce walked in with several other SVPD officers. All part of the team that had been watching the trailer park.

"Nika. You okay?" Bryce spoke and the other officers sported concerned and compassionate expressions. Nika loved this part of being a cop, when they all worked as a team on one op. The camaraderie wasn't unlike a big extended family.

"I'm good. I've finished filing my report, so I think we're done here." At her words, Bryce turned and dismissed the rest of the team. Nika waited for them to clear, each offering her a "Good job tonight, Nika," or "Way to work it, Nika." Their affirmations were better than her warmest sofa throw.

"How much of it did you see, Bryce?"

Bryce looked over his shoulder to make sure they were alone in the computer room. "Mitch provided forward eyes. He reported that you and Rachel were detained by three men when you tried to leave?"

She nodded. "We were, and it was beyond creepy. They didn't use any physical force. Instead they made us feel afraid by physical proximity and what I'd have to describe as programmed talking. They were trying to convince us to stay, to go back into the building."

"Why did you come out so quickly?"

"If we hadn't, we would have been stuck there. It's in my report." She filled him in on the pertinent details. "You know, Bryce, I have to say this is the scariest criminal case I've ever been on. Not the undercover part, or fear of being found out. It's how nice, how 'plain vanilla' they all seem, down to each person in that cult. It's difficult to believe the words that are spoken are harmful."

"Until Wise is impregnating underage girls."

"Exactly. It's clear to me that he's working with someone else, Bryce. He has to be. He's intelligent but not powerful enough to rig a mayoral election like we know he did last spring."

Bryce shook his head. "Not your concern. Just figure out who's throwing rocks at Mitch and you, and who wrote that pig's blood message." He didn't mention Trail Hikers—he couldn't. Not in the open bay of the station.

"Believe me, I'm working on it."

"Don't stay too late. They're going to shut down the main roads by midnight."

"So the weather forecasts are correct?" The local news had been reporting the chance of a snowstorm for the past week.

Bryce shrugged. "They're saying it'll be a blizzard. As long as it's not over New Year's, I'm cool with it."

Nika smiled. "The wedding plans getting a little stressful, Detective?"

"Zora knows I'll do whatever she wants to make this thing between us permanent and legal. But the constant checklists are getting to be a bit much. How am I supposed to get Christmas shopping done?"

"You'll manage."

"Good night, Nika." Bryce rapped his knuckles on her desk as a farewell. As she watched him go she wondered if Mitch had ever gotten that kind of joy in his eye when speaking about a woman.

The knock on her door wasn't unexpected and she allowed the warmth of pleasure to wash over her when she spied Mitch's face in her peephole.

"Hello." She spoke to a wall of white as snow blew in with Mitch, bringing the brewing storm inside. "How's the visibility out there?"

"Minimal." Mitch stomped his feet on her welcome mat, imprinted with a snowman family, before he stepped into the foyer and closed the door behind him. His hair sparkled with melting snow and Nika reached out. "Here, give me your jacket." He shrugged out of his ski jacket and handed it to her. "I'll hang it in the guest bathroom shower. It'll dry more quickly there. I've got hot cider on the stove. Help yourself and feel free to spike it if you want to."

When she returned Mitch had poured himself a mug of steaming cider and from the spicy scent he'd added a shot of spiced rum, too. She poured herself one and joined him at the counter.

"Thanks for being there for me, Mitch. I know you couldn't do anything, not officially, but knowing you were out there made all the difference."

"You couldn't have been certain I was there, Nika."

"No, no one told me you'd be, but I could feel it."

His eyes darkened and his jaw tensed. "Are you suggesting we have a connection that's more than the case, more than sexual attraction?"

Heat rushed to every single sensitive spot on her body. "Maybe." What the hell was she doing, admitting to Mitch that she felt connected to him in anyway other than sex and work?

"Stop it, Nika. You're trying to figure out how to take back what you just said."

"Not at all. A lot of law-enforcement folks have connected instincts. Partners work in sync for years and it has nothing to do with sexual attraction."

Mitch's laugh was low and resonated in the small kitchen. "With us, it will *always* involve the sexual chemistry between us."

"I can't argue that, Mitch." She turned away and sat at the kitchen table. The living room sofa in front of the fire would be cozier, but that was the problem. "We have a case to solve. I think our time is best spent breaking down what I saw tonight and what you've observed in your classroom and with the Rainbows."

"Yes, ma'am." His grin wrecked her with a sexy flash of white. Mitch's dark green thermal shirt matched his eyes, his irresistible dark looks. She let her fingers do what they wanted and brushed his dark hair off his brow. One concession to her need couldn't hurt, could it?

Mitch grasped her hand and placed his lips on her palm, his breath hot and his tongue tortuous as he traced a slow circle on her skin. He waited until she gasped before he let go and placed her hand on the table, his on top.

"We need to focus on the case, granted. But if the storm strands me here, Nika, we're going to do a lot more than work."

Nika didn't argue with him. His presence had already melted away any remaining barriers she'd erected to protect her heart from how he made her feel.

Mitch wasn't surprised by any of what Nika told him had occurred in Wise's base camp. What took his breath away was how much he hated the fact that she'd been there with no ability to reach out to him for help.

You're getting in too deep. Hell, he was already a goner when it came to Nika, but he couldn't let personal feelings inform how he handled his part of the op.

"When they started pressuring us to proclaim ourselves as New Thought believers, I knew that I had to get out of there and take Rachel with me. She's a strong young woman, Mitch. She came up with the period cramps ruse on her own and got us out of a very tense situation."

"You would have taken those three lugs out."

"Of course I could have, but it wouldn't have been easy or pleasant. As long as they weren't armed, I'd be okay."

"You would have disarmed them. But do you think they were armed?"

"Yes. I saw the outline of a knife under one pair of pants and they had rifles leaning against the porch as we came in, under the overhang."

"I couldn't make that out from where I was perched."

"So you really were in a deer blind?"

Mitch laughed at her wide eyes. "Yes, princess, I was in a deer blind. And, no, I'm not a hunter except for when I've had to, to keep from going hungry."

"It was the perfect cover story for Rachel. Good thinking on your part." Her eyes clouded with concern. "She's the most important person in this entire op, Mitch. By saving her we'll save potentially hundreds of young women that Wise and his cult want to hurt."

"I wish this was only about saving people from being recruited by the cult, but there's more, Nika."

"I read the same reports you have, Mitch, at TH headquarters."

"So you know Leonard Wise won't be happy until he takes over an entire region? Until he justifies his maniacal beliefs that he's the chosen one to lead people into whatever he thinks his kingdom is?"

She nodded and took a large swig of her cider, enjoying the hot beverage as if it warmed her not only from the snowstorm but the psychological chill of the case. He understood. Neither he nor she, from what he'd observed of Nika, used alcohol as a crutch or had a problem with it, but to be able to enjoy a warm mug of spiked cider on a cold night, as they faced an evil sociopath, was a welcome comfort.

"It was so damn disturbing, Mitch. Not how Wise behaved—I expected that. Heck, put on any news channel and it seems there are the same kind of crazy groups popping up in every state." She put down her mug. "It was how everyone in that room looked at him, how they were enraptured by his words. He wasn't making any sense but he was still able to exert an unnerving kind of power over them. They sensed they had to please him, to offer up new recruits. They knew that getting me and Rachel up on that tiny stage was what he wanted."

"You handled it well."

She shook her head. "I got us out of there, but Rachel broke us out from their grip." Lines appeared between Nika's brows. "I'm worried about Rachel. Since she's legally an adult, I can't make her go into the SVPD station. She still doesn't know who I am, Mitch. I want to use our friendship to protect her, convince her to get out of her house. But she has nowhere to go. Her father's abandoned her and her mother, and her siblings are older, living on the West Coast. She hasn't told them how bad it's gotten with Belinda."

"She's the adult in that relationship. The parent."
He understood all too well.

"You sound like you relate to that, Mitch."

Images of his brothers and especially his sister
flashed through his mind. His parents had been busy
trying to run their tavern, the same place they drank
together. Mitch, the oldest, had taken care of his three
brothers and his sister.

Nika placed her hand on his forearm and he covered it with his own. It felt so good, so right, sitting
with her at her tiny table as a blizzard raged around
them. "You don't have to say anything. I'm sorry if
I'm being too personal."

"Hell, Nika, we were as personal as two people
can get right here at that counter. There's nothing you
shouldn't be able to ask me."

Her blush delighted him. "Well, we didn't do everything. And that's beside the point. Sex is one thing,
emotions and memories are others."

"I grew up practically raising my younger siblings—
my parents were too busy with the family business to
be there." He wasn't ready to tell her about the booze-
fueled fights his parents had, or how he'd waited until
his next youngest brother was old enough to take over,
to make sure the rest were taken care of, before he left
for the Marine Corps. "My three brothers were easy—
as boys, they just needed someone to keep them in line.
My sister, she was such a little princess." He leaned
back, rubbed the back of his neck.

"When she was in high school she started to get
bullied. She didn't tell anyone and let some of the
girls in her class continue to bother her. Maria is gay

and had just figured it out for herself. The bullying got so bad that she, she…attempted suicide."

"Oh, my God, Mitch, I'm so very sorry."

"Yeah, well, it sucked. I took emergency leave from the corps and came home to help everyone get through the crisis. Maria wasn't successful, thank God, and is now an incredible, confident woman in law school. She wants to someday be involved in passing legislation to keep other kids safe."

"What about your parents?"

"The good thing of all of it is that they both got sober. It was their wake-up call that they had to make a change in their lives. After they sold their tavern they found other ways to stay busy than drink."

"Are you all close?"

He shook his head. "No. I mean, I spend holiday dinners with the entire family, but I tend to do more with my brothers or Maria when we can. It's hard to mend all those years of neglect and dysfunction."

"So that's why you've taken on the Rainbows."

"Yes. And because it's an important group for the kids who need it. Did you know that half of the Rainbows identify as straight, but participate to support their classmates?"

"Yes, I figured that out on the first day. That's something to be proud about, Mitch. I know it's about the kids, but if they didn't have a supportive faculty member like you, they might still be struggling to even start a group like the Rainbows. In all of this mess, you've lit a bright light."

He tried to absorb her praise, with little success.

"The real gift will be if we can get to the bottom of the attacks by Christmas. Are you still certain Rachel isn't involved in the blood writing or rocks?" He knew what he thought, but he needed to know what Nika believed.

Chapter 17

"Mitch, there's no way Rachel did any of it. I know it's easy to blame her because she's given up on her schoolwork. But she's doing the best she can with everything she's got going on. If we can support her through to graduation, she can get into college and start a new life."

"But it sounds like she won't leave her mother."

"There's that. But I'm heartened that she won't, and hasn't, fallen for any of Wise's traps. It proves her strong character. She's told me that she'll live alone before ever moving there." Nika knew as well as Mitch that what Rachel said was one thing. Actually leaving her mother in the hands of harmful people was another.

Mitch's presence next to her at the table made her feel so safe, so content. Nika almost didn't recognize herself. Her usual idea of a good weekend was wrapping up a case, catching up on paperwork at SVPD. Taking in a movie with Ivy.

"What, Nika?" His voice teased her, his slight grin letting her know that he was having the same wandering thoughts. Thoughts of how they would pass the night as the snowstorm kept Silver Valley's roads impassable.

"We have to find out who it is. I think Rachel has a good idea who, might even know for sure. But she's not telling me anything about it. All she's said is that I'd be surprised if I knew what some of the students were really like."

Mitch closed his eyes as if he were meditating. When he opened them, he shook his head. "It's hard to imagine that any of those kids would fall for such a kook. It was simpler when I was able to believe it was the actions of your average hater, period."

"The blood from the writing has been traced to a farm ten miles out of Silver Valley. It's part of a larger conglomerate that provides pork to the entire northeastern corridor. There's no going back with this evidence."

"What else have you figured out?"

"The owner of the conglomerate isn't local. But his CFO is. Daniel Donovan."

"Amy Donovan's father?"

"Yes. But I still don't know if he or his wife were at the cult meeting. I didn't have the blood results until tonight when I finally had time to go through my messages."

"You mean it's not like *NCIS* on television?" Lines radiated from his eyes as he smiled.

"No, I've never solved a case like this in a day. Or sixty minutes." As she spoke she realized she'd never faced such a complex case. "I'll bet you've solved way more complicated cases than this, in far shorter time."

"When firepower and money is on your side, yeah, it's easier to bring closure more efficiently. But that's not always the best way, Nika."

She wasn't convinced.

"What's getting your goat, Nika?"

"Whoever is committing the hate crimes and attacked you and me is escalating. They want to make a very clear message that the Rainbows aren't going to be tolerated. It made sense to go after me, as a new student, as I'd just joined the Rainbows and it was obvious the attack was aimed at me. It was a way to make a statement that was deadly, but not to a life-long Silver Valley kid."

"What do you think they'll do next?"

"I don't know, Mitch, but you have to agree that we've been very lucky so far. They haven't injured a student, or anyone else."

"You could have been killed." His voice was a growl.

"Mitch, if you'd been standing at the right spot, you would have been badly hurt from the rock that crashed through your window. People die from head trauma caused by smaller objects."

Her phone buzzed and she looked at the ID.

"Hi, Claudia."

"Nika, I want to thank you for the good work you did today, and tonight. I wouldn't normally call at this hour, but I wanted to verify your location for the storm."

"I'm at home. Do you need me to go anywhere?"

"No, no. Is Mitch with you?"

Nika met Mitch's eyes before she answered. "Yes, Mitch is here."

"Good. Tell him to stay put. I need you both together, ready to go as soon as we get a break in the snowfall. We'll either get a plow into your development or have SVPD on snowmobiles come get you."

"Where are we going, Claudia?"

"You're going to talk to Rachel Boyle and tell her who you are, let her know she can trust you both."

"Why? What's happened, Claudia?"

"Belinda Boyle never left the trailer park after the meeting tonight, along with several dozen other Silver Valley residents. There are reports that they're staying there for the storm. This is the prime time for Wise to pounce, to try to put the final sell on his ideas about impregnating young women. He has them as virtual hostages. I don't want Belinda Boyle to try to pull Rachel into this."

"So Rachel's alone at her house?" Nika needed to text her.

"Yes, but since no one's going anywhere with the snow falling this heavily, she'll be safe for tonight. It's noon tomorrow when the blizzard is predicted to end that I'm concerned about. Once the storm clears and folks can get around with four-wheel vehicles and snowmobiles, Wise could send his cronies for her under the guise of keeping her safe until the roads are all cleared."

"We'll go over there first thing and talk to her, Claudia."

"Good. Remember, she's eighteen and a legal

adult, but she's still Mitch's student. You have to let her know right away that she's safe with you."

"Got it."

After they hung up she looked at Mitch.

He raised a brow. "What on earth are we going to do until the storm ends?"

The snow was falling so fast and the wind was so strong that he was stumbling, barely able to stand up. The force blew him off the shoulder of the road, but it didn't matter. He'd followed her home from the Boyle girl's house the other day. He knew where she lived. And he'd get there if he needed to, if his plans didn't work out at the high school's formal dance.

Tonight was supposed to be the day he'd take care of both of them. Eliminate that annoying new girl, the one who'd forced the Boyle girl to leave the meeting. If she hadn't left the New Thought gathering she'd have stayed, just like her mother.

And he would have earned his place next to Leonard Wise.

No matter. He'd just have to take care of business on another day. This was what he was best at; having backup options. This was why he was out in the woods behind his development, training for all contingencies.

He stepped through the drifts and blowing snow for over an hour, practicing with his ski goggles and snowshoes. He could go anywhere on foot. But even he wasn't willing to hike the five miles to the evil new girl's house. Gaining attention from the Silver Valley losers who called themselves cops wasn't in his, or the New Thought community's, best interest.

It was imperative that he remain below the radar, above suspicion. At least until he delivered the ultimate gift to Mr. Wise.

He'd almost blown it with the car bomb. That had been overkill. That new bitch hadn't lost her cool at the wheel like she was supposed to. If he'd been the one dropping the rock, he'd have made sure it did more than smash her windshield.

The next time he would ensure real damage was done; an exploding car was kid's play. He'd finish what he'd meant to accomplish in the first place, and play for keeps. Let SVPD *try* to stop him.

It seemed natural to Nika to be sitting in front of her gas fireplace beside Mitch, watching the flames, as if they were on a date and not searching for insight into the case.

As if they had hope for a relationship beyond the incredible sex, beyond her self-imposed love-'em-and-leave-'em policy. She didn't even try to tell herself they were simply two law-enforcement officers taking shelter from a blizzard, not anymore.

It was getting too exhausting, arguing with her body. And now her heart was yearning to open up to Mitch, too.

Desire made her restless and as much as she tried to relax and tell herself they were enjoying companionable silence, her longing was like a snowball rolling down a mountain.

"We're not going to solve this in one shot, are we?" Her voice came out softer than she'd intended. As if he'd already kissed her beyond reason, the way she wanted him to.

His hand covered hers and their thighs were inches apart as they sat side by side.

"No. Wise has his legal tracks covered and where he's too stupid to deal with it, he's hired experts to keep him far from an easy arrest. As much as I'd prefer otherwise." Mitch's voice was low and sexy.

"I'm excited and honored to be a part of Trail Hikers, but I have to admit that I've learned more than I want to about Wise and his cult victims. Even if, when we get him back behind bars—and we will— he's infected enough people in Silver Valley with his venom that they might keep this new cult going. Hurt more people."

Mitch squeezed her hand. "It's easy to think it'll never end, and in some ways, it doesn't. There will always be another bad guy to take out."

"I know." She couldn't disagree.

"Nika." He turned to her, put his fingers on her face. "Life still exists, even when there's all this awful stuff going on. We have to take the joy where we can find it." His eyes were dark and intent on her lips.

"It doesn't take a rocket scientist to know how you want to enjoy life right now." She had to focus to keep her eyes open. All she wanted was to close them and let his lips meet hers.

"Hmm." His thumb caressed her lower lip. "But what about after, Nika? Will you let me in then, or am I going to be another casualty of yours?"

She pulled back. "What do you mean by 'casualty'?"

He ran his fingers along her jawline. "You leave men and the possibility of a relationship as quickly as they start. Ever since Ron, maybe before, as well? Am I right?"

Too right. His insight made her feel so exposed, so vulnerable.

It must have showed in her eyes because Mitch didn't push her, didn't insist on the kiss and what would come with it. He waited for her.

As she stared into his eyes she knew that no matter the very practical, very logical, reasons she used to convince herself she had to keep her emotional and sexual distance from him, she had to be with Mitch.

"Maybe. As you said, we've done enough serious talk tonight. It's time to let go and enjoy the moment." She leaned in and pressed her lips to his, knowing she'd never made such a smart decision.

Mitch's heart felt like it was going to rip through his rib cage as he waited for Nika to make up her mind. He couldn't pressure her to let him make love to her, not even with a kiss. Because kisses and even the lovemaking they'd done in the kitchen wasn't enough any longer. He had to be inside her, be one with her.

When she finally kissed him his primitive self did a silent whoop-whoop fist pump while his erection strained against his jeans, needing release he only wanted to find with Nika.

He wasted no time once she opened her mouth, and he'd never tasted anything sweeter. Desire, craving and the need for consummation of the emotional bond they'd formed in such a short time melded into a molten desire.

"Mitch." She breathed his name into his mouth

and he kissed her more deeply, loving the feel of her teeth, her tongue against his. He kissed her throat, sucked on her skin, his hand under her shirt, on her breast, teasing her nipple.

"Oh, my goodness, Mitch, don't stop." She eagerly shucked her top and bra, exposing her breasts to the warm air.

"You are so freaking beautiful, Nika." Her breasts were perfect in the firelight, her nipples erect and begging for his mouth. When he sucked on her, Nika's moans grew in intensity as her fingers ran through his hair. She arched her pelvis against his, rubbing his erection.

"You need to get undressed, Mitch."

"I do." He stood and let her hands unbutton his jeans, pull down his fly, tug at the waist. As he stepped out of his jeans and pulled off his underwear, he watched her expression. The heat in her eyes when she looked at him took him too close to the breaking point.

Not yet. He wanted to savor this first time with Nika.

"Your bedroom, Nika. Now."

She laughed, a rich, husky melody. As she stood she held out her hand and he took it. "Come on, Mitch. Let's go."

Nika wasn't a nun and she'd had men over before. But since Ron it had always been with the certainty that the relationship wouldn't last. She wouldn't let it. And frankly no one had ever kept her interest as long as Mitch.

He had her interest now.

They entered her darkened bedroom, where she'd left a soft LED candle on next to her bed. It flickered and made the room glow with the dark blue of the glass votive.

"Nika." The way he said her name was like an endearment. As if what he felt for her was more than this, this one night of lovemaking.

His hands came around her from behind and drew her up against his erection. As it pressed into her bottom she arched her neck back, leaning her head on his shoulder while he squeezed her breast with one hand and dipped lower, along her belly, to between her legs, with his other hand. When his fingers entered her she twisted and turned, needing satisfaction that only his deliciously bold touch would give her.

He kissed her and moved his fingers until she was on the verge of her climax. She gasped at the white-hot sensations and he pushed her back onto the bed as her knees buckled.

"Perfect timing. I don't think I could stand one more second." She put her hands on his head, drawing him to her.

"Less talk, Nika." Mitch poised above her, his forearms on either side of her head, his erection teasing her moist center.

"Mitch."

"Nika." He thrust inside her in one slick motion and Nika exploded as he filled her, stretched her to a point of sheer ecstasy. He continued to thrust as she absorbed the climax and her body readied itself for more. With Mitch there would always be more, she knew. This wasn't just another one-night hookup for her.

"Don't stop, Mitch." She encouraged his expert lovemaking, arching her pelvis as close as she could to him, meeting him and relishing the slam of their bodies together. His biceps and shoulders tightened under her fingers, his skin slick, and as he came in an explosion of release he called out her name.

They lay next to each other until sleep came, but not before Nika acknowledged that she'd never been so fully made love to before—and that she'd never allowed a man to take her so completely. Mitch was reaching her more deeply than her past lovers, and it had nothing to do with her G-spot. This was about her heart.

Chapter 18

Mitch woke to the soft sound of Nika's breathing. She lay on her side, spooned perfectly against him. The low roar of the winds hadn't stopped and he briefly wondered if he'd be able to leave her house at all on Sunday. It occurred to him that he didn't care if he ever left Nika's house.

He breathed in the scent of her hair, its long brunette strands curled between them. His training urged him to get up and check the weather conditions, check his phone for any messages from Claudia or TH headquarters. But his heart? His heart was…content.

He sat up with a start, the sudden movement waking Nika. "What?" She sprang into a sitting position as quickly as he had. "What's wrong?"

His laugh erupted into the quiet room. "Nothing's wrong. Nothing at all."

Nika ran her fingers through her hair. Hair that was beyond any grooming thanks to the two additional lovemaking sessions they'd enjoyed since coming to bed last night. "Then why did you wake us up like this?"

"I didn't wake us up. It's the wind." *Scaredy cat.* Yeah, he was afraid, all right. Afraid of acknowledging what his feelings for Nika meant. What they could lead to...or not.

"It's still snowing?" She got out of bed and padded to the window, peeking through her blinds. The dim votive light illuminated her naked curves and the inevitable erection he'd learned to accept whenever she was near stirred. "There's at least three feet out there, Mitch. We won't get out until they plow the street, and with this kind of visibility that won't be any time soon."

He looked at his watch: 0430. "Come back to bed, Nika."

Nika took her time in the shower, allowing the water to run in hot streams where Mitch's fingers, mouth and tongue had been all night. It should frighten her, this unbelievable bond they shared. Instead it puzzled her. How had she allowed it to happen, especially during such a difficult case? A case that was increasing in threat level?

She dried off quickly and made short work of getting dressed before she went into the kitchen. Mitch stood at the counter, holding a fork over the Belgian wafflemaker. He'd already showered and his hair was still damp.

"Good morning." She grabbed a mug from the

cupboard and poured a hefty amount from the full carafe he'd brewed. "Thanks for making breakfast, again."

"It's my pleasure." He grinned. "Really. I don't know how to cook much more than breakfast. I have omelets for dinner more than I care to admit."

She sat at the table and watched him. This was getting too familiar, too cozy, too, too comfortable.

"Stop it, Nika."

She didn't answer. Mitch took the last of five waffles off the iron and brought the stack of them to the table, where he'd set their places. He warmed up his coffee and then sat across from her. His expression was grave but the slight lift of his mouth at the right corner gave away his mirth.

"It's not funny, Mitch."

"Who's laughing?" He poured maple syrup on his waffle and helped himself to the bowl of fresh fruit.

"I see you found the grapes and melon. And banana." The guy was a regular gourmet.

"I did. And stop skirting the issue."

"I'm not skirting anything. We have a potential murderer on the loose. Silver Valley High along with the entire population of our town is at risk from a wacko cult. It's not the best time for us to be playing honeymooners. You don't disagree with that?" As soon as she said "honeymooners" she cringed. "I didn't mean—"

He placed his hand on her mouth.

Her lips pulsed under his fingertips, and she fought the urge to nip at them, suck them back into her mouth.

"No. More. Thinking. At least about last night. We

had an amazing time together, and it was because it was more than just sex. I know you're not going to want to talk about it now, and I suggest we don't. Let's refocus on the case and figure out our next steps."

"I thought that's what we were doing last night."

"We were, until other issues came up." He grinned. "That pun wasn't intended, but it works."

She got it. Mitch compartmentalized. It was essential to survival in the military and law enforcement. Personal issues had to be shelved until the mission was finished.

She dug into her waffle and groaned in delight. "Mitch, this is like pure butter. How did you do this with what I have in my pantry?"

"Chef's secret. More guarded than the Trail Hikers."

At his jest she swallowed and stared at him. "The Trail Hikers are going to take this case over completely, aren't they?" Disappointment welled; she'd really wanted SVPD to be at the center of bringing the cult to its knees. Especially in apprehending whoever was stalking the high school. She'd wanted to put the cuffs on the criminal as an SVPD officer, not work in the shadows as a Trail Hiker.

"Eventually the FBI and ATF will come in. They have to. But you'll be in it, Nika. It's going to take each and every one of us. And Trail Hikers doesn't exist, remember? Not on the surface, not under a rock. We're a shadow agency."

"Emphasis on 'shadow.'" She grabbed a slice of bacon from his plate. "Did they teach you to cook like this in the Marine Corps?"

"No, nothing like that. I used to make sure my

brothers and sister had a full belly before they went to school each day. I watched cooking shows on PBS long before it was cool to watch them on the Food Network."

She stood after she finished her waffle and helped him clear the table. "You go relax. You cooked, I'll clean up."

"You don't have to tell me twice. I brought some lab papers to grade. I had a feeling I might get stuck here with the storm." He looked through her kitchen window at the driving snow. "I had no idea it would last this long."

"Me, either. It's always a toss-up, central PA weather." She stacked dishes and filled the sink with sudsy water.

The warm, grounded feeling she had in her chest was peace. Being with Mitch allowed her to let go of the anxieties of her job and enjoy the moment.

There was no one she'd rather be stranded with.

The storm dumped three feet of snow on Silver Valley and it took two days to dig out. Mitch left early on Monday, as soon as the major roads were clear. One of Nika's neighbors had cleared their small subdivision with a snowblower. On Wednesday, Silver Valley had a full school day, during which Nika convinced Rachel to go with her to SVPD after school. Rachel was still vulnerable after their phone conversation the other night and Nika was relieved she didn't need to force the issue.

What concerned Nika most was revealing to Rachel that she was an undercover officer. Apprehension made her late lunch churn in her stomach, as if she'd had spicy chili instead of the leafy green salad from the cafeteria's impressive salad bar.

Rachel met her in the parking lot after agreeing in chemistry class that she'd go to SVPD headquarters with Nika to file a report about what they'd observed while at the New Thought gathering.

"Thanks for agreeing to go with me to the police, Rachel."

"No problem. I wish I thought I could help more. I don't have anything to tell them. What will the cops do, anyway? The people living out in the trailer park are all adults, with their kids. No one is being held against his or her will."

Nika listened to Rachel's complaints as she drove to the station. She considered it a small miracle that Rachel had allowed her to even bring her. She'd been very defensive about being able to take care of herself since her mother had gone to stay with the Wise cronies. Nika doubted Belinda would ever leave the campground of her own volition.

"You know more than you think you do. They just want to get your take on things. No one's going to make you leave your home, Rachel."

Nika adjusted her rearview mirror and wished she saw the reflection of Mitch's truck in it. He'd agreed to meet her, Rachel, Claudia and Colt at SVPD but she knew that a number of things could delay him.

She pulled into the gravel parking lot, as familiar as her own driveway, and parked the car. She looked at Rachel. "I know you haven't known me that long, Rachel, but you need to know that you can trust me. I'm more than just another high school friend." That was all she trusted herself to say before she got out of the car. She used her ID badge to buzz them into the station and Rachel's eyes widened.

"Wait—you're not—no freaking way!" Horror, shock, confusion raced across her expression before a grim comprehension settled over her features. "It figures. You wouldn't have wanted to be my friend otherwise."

"That's not true, and we'll settle this later. Right now, please come with me, Rachel. Silver Valley needs you."

Rachel stared at her. "You're not pulling me in here to narc on my mother, are you?"

"No. This is to protect you, and the other kids at school."

It seemed like hours but Rachel finally nodded, the early winter wind whipping her hair around. "Okay, I'll go in. But if I feel like it's getting too nuts, I'm getting a lawyer."

"That's fair." Nika slid her ID through the card reader again and the door clicked open.

Mitch sat waiting in the conference room with Chief Todd, Claudia and Bryce. He didn't think they'd get any new information from Rachel. Nika had been at the girl's side for the past couple of weeks. Save for Belinda Boyle's link to the cult, and the invaluable information Nika had gleaned from the cult's propaganda literature, he thought they'd eked out what they were going to get.

Nika appeared in the doorway first and, when her eyes sought his, satisfaction curled deep in his gut. She needed him, needed his strength. And it felt damned good. He prayed he wouldn't let her down.

The case still had a long way to go, the path fraught with danger.

"Good afternoon, everyone. This is Rachel Boyle." Nika moved into the room and Rachel came in behind her, a look of stunned anger on her face.

"Hi, Rachel. I'm Claudia Michaels, the SVPD social media and systems specialist." Claudia's smile was warm as she welcomed Rachel with a nod. Colt followed, as did Bryce.

"You know me, Rachel."

"Hi, Mr. Everlock. Are you a cop, too?" Rachel's eyes were sharp, the lines around her lips white with stress.

Ouch. If she only knew about the Trail Hikers, Mitch was certain she'd run from the station.

"No, Rachel. I'm still a chemistry teacher. I agreed to help with this case because of the threat to the Rainbows."

"Come on in and have a seat, Rachel." Bryce stood and pulled out the chair next to him, which Rachel took, her spine erect. Mitch knew she wasn't "his" kid but still, he was so damned proud of her.

Nika sat in the chair next to Claudia's, opposite Mitch. Her eyes were on Rachel. "Rachel, since Bryce is the lead detective on this case, I'll let him ask the questions. But first, we want you to know that your safety has always been paramount. And I want you to know that despite the obvious lying about who I really am, I do trust you and feel as if you're my friend. You can count on me in all of this."

Rachel replied to Nika's comment with a short nod. She was pissed off now but Mitch hoped that once she realized the scope of what they were dealing with she'd forgive Nika. Rachel's eyes were back on him. "Mr. Everlock, did you know about Nika from the beginning?"

He grinned. "I knew we were getting an undercover officer and I still had to look twice when she showed up in my classroom. She fits into the class, and the senior class as a whole, so well, that it was easy to think she was ten years younger than she is."

"You're twenty-eight?" Rachel's eyes were round.

Nika blushed. "Twenty-nine, actually."

Claudia put her hand on Rachel's. Mitch held his breath, waiting for Rachel to snatch it back and say something caustic to his secret boss. Instead Rachel closed her eyes and tears slipped from under her lids. "This is so scary."

"I know it is, honey, but you're not alone. Nika is the best friend you could have, even if she's almost as ancient as me." Claudia's comment made Rachel laugh through her tears.

"Rachel, whatever is going on with your mother at the New Thought trailer park, you must understand it has nothing to do with you. Your mom was vulnerable, as are all of the members of the cult."

"You think my mother's in a cult? I mean, they are a bunch of nut jobs, but 'cult' is a very strong word." Rachel accepted the tissues Claudia handed her and spoke through her quiet sobs. "I knew in my head that it's a cult, probably, but it sounds so awful to hear you actually say it, with everyone here. It makes my mother's craziness too real. So official, you know?"

Rachel's broken voice made Mitch's desire to put Wise back behind bars all the more pressing. He looked at Nika. If anyone ever hurt her like Rachel had been hurt, he'd…

You'd what? Like the rock that had sailed through the classroom window, Mitch was sucker punched by the ferocity of emotions he felt toward Nika. He'd accepted that they might have the start of a relationship, but not that he'd say that word aloud to Nika. Not yet.

His gut tightened.

Did they have more? He'd known Nika for only the better part of four weeks. Could you fall in love with someone in such a short time?

"Mitch." Bryce's voice cut through his thoughts and, from the exasperated expressions on each of his colleague's faces, it wasn't the first time Bryce had tried to get his attention.

"Sorry. I was working something out in my head."

"Anything you need to leave the room for?" Claudia's concern was palpable.

Mitch shook his head. "No, no, nothing like that, Claudia." At Nika's and Rachel's stunned expressions, he relented. Why not?

"I've had some PTSD symptoms that have lingered since I got back from the war years ago. Claudia has talked to me about them, since she was a Marine, too. But I have to say, since having this cult issue come up, I haven't once had to talk myself through one iota of anxiety." No, his concerns had revolved around keeping Nika safe. *Shit.* His old excuses didn't hold any longer. He'd fallen for Nika in the way poets described. Completely.

At everyone's silence, Mitch looked at Nika. Her eyes brimmed with—compassion? Pride? The same emotion he was struggling with?

"Mr. Everlock, is that why you're the teacher representative for the Rainbows club? Because you know what it's like to not fit in?"

"No, Rachel. I support the Rainbows because it's the right thing to do. Also, I have a sister who happens to be gay, so I understand the kind of hell high school can be for anyone who feels different from the crowd."

Nika cleared her throat. "The most important thing for you to know is that you're safe, and we're going to keep you safe. Since your mother has moved to the trailer park, and your father has left town, we think it's a good idea for you to move in with me."

"What will I tell the other kids? What about paying the bills at my house?" Rachel's worries should have been about what to wear to the holiday formal and how to study for the chemistry exam. Not how to run a household.

"We'll take care of it for you, Rachel." Claudia spoke up. "Your father is still sending your mother alimony and child support?"

"Yes, and I have all the passwords for my mother's checking account. She's not in a place to manage numbers and let me take it over months ago."

"How long have you really been doing this, Rachel?" Chief Todd chimed in.

Rachel's face reddened. "Since freshman year. My dad was around less and less, and my mom wasn't feeling well even then. But she didn't get really crazy until after last Christmas. We were at the Silver Valley Community Church when the fire broke out. She saw it as a sign that she was supposed to stop going there and spend more time with her new friends."

"The New Thought folks?" Bryce had been taking notes in his laptop the entire time. Mitch hoped like hell Rachel's bravery was going to pay off sooner than later.

"Yes. But last year they were calling themselves the True Believers, and then after we found out about the undercover minister, they changed their name to New Thought."

"That makes sense because the undercover minister was Zora, who happens to be my fiancée." Bryce's tired eyes lit up at the mere mention of Zora. Mitch understood why.

"Silver Valley is incestuous." Rachel frowned and turned to Nika. "And I don't want the whole school to know my mother is cray-cray. Are you going to let my classmates know you're a cop?"

"No, not yet. After we're done with the school's part in this, after we figure out who's been targeting the Rainbows and Mr. Everlock, I can either disappear or let the few kids in the chemistry class know. You don't think anyone suspects I'm a cop, do you?"

Rachel shook her head. "Not at all. They'd be talking about it, believe me. We know there are undercover cops in the lunchroom and after school, behind the Dumpsters." Rachel looked at Colt and Bryce. "That doesn't take a rocket scientist to figure out."

Nika laughed. "No, not when that's where the kids go to get their pot."

"And other things." Rachel didn't budge.

Colt grunted.

"We know there's a big drug problem at school but we're not the team focusing on that. Not now. Our job is to keep the Rainbows safe. We have to find out who the bad guy is here, Rachel, and we need your help. Are you willing to join our team?"

Rachel considered Colt as if he were a bug. "Do you mean am I willing to turn in my classmates for anything illegal?"

Colt shook his head. "Hell, no. That's our job to find out, anyway, isn't it?" He looked at Bryce and Nika for affirmation. "Just like Nika said, we're in this to solve one issue—find out who wrote the blood messages on Mr. Everlock's board, and who threw the two rocks, one through the classroom window and one off the pedestrian bridge into Nika's windshield. It could be the same person. It could be three different thugs."

"But you think it's the same person, don't you? And you definitely think they're related to the cult my mother's in." Rachel stilled. "It's not my mother. Is that what you think? Is that why you pulled me in here?"

"No, we don't suspect your mother. I met her, remember?" Nika's voice was calm, soothing. "But it could be someone in our chemistry class. The fact that they are going after Mitch as well as targeting me as the 'new kid' makes us think so. Do you disagree, or have any other ideas?"

Rachel sat quietly for a moment. In the silence, Nika's gaze met his and Mitch wanted to be alone with her blue eyes, her full lips. If he could go back in time to the two of them in her bed during the storm he wouldn't hesitate.

Except they wouldn't be any closer to catching their criminal. A person who had wanted Nika dead.

"I don't know anyone who would do this. There are

a lot of parents going to these meetings in the trailer park, but most of them only show up once or twice a month. Some never come back. I'd have to figure out who the regulars are. And, believe me, you can trust me. I want you to get these crazy psychos out of Silver Valley more than anyone. They took advantage of my mother and the weak state of her mind."

"If you can do that for us, that would be huge, Rachel. But we don't want you to go back to the trailer park under any circumstances. You and Nika are going to have to work as a team at school and find out what you can."

"Is there a deadline we have to meet to do this?" For being the youngest and only person in the room who hadn't taken an oath to serve and protect, Rachel's commitment was impressive.

"As soon as possible." Bryce spoke with authority and Mitch bit his lip to stay quiet. Rachel was legally an adult at eighteen, but she didn't need to know every frightening detail of the case. "We have one more Rainbows meeting before holiday break—the Silver Bells Ball, where we'll have a table—and then our big welcome reception for new members in January. We need to get the criminal before then, because as much as we will always support the Rainbows and keep the club going, we can't put students at risk."

Rachel looked at Nika. "So what do we have to do?"

Chapter 19

"This is delicious, Nika." Rachel gobbled up the pasta dish as if she hadn't eaten in weeks. Nika wanted to weep at how alone Rachel must have felt, how afraid she'd been as she watched her family fall apart. And yet she'd managed to survive it all and was still willing to help SVPD catch a criminal.

"Thank you. It's an easy recipe I can teach you. It'll be perfect for when you're in college. You can make it for your roommates."

Doubt clouded Rachel's eyes. "I don't see how I'm going to be able to go to college, Nika. Not until I work for a few years and put money away."

Mitch put his fork down. "Rachel, we're going to get you into the best school we can. Now that we know why your grades have suffered, we'll work around it. Your SAT scores are off the charts, and I have some contacts at Penn State. I know you origi-nally wanted to go out of state—"

"Penn State would be wonderful, Mr. Everlock!" Rachel's enthusiasm, and Mitch's thoughtfulness, brought tears to Nika's eyes. She sniffed and found both of her dinner companions staring at her.

"I...um, it's allergies."

"To fettuccine Alfredo?" Mitch teased.

Nika came back to the living room after showing Rachel the spare bedroom and bathroom.

"She's going to take a long hot bath. Says she's missed it since she and Belinda have had to cut cor-ners and it wasn't an option to use hot water for some-thing as frivolous as a bath."

"That's awful. The poor kid. It makes me sick to think about how many other students of mine are going through something similar."

"I know."

Mitch walked to the coatrack and reached for his leather jacket. "I need to get a move on it. Tomorrow is going to come bright and early."

He filled her foyer and Nika realized he'd filled her life. In four short weeks she'd gone from never thinking she'd be able to trust a man, especially one in law enforcement and former military, to wonder-ing how she ever lived without him.

She didn't think she'd ever be ready to commit to a man for the duration, but if she was, it'd be Mitch. The thought jerked her from her study of him and she crossed her arms in front of her.

Focus, focus, focus!

"What?" He stood with his hands on his hips, his

leather jacket open and his scarf wrapped around his neck.

"You need to go. The next few days are going to be long."

"They might not be. Now that Rachel trusts us— you do think she trusts us, right?"

"Yes." Nika loved how Mitch said "us."

He closed the small distance between them and wrapped his arms around her waist. "Then there's a good chance we'll get to the bottom of the Rainbow Hater before the Silver Bells Ball."

"And that's significant why? Other than keeping the student body safe, of course." She reached up and tugged on his scarf, bringing his face closer to hers.

"I don't know. Maybe it'd be nice to spend the holiday free from this case, free to celebrate?" He lowered his lips to hers and used his mouth, his tongue and the hands that cupped her buttocks to communicate exactly what he meant. When he lifted his head Nika kept her eyes closed, savoring the moment.

"Look at me, Nika." His eyes shone with an emotion she couldn't name. Not yet.

She pushed him away and stepped back, hating how easily he let go, his arms dropped to his sides. "Rachel's going to suspect we're doing more than working on this case together if you don't get out of here pronto."

"I know. See you in the morning, babe." He left and she stared at the door for a good while, as if willing him to come back and go to bed with her.

Of course he didn't, and she had to face facts. If they had all the time in the world to spend together, would she ever be the kind of woman a man like

Mitch Everlock would settle for? A woman who put her life on the line every day, as Mitch did when he was on a Trail Hikers' mission?

"Nika?" Rachel stood in the living room, wrapped in the old terry robe Nika had lent her, the wise-old expression on her face incongruous with her teenage years.

"Hey. Mitch, um, I mean Mr. Everlock just left."

"I figured that out. Are you two a couple?"

Nika could tell her no, could justify the lie with the needs of the case. But if she were to be Rachel's real friend, it started now.

"Not a couple in that we're not officially together. Are we dating? I guess we're not really doing that, either. But we've spent time together, outside of the case."

"And you'll spend time with him after the case is solved."

"I don't know. Maybe." Rachel pursed her lips and raised one eyebrow in a manner befitting a Hollywood actress. Nika relented. "Okay, yes. Hell, yes. But it's not the priority now. Catching the Rainbow Hater is." She looked at Rachel's dry hair. "You didn't take a bath?"

"I wanted to make double sure it's okay." In an instant Rachel looked five years old, afraid of being punished.

"Yes, yes. I never use up my hot water, even when I have guests. It's an extra large heater for a town house. There are lavender bath salts in there, too. Please, help yourself."

"Thanks, I will. And, Nika?"

"Yes?"

"It's hard for me to take all this in, but thank you. I know it can't be the most fun, having a high school kid shoved into your lap like this."

"For the record, Rachel, this is my choice. You could have stayed with another friend, or one of your other relatives that live in the area. But since we're friends I want you to know you can count on me not just now, but after we catch the son of a bitch who's got a hard-on for the Rainbows. I'm here."

Rachel took the three steps that separated them and gave Nika a bear hug. Her arms and rib cage were dreadfully thin, something Nika hadn't noticed under the heavy sweatshirts and sweaters Rachel normally wore. No wonder she'd devoured dinner so ferociously.

"Thanks, Nika." Rachel stepped back and wiped her eyes with the sleeve of the robe. "I may sit in the tub for a long time, if that's okay."

"Of course. I have wireless speakers if you want to borrow them for your phone. Do you have music on your phone?"

Rachel laughed. "Yes, I always did put a couple of bucks away for music. And there's a lot to stream for free, too."

While Rachel took her bath, Nika sat in front of the fireplace with her yellow legal pad and started brainstorming. Someone they saw every day at Silver Valley High had to know who the stalker was.

Sunday afternoon Nika invited Mitch, Claudia, Bryce and Colt back to her house with Rachel. She knew it would have been easier to meet at SVPD but didn't want anyone seeing Rachel around the station. They were too close to getting to the core of this case.

"Thank you all for coming over on such short notice. And thank you, Colt, for the doughnuts."

"Hells yes!" Rachel fist pumped the air as she bit into a maple-glazed, old-fashioned cake doughnut. She looked around at everyone at the sudden silence and her cheeks turned red. "Um, sorry. I just love doughnuts, and maple is my favorite."

"No worries, Rachel." Claudia helped herself to a doughnut and Nika wondered if she was doing it to put Rachel at ease. Claudia was fitter than most people twenty years younger and didn't look like she indulged in sweets very often.

"What's up, Nika?" Bryce looked the most put out to be in her living room on a Sunday afternoon. She didn't blame him; with his wedding less than two weeks away, his time was precious.

But so was everyone's, with Christmas just next week.

"I was brainstorming, and going over every piece of evidence that we have from the multiple SMART Board messages, the two rocks—the classroom and the one through my windshield—and I still can't find a way to determine the person doing this. So that leaves the most tried-and-true method."

Everyone stared at her and she smiled. "A stakeout."

Bryce groaned. "What, are you going to dress like a Navy SEAL and camp out in Mitch's classroom?"

"We already have surveillance cameras in the chemistry classroom and lab, Nika." Colt spoke evenly, obviously trying not to embarrass her.

"Yes, we do. But so far we haven't captured anyone on the cameras, have we?"

"They're too obvious." Rachel spoke up, wiping her mouth with a napkin. "There were never potted plants in the chemistry room before. It's too much of a coincidence that they were put there after they wrote that last message."

Nika nodded. "Exactly. And the culprit can easily cover them when they come in the classroom, without being caught on camera. I'm more concerned about the time line. The previous incidents, except for the rock through the windshield, happened on the same day as the Rainbows meetings, right?"

"Go on." Mitch spoke.

"Mitch, you can't be in the classroom or your office because he'll know you're there. The writing has never happened when you're in your office, even with the door closed. It's always before school starts or when you're very obviously out of the building."

"True."

"I'm going to hang out in the lab cupboard, under the counter and in front of the whiteboard. I'll see whoever comes in and stop him." Nika watched everyone's expression as she spoke, waiting for argument.

"That's brilliant, Nika. But whoever is doing this is escalating the stakes. How can we be certain they'll stick to something as innocuous as writing on the wall again, or that they won't be carrying?" Bryce sat on the arm of the sofa.

"We can't. Let's face it. If someone wants to, they can get around the tightest security measures in place at the school, including the metal detectors. There are too many ways to get in and out of such a huge campus. Which is why I need to do this. I may wait there for nothing. But since the last few messages were left in the morning, my bet is that the writer will do it in the afternoon, like they did when they started a few months ago. Mitch has a teacher conference day that's been on the schedule for months. He'll leave at noon and be back for the Rainbows meeting after school. It's the perfect time for the hater to strike again."

"Is it well-known that the Rainbows are going to meet on a Friday instead of Tuesday or Thursday?" Claudia spoke as a true social media person would, but Nika saw her Trail Hikers CEO strategy.

"All it takes is a few Snapchats and everyone will know. And most groups that have raised enough money to have a table at the dance will be meeting then, too." Rachel looked at Claudia. "You know what Snapchat is, right?"

Claudia smiled. "I sure do."

Rachel turned back to Nika. "This is perfect, Nika. I can be in the hallway and text you if I see anyone hanging around outside the classroom—"

"No. No way. You are not going to be anywhere near where the culprit could be." Mitch spoke, his protective tone startling. Rachel looked like she was going to protest, but remained quiet.

"Mitch, Rachel has proven she's able to handle herself in sticky situations." Nika needed to stick up for Rachel, but she did have the same reservations as Mitch. "What would help me more, Rachel, is if you get the word out that I'm out of school for the afternoon for a dental appointment, a follow-up for the one I had earlier. Make it clear that the chemistry classroom is closed until the Rainbows meeting. We'll put more signs up in the hallway encouraging people to visit the Rainbows dessert table at the Silver Bells Ball. That will give us the exposure that whoever the Rainbow Hater is doesn't like."

"It's your op in the high school, Nika. I support your decision. As long as you're not putting any other students at risk." Colt looked at Bryce. "You okay with it?"

"Yes, sir. I'm not sure we'll get them, but it wouldn't be the first time the most simple tactic took down the bad guy." Bryce mirrored Nika's enthusiasm. They'd worked for so long on this case, and with the probable tie to the New Thought cult, they might be solving more than one crime this week.

"You should be armed if you're going to face this bad guy. They're playing for real, Nika," said Mitch. "But you'll also be in the midst of a lot of volatile chemicals."

"I know." She looked at him and it was as if no one else was there; her whole world shrunk to Mitch.

Colt coughed. "Make sure you have what you need to arrest them, and I want two SVPD units on standby to assist. They can wait in the middle school parking lot—it's Anti-Drug Day for the middle school, so no one will think twice about the cruisers."

"Yes, sir." Nika couldn't look at Mitch again in front of everyone. She didn't want anyone to think she'd allow a distraction from the case.

Problem was, Mitch was more than a distraction. He had somehow become her reason to solve the case. Mitch saw her police-officer side and all the hard parts that came with it, and still wanted her in his bed. God, thinking of Mitch and bed was not beneficial to the case at hand.

First, she needed to practice apprehending a suspect in a two-foot-wide space between the counter and wall that the SMART Board was on.

On Friday morning Nika still hadn't had a break in the case, so her stakeout plan was a go. As she sat in Mitch's class she looked around at the chemistry students and tried to place the parents that Rachel had pointed out at the New Thought. There'd been at least three parents of kids in Mitch's highest level chemistry class, unbelievably. But none of the students fit the mold of a child being taken advantage of, and all had very vocal plans to still go to college.

"That's going to wrap up our lessons until after the holiday break. All next week will be review for the exams in January. I'm going to cut you loose a few minutes early today. I've got a seminar I have to attend this afternoon, but I'll be back for the three o'clock Rainbows meeting, and if you're not going to that, I'll see you at the holiday formal tonight." Mitch shut down the interactive whiteboard. Nika mentally reviewed the messages that had been written there. She'd pored over the photographs and lab reports collected by the forensics team, willing the files to give her an answer.

So far, no luck.

"See you after school, Mr. Everlock." Rachel spoke up and a few of the other students who were in the Rainbows murmured their agreement. They were having a quick meeting to verify the funds spent by the Rainbows for giveaway bakery goodies and imprinted souvenir items at the Silver Bells Ball tonight.

Nika didn't bother to say farewell. She'd be here after school, too, hopefully with an apprehended suspect on their way to SVPD.

"Nika, can you stay for a minute?" Mitch didn't look at her as the students filed out. It was getting harder to pretend she didn't know Mitch as more than "Mr. Everlock." A longing tugged at her, right in the middle of her chest. She yearned to be known as Mitch's partner. Lover. Girlfriend.

She was in big trouble. More than any case had ever gotten her into.

"Come into my office. I have some research findings to show you." Mitch kept a straight face as he turned and headed for his office and Nika wished they were walking into her bedroom instead of Mitch's office.

She'd never allowed a man to interfere with a case before.

Mitch turned and faced her. "I really wish we could shut the door."

"We can't." Her reply was loud in the small space and Mitch's eyes narrowed.

"What's going on, Nika?"

"Nothing. I need to focus, Mit—Mr. Everlock."

"You do." He looked away and she saw his chest rise as he took a deep breath, expelled it forcibly. "I don't like this one bit, Nika. It goes against every instinct to leave you here to face a dangerous criminal." His voice was low, his tone beyond tense.

"We don't have a choice. Worse case—I look like an idiot waiting in the cupboard. Best case—we catch the culprit and can breathe a sigh of relief." She kept her voice low, too, as she fought against the urge to hurl herself against him and hug him, let him know she'd be okay.

"For now. This is only the beginning with this cult. We've already been trying to crack them for over a year."

"We'll deal with that as we have to, Mitch. Right now we have to keep the students safe." When his expression didn't soften, she risked touching his forearm with her hand, briefly. "I'm trained, Mitch, as much as you. Well, almost as much. I might not know how to use all of your superspecial spy stuff, and I didn't serve in the Marine Corps, but I can take out the biggest, meanest culprit. Don't worry."

Her attempt at humor had no effect as she watched the conflict play out across Mitch's expression. A bell rang and the noisy hallways were quiet beyond the classroom, the silence an unexpected omen of the danger lurking in the school.

Finally he met her eyes. "You can't tell me to not worry, Nika."

"This is where you have to trust me. I know what I'm doing."

"Of course I trust you."

But not enough to believe she'd handle whatever came her way.

"Do you? And please don't say it's the bad guys that you don't trust. That's pathetic, Mitch. I know you served alongside women in the war."

"You'd better stick to 'Mr. Everlock.'"

"Mr. Everlock, do you have a minute?" Gabi stood in the threshold of the classroom, her books a huge pile in her slim arms. Nika was grateful Mitch had warned her as she'd been too worked up to notice Gabi's approach.

"Thank you, Mr. Everlock. I'll look at those studies. Hi, Gabi." She left the classroom, wishing she and Mitch had had another few minutes to settle this.

Who was she kidding? If they had five years it wouldn't be enough. Mitch was a man who was used to running an operation. And while she'd never felt he doubted her abilities, he'd never relent when it came to her safety.

Chapter 20

Nika wanted to be in place for her surveillance well before the end of the school day, so an hour before the Rainbows were to meet she positioned herself inside the cupboard at the base of Mitch's counter. In the front of the class, the doors faced the whiteboard and a small crack allowed her a narrow but sufficient field of vision. If anyone came in to write on the board she'd see their feet and be able to apprehend them.

Mitch had helped her by clearing out the cupboard during his lunch hour. He'd thoughtfully placed a blanket at the base of the cabinet, which she'd have to thank him for later. The best thing was that he'd taken out all of the shelves so that she wasn't as scrunched up as she'd have been otherwise. She sat in a cross-legged position and waited.

Her vigilance was rewarded fifteen minutes before

the end of the school day. Soft footsteps fell on the linoleum floor and she identified white athletic shoes and school-colored knee-high socks. A cheerleader?

As silently as possible, Nika let herself out of the cupboard. The girl didn't hear her until Nika was standing behind her. Nika made a split-second decision to stay undercover.

"Amy? What are you doing?"

Amy jumped at Nika's voice and, as she turned to face her, Nika identified a paintbrush in one hand and a jar of red liquid in the other.

Amy Donovan.

"Nika! Where did you come from? You shouldn't sneak up on people like that! I'm, I'm just about to write a surprise message for Mr. Everlock. To thank him for all he's done for the Rainbows."

"Is that right? But you're not in the Rainbows, are you?" She feigned getting a text. "Hang on—my mother's asking where I am." She used the time to text Bryce. SVPD officers would be here in minutes if not sooner.

"Yes. What else would I be doing?" Amy looked shaken but was trying valiantly to appear annoyed, aloof. Nika wanted to have compassion for her but if this child had fallen for the hate her mother was absorbing at the New Thought meetings, then compassion wasn't the ticket. Not right now.

"I don't know. I've never seen anyone write in paint on the SMART Board. Won't that ruin it?"

"No, I don't think so." Amy put the brush down and screwed the lid she'd left on the counter back onto the jar. "You know, I need to go. Practice starts early today."

"Answer my question, Amy. Are you in the Rainbows? Because I've been attending since I enrolled at Silver Valley and I've never seen you at one meeting or fund-raiser."

"You did, too. You saw me buy baked goods from you last week!" Amy's desperation was spiking and her skin boasted a sheen of sweat.

"As I recall, you stopped by to harass us. You didn't drop one cent in the donation box." Nika had no doubt Amy was their writer. But why Amy? Had she thrown the rock off the pedestrian bridge, too?

"Stay right there, Ms. Donovan." Two officers walked into the classroom, followed by Mitch. Nika feigned ignorance and took several steps back, away from the front of the room.

"What's going on?" Amy's voice rose to a high pitch and Mitch placed himself between Amy and the officers.

"Amy, you know what's going on. It was you who moved the silk plants that held the security cameras today. We have you on tape. You neglected to cover the lens before you reached up to disable the cameras. And judging from what you've got in your hands— can I smell it?" Mitch held out his hand.

Amy stared at him then gave him the jar. Mitch opened it and sniffed. "It's pig's blood, isn't it? What were you going to write today, Amy?"

"Wait, I can explain all of this. It was just for fun. I didn't mean anything by it."

"Just like you didn't mean anything by throwing a rock through my classroom window?"

Amy's eyes widened. "I never did that! I don't know what you're talking about."

"But you know about the pig's blood, the messages."

Amy started to sob. "Yes."

"You'll have to explain the rest down at the station." Mitch nodded at the two uniformed officers, who proceeded to read Amy her rights and then cuff her. As they led her away, Nika stood in place near the back of the classroom. Amy didn't look up as she walked out.

Mitch stayed behind and spoke to Nika.

"You'll have to run the Rainbows today."

"Gladly."

"I only know what I saw. They took Amy away and she looked really upset." Nika stuck to the script she and Bryce had agreed upon to inform the students without causing any extra upset. Since Amy was already eighteen, it wasn't illegal to report what she'd witnessed regarding Amy's arrest. Nika could have told the other students what had really happened but it wasn't her place. Amy deserved a chance to explain herself.

Several members of the Rainbows had their own opinions.

"It doesn't surprise me. Amy's mother has been getting nuttier and nuttier. She's got, like, dozens of brothers and sisters."

"I always thought she might want to join the Rainbows but her parents are so lame. Very repressed and unwilling to see reality."

Nika wondered if Amy could have used the support of the Rainbows but her parents wouldn't let her. That made her sad in ways these kids understood all too well. And might be a lead to another critical part of the case. Another suspect.

"There's not a lot we can do about it right now, so Mr. Everlock suggested we finalize our game plan for tonight."

"We've got the schedule here." Rachel pulled out the spreadsheet they'd created last meeting. "Each of us only needs to work the table for twenty minutes. That's not bad over a three-hour event."

"I'll be leaving here to pick up the cupcakes and cookies from Silver Bites Bakery that we're giving away along with the water bottles. Who has the original order?" Nika had volunteered to get the large order. As she looked around at the Rainbows, she didn't notice anyone staring at her or giving each other looks about her. They still thought she was a student, as had Amy.

And Rachel remained steadfast in her commitment to the operation against the Rainbow Hater.

"Do you know how many kids will want our water bottle?" One of the members held up a rainbow-colored water bottle with Silver Valley High School, a silver bell and Holiday Formal emblazoned on it. They'd ordered ten dozen with the extra funds they'd raised beyond the cost of buying a table at the ball.

"Are you kidding? They'll be one of the first things that run out from all the tables."

"But some kids wouldn't be caught dead with a Rainbow on anything."

"That's their problem. Look how well our bake sales have done. We've changed the attitude of most of the school over the past four years. Remember when we were freshmen and everyone was afraid to

join? Mr. Everlock took care of us even back then."
Rachel spoke with sincerity and Nika fought the tears
back. *You're on duty. Get it together.* There would be
time to "feel her feelings" later.

"When will he be back? Oh, yeah, he's at the police station. Is this going to be the end of the hate
crimes against the Rainbows?" Neel asked the question to the group.

Nika waited before she responded, not wanting to
seem to know too much for a newcomer.

"There will always be haters. But if Amy's the
one who's been leaving the ugly notes, and trying to
disrupt the club's activities, then I'd say we're in the
clear." Several heads nodded in agreement.

"So, what's everyone doing before the formal tonight?"

Chapter 21

Mitch stood next to Colt in front of the one-way mirror to observe Bryce and Claudia interviewing Amy Donovan. He glanced at his watch. The formal would be starting within the next hour and he needed to be there as a chaperone.

And to keep an eye out for Nika, if he was being honest with himself. They had Amy in custody but he knew there could still be danger lurking in the crowd at the holiday formal.

"Nika did right by SVPD, and the high school." Colt's voice held a note of pride, as it should.

"There's no doubt that you have the best team here, Colt." Mitch spoke more familiarly since it was just the two of them.

Colt nodded toward the ongoing interview. "And we're lucky we were able to work Claudia on to it in a legitimate, *official* unofficial way."

Both men laughed.

"Watch Bryce go in for it here. I've seen him do dozens of criminal interviews and he warms them up, like he's been doing for the past hour. Then he zings them." Colt beamed and Mitch shook his head in mock dismay.

"They're not your children, you know."

Colt turned to him, his face wrinkled his own smile, his eyes bright. "No, but they're the best damn law-enforcement officers I've ever known. You know as well as I do what they've both gone through."

Indeed, Mitch knew that Claudia had survived war and now several Trail Hikers' operations, many of which he had no knowledge of. TH followed a strict need-to-know policy. And Bryce, besides being in TH along with his fiancée Zora, had been through hell last Christmas when the Female Preacher Killer was loose. Bryce had almost lost the love of his life during that case, right after they'd been reunited after years apart.

"Here he goes." Colt's voice was hushed, almost reverent.

Claudia put her hand on Bryce's forearm, as if to restrain him from being so "mean" to Amy.

"Amy, what Detective Campbell is asking you isn't a reflection on you, or even your mother. A lot of Silver Valley residents have gotten caught up in the cult group you mentioned. Did you call them New Thought?"

When Amy nodded, Mitch felt his own surge of pride. Claudia had been the best Marine Corps General he'd ever reported to while on active duty, and now her skills parlayed into a far more subtle way of smoking out the enemy.

"My mother goes to the meetings all of the time. She's made all of us—my brothers and sisters—go, too. But my father told her that I didn't have to go."

"Why not?" Bryce took over.

"I… I agreed to do whatever he wanted me to if I didn't have to go and join the New Thought group. And I made him promise I'd still get to go to college next year. That he wouldn't make me stay home like my mother wanted, and become some kind of slave to her and my siblings."

"Does your father attend the New Thought meetings?"

Amy shook her head vehemently. "No. But he agrees with them on a lot of things. Like the Rainbows and what they stand for. He doesn't think it's right that Silver Valley High School protects the LGBT kids."

"And do you agree with him, Amy?" Claudia's question was soft, as if she were Amy's long-lost aunt.

Perfectly volleyed, Mitch thought.

"I don't care about who someone is. We all have the right to live our lives freely. I think the cult group is crazy, and I don't care whether the Rainbows meet or not. I only wrote the messages because I had a deal with my father. Plus, it was kind of fun, I guess, at first. Like playing a prank. Until the messages got uglier." Her lower lip wobbled. "I never wanted to make Mr. Everlock worry that he was really going to be hurt. But I had to do it, so that I can get out of Silver Valley after graduation."

"So why did you keep writing the messages, Amy?

If you thought the messages were 'uglier'? You had many avenues to pick for help. School counselors. Principal Essis. SVPD." Bryce was playing his "bad cop" persona perfectly.

"I already told you—my father promised I wouldn't have to go to any of the meetings as long as I did what he told me to. It was easy enough to put them there in the early mornings, before anyone was in school. I was in early for cheer practice, and it was a no-brainer for me to say I was going to the bathroom and then run up to the classroom and write the messages." She sobbed, her cries getting louder, her gasps for air pitiful.

"What about the rocks, Amy?"

"I never meant to hurt anyone. I mean it when I say I didn't know about the first rock, through the classroom window. Not until one of the kids who came into the classroom when the cops were there told me. I heard about when the rock was dropped on Nika's car, and she almost died..." She buried her face in her hands. After a while, she looked up.

"I didn't want *anything* to do with the New Thought meetings. My mother started to go all of the time, and she was bringing home information to my father after he stopped going. I didn't want them to change their minds about me going away to school. I have to get out of Silver Valley and when I was accepted early decision to Temple University I knew it was my ticket out. But then my parents started making me stay home more. The only way my father let me leave the house was if I agreed to do something to discourage the Rainbows. And he wanted the list of names of students who were in the club, too."

"How much does your mother know about what you've been doing?" Bryce didn't relent.

"I don't think she knows anything about it. We don't talk very much anymore. I don't go home until I absolutely have to, because once I'm there, I'm stuck."

"What about your brothers and sisters, Amy? How much of the New Thought propaganda are they absorbing?" Claudia was pressing for the purposes of the Trail Hikers' op with this one.

Mitch felt Colt tense next to him.

Amy sniffled and accepted the tissue Claudia handed her. "They're all so much younger than me. My parents had me, and my sister, who's in middle school, was born five years later. The rest are in elementary school. I love them, and I'd do anything for them, but I can't stay here. We'll all suffocate under this crazy group if I do." Tears welled and streamed down her cheeks, dripping off her chin. She grabbed another tissue.

Amy looked nothing like the put-together student and cheerleader she portrayed at school. Compassion welled for the young woman, the student he'd taught for the past year and a half. Still, she'd been complicit in criminal acts and, at age eighteen, was considered an adult.

Bryce's face was set in a grim expression that only hinted at the frustration Mitch knew he experienced. If Amy was only involved with the blood writing, who had thrown the rock through his window? And was it the same person who had targeted Nika's windshield?

"Amy, let's go over what we have so far. You've told us that you were the one who wrote the warnings on Mr. Everlock's SMART Board, including the threat on his life?"

Amy nodded. "Yes. But he isn't in real danger. They're just words. Just a way to get to the Rainbows and make the group break up."

"And you had nothing to with the rock throwing, no knowledge of whoever did that?"

"No, it wasn't me. And I know you're going to think it was my father, but it couldn't have been."

Mitch's gut tightened as he watched Claudia and Bryce sit straighter.

"Why couldn't it be your father, Amy?"

"Because he was out of town when Nika's car got hit."

Mitch looked at Colt. "Are you thinking what I'm thinking?"

"That Daniel Donovan may not have been out of town as much as she thinks? Yeah." Colt pulled out his phone. "I'm texting Nika. Can you use your TH systems and get a decent photo of him, and text it to her?"

Mitch nodded. "I need to leave, anyway. As much as I'd love to hear the rest of this interview, I've got to be at the dance."

Colt looked up from his phone. His eyes were knowing, unflinching. "You know you have orders to stay out of it, right?"

"Yes." Mitch didn't report to Colt, but they were on the same side—the same team, when it boiled down to it.

"I'm not saying don't use your skills if you're called to, but you can trust my officers who'll be there, and above all else, trust Nika, Mitch."

"I do. I know she's the best, Colt."

"Sometimes we can forget these things in the heat of danger, when someone we care a lot about is threatened. Do we understand each other?"

Mitch knew that if he thought Nika was in danger he'd fight through hell to save her. Whatever it took. Colt knew it, too, but it wasn't what Colt wanted to hear and not what he needed to express to Nika's boss.

"Yes, sir."

Chapter 22

Friday night at the Silver Bells Ball

"It's a miracle that we're here and look halfway decent." Rachel sipped the bottle of water she'd gotten off the beverage table. She held the bottle up to the sparkling lights and sighed. "I wish they'd have let us use the Rainbows water bottles instead of these ugly, environmentally offensive containers."

Nika laughed. "It's a good school policy. There would be booze and other things in everyone's Rainbows bottle in no time."

"Probably. But they look so much nicer."

"How is the sale going so far?" They were across the gym from the long line of tables where different Silver Valley High School clubs and organizations sold everything from cookies to security whistles.

Rachel did her trademark shrug. "Okay, I guess. We'll know more when we stand our shift."

Nika looked at the clock on the gym wall, behind where the basketball nets had been folded away for the big bash. They had ten minutes until their shift, the third of the evening.

The dance was almost a third of the way through and still no Mitch. She had to stay vigilant in case anyone tried to disrupt the dance, but her mind wanted to wander to the what-ifs of the situation at SVPD. Had Amy confessed to all of the incidents? Had she pointed the finger at someone else?

There was no way to know until Mitch showed up.

"Stop worrying about him. He'll be here." Rachel grinned at her in the dim light of the huge room, the glittering Christmas lights twinkling all around them.

"I'm not worried."

"Yes, you are. And, honestly, we caught who was writing the words on the board. She's probably the same person who threw the rocks, right? All's safe for now." Rachel looked like a mature woman, far beyond her years.

"We can't ever let our guard down. Not with—" Nika cut herself off. This was Rachel's senior Silver Bells Ball. Her last holiday dance as a high schooler. "Rachel, we haven't really talked about this, but is there anyone you'd like to dance with?"

Rachel rolled her eyes. "I know you're trying to be all sensitive and everything, and I appreciate it. There's no one special, not really."

"I've seen how you look at Neel. And how he looks at you." Neel had a gay older brother and had joined the Rainbows because of the struggles he'd witnessed.

Nika didn't think she was too far off the mark to try to fix these two up.

A bare ghost of a smile flitted at Rachel's lips. "He is kind of cute, isn't he?"

"Why don't you go ask him to dance? It doesn't have to be a slow dance."

"Hell, no! I don't want to be in that sea of disgusting pubescent children, gyrating and grinding for everyone to see."

Nika raised her eyebrows but remained silent. She didn't want Rachel to know how worried she'd been about her with the revelations of the past few weeks. It was a relief and empowering to see that Rachel still had some healthy teenage emotions going on.

"I have to agree, it is pretty gross. But you should ask him, anyway. You can dance at the side of the floor, away from the 'ickiness.'" Nika made a pretense of looking at the decorations, but she was doing a security sweep. Nothing looked amiss or warranted extra inspection. "Tell you what, I'm going to head over to the basketball table and get one of those homemade Amish root beers they're selling. I'll meet you at the Rainbows table in five minutes, when our shift starts."

"Don't be late." Rachel tried to sound bored but Nika saw her scouring the crowd. For Neel, perhaps?

She understood completely, for the minute her eyes found Mitch, standing at the entrance to the gymnasium, she breathed a sigh of relief. It would be okay, no matter what. Mitch was here.

Mitch spotted Nika the minute he walked into the gym and hadn't let her leave his peripheral vision since. She played the part of a student well, and from his vantage at the bleachers she looked like she was handling the horny teenaged boys with aplomb. He met her gaze and allowed the instant chemical reaction that always accompanied being near her jolt along his nerve endings. But he'd have to wait until well after the dance to do something more concrete about his physical need for Nika.

They had students to protect. He checked his cell phone, frustrated that Bryce hadn't sent word yet on Amy's continued questioning. There was always the chance that Amy wouldn't divulge more about her mother and father's involvement in New Thought, but his instinct told him otherwise. The question was *when* Bryce got Amy to confess all.

Finally his phone dinged with a text from a Trail Hikers' IT technician. A photo of Daniel Donovan, Amy's father. He immediately texted it to Nika and watched as she looked down at her phone. He knew exactly what she was thinking, what she was feeling. If Daniel Donovan was involved in this mess they were going to get him.

"What are you doing this weekend?" Kristine, the PE teacher Nika had seen at the New Thought meeting, broke through his concentration as she breathed into his face. Mitch quickly put his phone away.

"Hanging out, grading papers." He knew not to reciprocate the query. Kristine had been too familiar with him since he'd started working at Silver Valley High, always trying to get him to have a drink after school. She wasn't his type. But she had let up on getting him to go out with her over the past several months.

"I was thinking of having a *Breaking Bad* marathon at my place. Interested?"

"Uh, no. You know, Kristine, that not all chemistry teachers are secret meth cooks, right?" He tried to keep his tone light while making it clear they were never going to date. He didn't think dating another teacher was a good idea to begin with, and unless it was someone he could get very serious about, not worth the stress. Kristine would never be more than a work colleague to him. But if she was part of the New Thought group, maybe he should try to see what she saw in it.

No. Way. He'd let Bryce and Claudia know she'd approached him here, but other than that, he wanted nothing to do with Kristine.

And now, with Nika in his life, there would never be another woman he'd look at in that way. The realization hit him in the gut.

"Are you hitting on our favorite chemistry teacher again, Kristine?" He breathed a sigh of relief as Ken Thomas, the agricultural studies teacher, teased Kristine.

"No, just trying to find someone to spend a lonely Saturday night with." Kristine didn't miss a beat. And Mitch didn't miss the look in her eyes—it wasn't her usual friendly spark. It was flat. As if she was thinking about something else.

"Why don't you ask me? I'm single. And I'm not a geek like Mitch." Ken smiled at Kristine. She ignored him.

"We're supposed to be watching the kids, aren't we?" Mitch spoke as his mind worked overtime like it did when he was trying to solve a complicated chemistry equation.

"They're either standing in a corner afraid to talk to anyone or grinding up against each other." Ken made a salacious face at Kristine.

"Spoken like a true farmer." She wasn't impressed. "Stop looking at the kids for a minute and you'll see something funnier, over there." Kristine nodded over at the snack tables, stretched along the side opposite of the DJ's stage. "Check out the parents. They're more into the music than the kids."

Sure enough, several sets of parent chaperones jiggled and moved around to the heavy hip-hop beat. As Mitch watched them he wondered if his parents had ever looked as silly.

As lights blinked and the crowd swayed to the beat, he saw Nika in her formal wear that was supposed to be teenage sexy but her body reminded him of her very adult moves when they'd been alone. He knew she had a hidden mike so that Bryce could communicate with her as needed. She wore her long hair down, covering her ears and earpiece. He thought he could make out her lips moving and with no one close to her, he wondered if Bryce was talking to her. Screw pretending to be here as a teacher. He had to know if Amy had confessed more after he'd left the station.

"Mitch, where are you looking at?" Kristine's voice was sharp. Too sharp.

"I'm looking at my favorite chemistry student. I need to check in with the Rainbows, so I'll take a walk around the room. Do you have a problem with that?" He stared at Kristine, hard. She lowered her eyes and walked away without saying a word, as if in a trance.

"Mitch, what the hell?" Ken looked at him like he was insane. Maybe he was.

"Trust me for a minute, Ken. Keep an eye on her and don't let her leave your sight."

"Does this have to do with the writing on your SMART Board?" Ken, as well as every other faculty member, knew what Mitch had dealt with. Principal Essis had briefed them so that they'd all be on board with SVPD investigating the threats. Of course, no one had known there would be an undercover officer involved, or that there was a tie to the cult.

"I'm not sure, but she's not acting her usual self, is she?"

Ken stared at Kristine's retreating form and shook his head. "She hasn't been herself for the past few months. Since school started this year. I thought it was maybe because she'd been taking care of her mother, who moved in with her last spring."

"Her mother's an odd duck." Mitch couldn't mention New Thought, not now and not where any student could overhear. "Just keep an eye on her."

"Will do." Ken was also prior military. Navy, if Mitch remembered right. Kristine wasn't going anywhere without Ken following her.

Mitch looked back around the room and at first he couldn't find Nika. All too familiar feelings of powerlessness and anxiety rushed at him.

No. Breathe.

He envisioned Nika as he'd last seen her. The edges of impending panic subsided and, when he opened his eyes, there she was. At the Rainbows table, selling the cupcakes with candy snowflakes on them.

As he approached the table he enjoyed seeing her acknowledge him with her eyes, the slight smile that she kept friendly while detached as a student should be from a teacher. He wished her aloof appraisal of him could turn into a warmer welcome. The kind a woman gives a man she's interested in. The kind she gave him when they were alone, in her bed, making love.

Hell, where was that coming from?

He'd always been able to keep his mind on his work no matter what. With Nika, all the rules were off the table. She'd somehow gotten not only under his skin but into his every thought, his dreams, his... *shit*. His heart.

You're in love with Nika.

"Thanks for the text. Hey, what's wrong?" Her eyes were large, her beautiful lips parted.

"Nika, I have to tell you—"

"Wait a minute." She pressed at her ear, listening. Her eyes met his and he saw acknowledgment, a flare of concern and then grim determination.

"Copy. We'll get on it."

"What's going on? Was that Bryce?" At this point he didn't care who heard, if he blew her cover wide open. All he cared about was keeping her safe.

Nika's expression warned him to back off. Calm down. She had this. "Come over to this side of the table." Louder, for the benefit of the three boys walking up to the table, she said, "Mr. Everlock, we've saved you some cupcakes for the teachers, back here." When she bent over to reach under the tablecloth for an unopened box of baked goods the boys snickered. And Mitch's control was pushed to its limits. They were all staring at the same thing—Nika's ample cleavage, her breasts straining against the white silk of her strapless dress.

"Boys, are you here to order something?" He used his best teacher voice and was rewarded by their nervous coughs and immediate focus on the assortment of cookies and cupcakes.

"Hey, Rachel, can I have one of those water bottles with a cookie?"

"Me, too."

"Same."

All three boys pulled out money to pay and Rachel kept them busy as she played the consummate saleswoman. Mitch used the opportunity to walk around the table and stand next to Nika.

"What's going on?"

"Amy's still denying she knows who threw the rocks." She leaned toward him, her arms crossed across her beautiful breasts. "So there's nothing from Bryce on that. But as I told him, some of the girls have told me that a group of kids have planned to crash the dance with liquor and drugs."

"What kind of drugs? Which kids?" He knew the school had a growing heroin problem; he'd referred two students to the specialty counselor for showing up high to class.

"It doesn't matter. The fact that they think they can get past Principal Essis's gauntlet, as well as police security, is what bothers me." She looked away, a bored expression on her face as two parents walked by and nodded at Mitch. He admired her professionalism, her ability to handle the undercover op, her dedication.

He admired *her*.

"Did you tell Principal Essis?"

"I haven't had a chance." She jumped a little and he knew Bryce must have said something.

"Was it something I said?"

She lifted one side of her mouth and rolled her eyes. "Bryce says 'hello.' And tells me to inform you that he's got it under control. He's let the officers on duty out front know, and they've informed the principal. He suggests you might want to stick to chemistry tonight."

He grinned, but didn't say anything. They were all in this together. "Tell you what, I'll head over to the main entrance and keep an eye out for trouble. Let me know the minute you hear anything different. And if you see a man who looks like the photo I sent you... well, never mind." Hell, he'd been about to tell her to call him. What would it take for him to get it through his skull that this was Nika's op? Bryce's, as well, and Silver Valley PD's. Not Mitch's, not Trail Hikers'. He felt so goddamned powerless and he hated it.

Hated that Nika was in danger and he had to step back.

Nika watched him and he knew she saw right through him. Classic Nika, though, she didn't call him on his almost slipup. Instead she shot him a dazzling smile.

"Will do. Any reason you're looking down my dress, Mr. Everlock?" Apparently Nika didn't care if Bryce heard her. In fact, she was probably having fun at his expense. Cop humor was similar to military humor, from what he'd observed. Bryce was probably groaning on his end of the connection, rolling his eyes at the flirting. But Bryce couldn't call them on it, as he'd fallen for his fiancée during a similar case. A case that had endangered a large part of Silver Valley before it was solved.

Mitch hoped to hell this case ended with less drama.

"Just making sure your wire isn't exposed, Nika. There's a dress code at Silver Valley High School, young lady." He dropped his voice as low as he could while being sure she heard him.

Nika's face flamed rosy pink and it wasn't from the red laser snowflake that flickered over her. Satisfaction wrapped around his gut, which he expected. It was the instant erection that threatened to throw him off. He didn't need to sport a raging hard-on for a "student," not if he wanted to keep his job at Silver Valley.

Damn it. He wanted—*needed*—time alone with Nika, to tell her that not only was she the hottest undercover agent he'd ever met, he was in love with her.

"Go do your job, Mr. Everlock. Bryce suggests you take a walk through the locker room showers on the way." Her firm tone didn't match the smoldering look in her eyes, and he wondered if maybe there was a chance she felt the same depth to their connection that he did. A man could hope.

Awareness of Mitch made Nika's skin as hot and sweaty as if she were one of the teens grinding on the dance floor and not a twenty-nine-year-old undercover operative. So many thoughts raced in her mind and she needed to tell Mitch, but not here, not while she was working.

Besides, how was she going to start the conversation? *Hey, Mitch, I think I'm falling for you. And while I don't see myself settling down and having babies, not with this job, I'd really like to commit to you for longer than a few hot nights.*

No, that would never fly with Mitch. Mitch carried a silent strength with him. She knew he wasn't the kind of man to ever harm a woman; she'd sensed his kindness and gentle side the minute she'd met him. And the way he'd reacted when the rock came through the window had proved his instincts were to put her safety first. And the way he'd made love to her, with both gentleness and ferocity, only stressed how much he cared, how much he controlled himself for her pleasure.

What intimidated her about Mitch was how he made her feel.

Mitch had served in the military, in one of the most elite units. He'd had to make hard decisions, she was sure. And while her family's struggles had taught her that no matter how kind a man was in a regular, peaceful setting, one never knew what they were going to do when the crap hit the fan, it didn't apply to her and Mitch.

Mitch wasn't a man she ever had to fear, ever.

Who was she kidding? She'd spend forever with him if he asked.

What had he been about to tell her? She ran her finger through the thick frosting on one of the cupcakes and licked it. Sweet and salty, as the cupcake was salted caramel. *You have to take the pain with the joy*. She laughed and Rachel looked at her like she was crazy.

"What's so funny, Nika?"

"My life. When you're older, you'll get it."

"I think the sugar is getting to you."

"Nika!" Bryce's voice boomed in her ear. "Quick! Go out to the front. There's a group of at least twenty kids trying to break through the security checkpoint. They're throwing rocks at our uniformed officers."

Chapter 23

Loud screams followed by a huge roar drowned out whatever else Bryce was trying to say. Nika repeated what she'd heard so that Bryce and the team in the van knew what she'd been able to hear. She turned to Rachel. "Stay here, and keep our group close together. If anything starts flying, hit the deck."

"Why can't I go with you?"

"Police business."

Nika ran for the gym exit, the doors that led into the large corridor where two metal detectors were set up and operated by several SVPD officers.

Total chaos was breaking out in the gym and she forced her way past sweaty teens, hearing more than one girl squeal as she stepped on toes. She'd dressed in typical rebellious teenaged fashion with a formal dress and Doc Martens boots. The boots were perfect as far as adolescent fashion went but she'd chosen them for this eventuality.

"Sorry, let me through!" She wasn't about to pull her weapon from her thigh holster unless she knew the students were at risk. Then she'd do what she had to.

The lights went out. The students let out a cry of dismay as the music stopped and the emergency lighting came on, harsher and far less sexy than the dance illumination.

"Nika, if you can get some of the kids to leave the gym from the back doors, do it. Otherwise just get out of there. We've got a big problem at the entrance. Six more units are en route." Bryce's voice rapped in her ear but Nika ignored it.

She found Jon, the Rainbows president, near her and grabbed his upper arm. "I need your help. It could get really messy. Let's try to get everyone out the back doors."

"We'll be expelled for opening those doors!"

"Not in this instance. Get everyone outside, out of the gym."

Mitch was in the hallway and she wanted to go to him. She knew he could handle himself, but he didn't know what they were up against. None of them did.

Why was she worrying about a specially trained operative when she had her own mission to worry about?

It took all of her training to put Mitch out of her mind and focus on the task at hand. As she made one last sweep of the gym before she went out to the corridor, her eyes froze on a police officer's most dreaded sight.

Rachel was being dragged toward the bottom of the folded bleachers by a man who had his arm wrapped around her neck. She wasn't struggling and as Nika looked more closely she saw why. The man had a knife to Rachel's neck.

"Bryce, Rachel is being kidnapped by a man with a knife. I can't make out his face from here."

"Where? Where is she, Nika?"

Nika started running toward Rachel, sticking to the side of the gymnasium, up against the wall and now the bleachers.

"Nika! Answer back."

"I've got eyes on them. East side of the gym, under the fifth section of bleachers. I think he's going to try to drag her into the boys' locker room."

"Keep eyes on them, Nika, but do. Not. Engage. Wait for backup. I'm sending in our hostage negotiator."

"I've had the same training, Bryce." Nika was ten feet from them and peered through the bleacher's steel girders to see the man's face lit up by a side spotlight.

Daniel Donovan.

"It's Daniel Donovan. I'm going into the locker room with them, Bryce. I can't risk that he'll get her out of the school building. If I lose them we might never see Rachel again. I'm cutting out." She yanked the earpiece out, needing to rid herself of the distraction. Bryce would still hear whatever her mike picked up.

As she neared the door to the boys' locker room

Nika had a brief thought of Mitch and whether he'd be okay with her doing this. She knew he would. Mitch believed in her.

The locker room was damp and dark, the only light coming from the emergency lighting system. The rasp of heavy breathing echoed over the metal lockers and Nika followed the sound as silently as possible, her weapon drawn, its safety off.

"What do you want from me?" Rachel's voice was strained but steady.

"You need to learn to listen to your mother, little girl. If you would have just joined her with the rest of us at the community home, then none of this would have had to happen."

"None of what? Let me go!"

"Move any more and I'm going to have to hurt you."

Rachel's whimper was as effective as any other call to action Nika had received as a police officer. She held her pistol firmly in both hands as she turned into the aisle where Daniel had Rachel pinned up against a locker, his hand on her upper chest while he held a knife to her throat.

"Silver Valley PD. Drop the knife, Donovan."

His pale face turned toward her and he grinned: a sick, menacing stretch of his thin lips. "You think you can get me? Right."

"Drop the knife."

As he focused on her, distracted, Donovan's hand moved infinitesimally as did the knife. Nika held her aim steady as she watched Rachel push Donovan's arm as she kneed him in the groin. He stumbled back and Rachel ran to Nika.

Donovan didn't let go of the knife, didn't fall. Gasping, he roared, "Come back here, you bitch!"

"Get out of here. Go to Mitch." Nika spoke low and quickly, hoping Rachel had the strength to listen.

"I'm not leaving you with this psycho piece of shit."

"You do not know your place in this world. You will learn!" As Donovan lunged at them, Nika shoved Rachel out of the way and kept her weapon trained on him. She heard Rachel scream for help as she left the locker room.

Nika faced Donovan. His twisted expression was a face of the cult, the source of so much hate and family destruction.

"I am going to take you down. You are nothing more than another teenage slut." He waved his knife around like the madman he was.

Nika held her ground, her focus entirely on the knife. She wasn't wearing body armor and even if she was, a knife was a cop's worst enemy as blades could pierce Kevlar that bullets merely dented. The dim light reflected off the blade and the crimson blood—Rachel's blood—contrasted against the silver.

"Drop it, Donovan. I promise you I'm a sure shot."

"You're part of the problem, you lying excuse for a woman!" His screams reverberated around the locker room. "You belong in the family, making family. Not trying to be a man in a man's job."

Son of a bitch. Donovan had really broken with reality.

"You can drop it for me, Donovan, or wait for

more officers to show up and take you out. What do you want?"

The knife steadied and Donovan swayed, as if he were about to pass out. Nika registered that he raised his arm to throw the knife as she saw the flash of the blade arc toward her. She ducked and the knife flew by. She heard a muffled grunt behind her but had to ignore it. Until she heard a body hit the ground.

"Mitch!" Mitch lay on the ground six feet behind her, the knife impaled in his shoulder.

"Go get her, Nika." His gaze was steady, purposeful, but he had to be in shock, referring to Donovan as "her."

"Leave the knife alone, Mitch. Help is coming."

Then she ran after Donovan.

Donovan had already run for the back of the locker room to the entrance that opened into the main school corridor. Where there were hundreds of students.

"Stop!"

Donovan reached the door and had his hand on the handle and turned to look at her. His other hand was outstretched, holding a second weapon he hadn't used against Rachel.

A gun.

Nika saw his finger move as he squeezed the trigger. The sound of the bullet firing from his weapon was deafening in the small space, but she was expecting it as she hit the ground and rolled, shooting at him.

Donovan dropped his pistol as he grabbed his thigh and fell to the concrete floor, screaming.

Nika scrambled up and kicked his weapon away.

A cold metal barrel pressed against her temple as

a familiar female voice spoke. "You're done here, Nika. Drop your weapon."

Kristine Rattner. Mitch's meaning when he'd said "her" crystallized in dreaded comprehension.

"Let me kneel down and place it on the ground, Kristine. You don't want it to go off and kill your boyfriend over there."

"Shut up and do it!" Kristine's hands shook and Nika waited for a chance to throw her to the ground.

Nika knelt and placed her weapon on the floor, going as slowly as possible. Kristine forced her to move, on her knees, closer to Donovan's writhing form, in front of the door. "Daniel, you hang in there. I've got this bitch in hand, and I'm going to get you out." She put her mouth near Nika's ear. "You are going to get what you deserve. I'll bet you thought I was so stupid, not recognizing you in the bathroom. Then when you showed up at our meeting, a meeting for True Believers, I knew who you were. You're evil. You think you're so superior. You don't know the *truth*."

Nika prayed she could keep Kristine distracted long enough for SVPD to get there and rescue Mitch. Bryce heard everything through her concealed mike.

Where the hell was her backup?

Donovan made a feeble attempt to grab her ankle but as he did the door burst open behind him, smacking his head and forcing his body to bend in two. He grunted as several SVPD officers entered, all with weapons drawn and on him.

Nika felt Kristine jump in surprise and used the opening in her defenses. She grabbed the hand holding the gun to her head and forced it up. Kristine cried out as Nika twisted and squeezed Kristine's hand until she dropped the gun. And probably broke a few of Kristine's wrist bones.

"Don't move!" Two uniformed SVPD officers separated from the group attending to Donovan and arrested Kristine.

Nika's legs shook but she had to keep moving, to get to Mitch.

"I need EMTs for Mitch Everlock. He's down, over in the next row of lockers. This is the shooter and the one who had the knife—Daniel Donovan. This woman is Kristine Rattner. You saw what she tried to do. Take them both in."

Nika ran to be with Mitch as the officers got to work. And practically ran into him as he stood in the aisle, leaning heavily on one of the lockers.

"Nice work, Officer Pasczenko." His deep voice was steady but strained and she searched his face for signs of shock or pain.

"Are you okay, Mitch?" His shoulder was bleeding, the knife gone. "You pulled the knife out?"

"Just a surface abrasion." He held his hand to his shoulder where the dark stain on his dress shirt was widening.

"Let me guess. You take your hand away and the blood starts gushing."

"I love a woman who can handle gore." He smiled and she wanted to slap him and hug him at the same time. And then she remembered.

"You were supposed to be out front, handling the rowdy kids. What were you doing in here?" Anger and resentment boiled into an ugly mix. She felt like a fool. She'd actually believed that he trusted in her ability to solve this case, to handle whatever went down tonight. That he'd trusted *her*.

"SVPD had it under control. It was Kristine. She let a bunch of kids in who hadn't bought tickets. There are going to be at least two-dozen underage drinking arrests. We called in backup units. Rachel found me and begged me to come in here."

Rachel.

"Where's Rachel now?"

"EMTs are looking her over. They'll take her to the hospital to make sure the knife wound on her throat is minor."

Nika wasn't going to let him off the hook. "Why are you really here, Mitch?"

"Why do you think I'm here?"

"Because you...you didn't think I could handle this on my own," she whispered, not wanting it to be true but knowing it was.

"Is that what you think of me, Nika? That I wouldn't have your six in the middle of an op that you're in charge of?" His gaze narrowed and she wanted to focus on her anger, her sense of betrayal, but she noted the white lines around his eyes.

"Mitch, do you feel okay?"

"Sure." And then all six feet three inches of Mitch Everlock dropped to the locker room floor like a lead weight.

Chapter 24

Christmas Eve

"I'll have everything ready by six, Mom. Come over then." Nika spoke to her mother on the phone as she traced her finger around the glass icicles she'd hung on her Christmas tree. Convincing her mother that she had enough food for the entire family's Christmas Eve dinner was always a challenge. "Ivy will be here, too." And Mitch...she'd hoped to invite him but hadn't heard from him since the Silver Bells Ball. Since she'd broken her undercover role and gone back to her regular role as an SVPD officer.

She'd made sure he was okay, of course. The ER doctor had let her stay by his side the entire time he'd been worked on. Mitch's stab wound had only required stitches, thank God. *And a pint of blood.* Nika hadn't been able to shake her culpability for Mitch's brush with death.

Mitch could have died because she hadn't taken out Donovan soon enough.

After she hung up with her mother she checked on the roast and added some broth to the bottom of the pan. It was still only half past eight in the morning; the roast would slow cook for the next eight hours. Her kitchen counter was crammed with all of the ingredients for the holiday meal. A meal she'd wanted to share with Mitch more than anyone.

At least Rachel was going to be here. She was staying with Nika for the rest of the school year, by choice. She was out with a few of her friends this morning, doing last-minute shopping. Rachel's popularity had exploded once the story came out about how she'd escaped a madman with only butterfly bandages on her throat.

The deeper wounds Rachel had would take longer to heal.

Rachel had asked Nika to join them but she had to make it clear that she wasn't a student. Her cover had been blown and, besides, she needed time alone to nurse her broken heart. A break only one man would ever be able to fix.

Mitch.

It made sense that Mitch hadn't called her. At first she'd assumed it was because he was embarrassed that he'd fainted. But she'd seen far less serious wounds take down the most macho men. He'd had a decent stab wound that had nicked an artery. She'd applied pressure to it until the EMTs came in, which was within minutes. Mitch had been conscious and grumpy by then.

It had been his own fault for standing behind her when Donovan was wielding that blade. Or so she thought. And thought. She had barely slept in a week and had finally admitted to herself that it wasn't anger that kept her up. It was her own damned guilt. Guilt at not trusting him, not seeing that he'd been there at the dance, in the locker room, fully capable of stepping in, but instead he'd allowed her to do her job. Mitch had watched as she'd taken out Daniel Donovan because Mitch had trusted her capabilities.

And she'd doubted *his* motives.

The doorbell rang and she put down her coffee, wondering who'd be here so early on Christmas Eve. She opened the door to Claudia, who appeared far too festive as far as Nika was concerned.

"Merry Christmas, Nika!" Claudia held out a huge basket in her arms.

"Oh, my goodness, please, come in." Nika took the wicker container and placed it on the coffee table, the only place that wasn't covered with a decorative dish of candy, cookies or mints.

"Can I get you a cup of coffee?"

"Oh, no, I just wanted to play Santa's elf and bring you this. A personal thank-you from me for all you've done for the True Believers–New Thought case. We wouldn't be as far as we are with it if you hadn't dug up all the details and evidence you did with Rachel. Not to mention you brought down two of Wise's henchmen."

"I wish it had been Wise." It still galled her that the New Thought meetings were still going on and that Leonard Wise was free to preach his gospel of demented hate.

"As do I, but until he gets caught actually harming or threatening a minor, we have to bide our time. We'll get him, Nika." Claudia's confidence buoyed her own regrets.

"Do you still think the cult will try to bring down Silver Valley?"

Claudia nodded. "Of course they will. They'll lie low for a month or two, wait for Donovan and Rattner to be sentenced and put in jail. We're lucky they both pled guilty, and that Rattner confessed that she dropped the rock from the bridge. It is a damn shame we can't tie them to Wise, but it's to be expected. He knows what he's doing."

"Yes, he does." Nika spoke quietly, not wanting to swear on Christmas Eve.

"Today and tomorrow are not about bemoaning the likes of those crazies. The school and town are safe for the time being, and you need to celebrate, Nika. You got your man. And woman, I might add." Claudia's smile faltered when she met Nika's eyes. "The bad guys aren't the catch you really wanted, though, are they?"

Nika couldn't answer. A big, fat tear slipped down her cheek and she damned her emotions. Of all times to lose it, she was doing it in front of her new Trail Hikers' boss.

Claudia's expression softened. "Nika, love never appears at the right time, especially when you've chosen the career path we have. Things will work out with you and Mitch if they're supposed to. And I do have a sixth sense about these things. By the time we're working on the next phase of taking out Leonard Wise and his followers, I daresay you and Mitch will be together more than as work colleagues."

"I don't agree, Claudia. I really messed up with him."

Claudia smiled. "I thought I messed up with someone special to me, too, but we worked it out. I hope you do, too." She stomped her feet on the doormat. "Now, I'm sorry to drop and run, but I have more Christmas baskets to deliver. Merry Christmas, Nika!" With a jaunty wave Claudia was back in her car and off to play Santa for her next holiday target.

Nika reached to close her front door but saw a familiar vehicle pull up in her driveway.

Mitch.

He strode up her walkway and stopped at the door, his expression unreadable. His color was back and he didn't move as though he'd been injured.

"Merry Christmas, Nika."

"Hi, Mitch."

"There's something—"

"I want to apologize—"

They both spoke at once and stood there staring at one another. Mitch's eyes blazed with heat that didn't come from anger or resentment. It was the same light she'd seen in his eyes as he'd made love to her all night.

Before either of them spoke again he pulled her into his arms, crushing his mouth on hers. His lips and tongue told her what he wasn't able to before now. She hoped her hot response did so, too, but she had to look at him.

Nika was done with assuming anything. She pulled back and Mitch groaned.

"Mitch, listen to me. I'm so sorry. I'm a jerk. I should have realized you were there to back me up, not take over from me. You let me handle the op and I was so worried about your injury, so upset that I'd let Donovan hurt you, that I wouldn't slow down enough to see I was wrong. I was scared out of my mind, Mitch. He could have killed you because I didn't shoot sooner."

He didn't let her go, kept his arms around her as he placed his forehead on hers. "Nika, I'm a stubborn fool. I know that. But it took me the better part of a week to figure it out." He leaned back and lifted her chin with his finger. "None of that matters, Nika. What matters is that I love you and I'm not going to let you go. We belong together. It's only been three weeks but we're like sodium and chlorine. We fit together perfectly."

Nika's joy bubbled up through her chest and burst out of her in a loud laugh. "Did you just say we're like table salt? I thought that was a 'normal' compound? Ordinary."

"What we share is solid, Nika. A pure chemical reaction with a bond that will last forever. If you'll give it a chance. Give me a chance, Nika."

"Mitch, I love you. I've been fighting it since the day I walked into your classroom. We need to talk. I need to tell you how much you mean to me, how stupid I've been. I'm so sorry, Mitch."

"I love you, Nika. We have the rest of our lives to talk about whatever you want. But, right now, I need to hear you say it again." His eyes burned with the promise of tomorrow and her knees shook.

"I love you, Mitch Everlock. Every geeky part of you."

He pulled her close, his pelvis crushing into hers as he kissed her until she couldn't think, couldn't breathe.

Several minutes later, or it could have been hours, a cough broke through their make-up kiss. Nika ignored it, but she couldn't ignore the laughter.

"Looks like you have your date for our wedding, Nika." Bryce stood in the driveway, holding what looked like a wine bottle in a gift bag, with his fiancée, Zora, at his side. "We're just dropping off last-minute Christmas gifts. Maybe you two should take it inside and light a fire."

Nika smiled up at Mitch, who answered her with a quick kiss on her nose before he turned to Bryce.

"Hi, Zora. Hi, Bryce. Yeah, we'll be attending your wedding. Together."

* * * * *

#1927 UNDERCOVER IN CONARD COUNTY
Conard County: The Next Generation
by Rachel Lee

Kel Westin is assigned an undercover role to draw out illegal trophy hunters in Conard County, but his feelings for the beautiful yet wary game warden, Desi Jenks, are anything but a front. When signs point to an inside job, can Desi and Kel learn to trust each other before they wind up dead?

#1928 DEADLY FALL
by Elle James

Billionaire Andrew Stratford, desperate to keep his small daughter safe, hires tough-as-nails—and sexy-as-hell—Stealth Operations Specialist Dixie Reeves as a nanny to protect his daughter, but sparks begin to fly when they are forced to set aside the walls they've hidden behind for years in order to save little Leigha from a mysterious threat.

#1929 SPECIAL FORCES SEDUCTION
by C.J. Miller

Alex "Hyde" Flores had hung up her spy gear for good, at least until her currently off-again lover Finn Carter shows up with one last mission in mind. But taking down the drug lord who killed their friend isn't Finn's only objective. He's determined to win Alex back, whatever it takes.

#1930 DR. DO-OR-DIE
Doctors in Danger • by Lara Lacombe

Dr. Avery Thatcher was sent to investigate a mysterious illness at a research base in Antarctica. Instead, she finds a deadly new bioweapon—and help in the form of her ex-boyfriend, Dr. Grant Jones, the senior doctor on staff. Will they be able to stop the spread of a deadly disease *and* face the never-quite-forgotten feelings bubbling back to the surface?

Her eyelids fluttered. "I didn't know," she murmured, her
voice breathy.

"Didn't know what?"

"That a kiss could be so nice."

At once he found his self-control. It snapped into place
like the jaws of a crocodile. She didn't know a kiss could
be so nice? Her words speared him until his chest ached
for her. My God, what had this woman been through?
Had her rapist been her first and only?

Forget his attraction to her, he had a strong urge to
rend something, smash something, hunt down the SOB...

"Did I do it right?"

He closed his eyes, battling fury, battling pain for her.
"You did it right," he said. "Very right." That she should
have to wonder about the smallest touching of lips?
That guy must have assaulted her in ways that weren't
physical. She might say he wasn't able to walk for a week,

but that wouldn't remove the experience or stinging words. Only fresh experience would, and she apparently hadn't allowed herself any.

Opening his eyes, hanging on to his temper, he gave her another soft kiss. "I want to do it again. But like I said, let's take it slow."

"Because of me?"

Double damn. Was he messing this up? "Because I want it to be perfect and right for both of us. Okay?"

She nodded, then let her head fall against his shoulder. Relieved, he snuggled her in, astonished that this self-assured woman had exposed so much vulnerability to him. Vulnerability he had never imagined could be part of a woman who presented such a confident face to the world.

He felt a little shiver run through her, then she softened completely. Staring at nothing, he held her and wondered what he was walking into. What he might be dragging her into. Because something was rotten, and it was easier to think about that than to think about the ache in his groin and how much he wanted Desi.

Don't miss
UNDERCOVER IN CONARD COUNTY
by Rachel Lee, available January 2017
wherever Harlequin® Romantic Suspense books
and ebooks are sold.

www.Harlequin.com

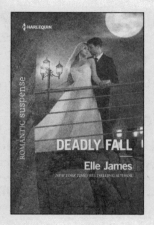

JUST CAN'T GET ENOUGH?

Join our social communities
and talk to us online.

You will have access to the latest
news on upcoming titles and special
promotions, but most importantly,
you can talk to other fans about your
favorite Harlequin reads.

Harlequin.com/Community

Facebook.com/HarlequinBooks

Twitter.com/HarlequinBooks

Pinterest.com/HarlequinBooks

Turn your love of reading into
rewards you'll love with
Harlequin My Rewards

**Join for FREE today at
www.HarlequinMyRewards.com**

Earn **FREE BOOKS** of your choice.

Experience **EXCLUSIVE OFFERS** and contests.

Enjoy **BOOK RECOMMENDATIONS**
selected just for you.

PLUS! Sign up now
and get **500** points
right away!

Earn
FREE
REWARDS
Join
Today!
HarlequinMyRewards.com

MYR16R